Here's

MW01257824

"With an irreverent, tell-it-like-it-is, suburban-mom-assassin narrator, Leslie Langtry's *'Scuse Me While I Kill This Guy* delivers wild and wicked fun."
—Julie Kenner, USA Today Bestselling Author

"Darkly funny and wildly over the top, this mystery answers the burning question, 'Do assassin skills and Girl Scout merit badges mix…' one truly original and wacky novel!"
—RT BOOK REVIEWS

"Those who like dark humor will enjoy a look into the deadliest female assassin and PTA mom's life."
—Parkersburg News

"Mixing a deadly sense of humor and plenty of sexy sizzle, Leslie Langtry creates a brilliantly original, laughter-rich mix of contemporary romance and suspense in *'Scuse Me While I Kill This Guy.*"
—Chicago Tribune

"The beleaguered soccer mom assassin concept is a winner, and Langtry gets the fun started from page one with a myriad of clever details."
—Publisher's Weekly

BOOKS BY LESLIE LANGTRY

Merry Wrath Mysteries:
Merit Badge Murder
Mint Cookie Murder
Scout Camp Murder (short story in the Killer Beach Reads
collection)
Marshmallow S'More Murder

Greatest Hits Mysteries:
'Scuse Me While I Kill This Guy
Guns Will Keep Us Together
Stand By Your Hitman
I Shot You Babe
Paradise By The Rifle Sights
Snuff the Magic Dragon
My Heroes Have Always Been Hitmen
Four Killing Birds (a holiday short story)
Have Yourself a Deadly Little Christmas (a holiday short story)

Other Works:
Sex, Lies, & Family Vacations

Hanging Tree Tales YA horror novels:
Hell House
Tyler's Fate
Witch Hill
The Teacher

MARSHMALLOW S'MORE MURDER

a Merry Wrath mystery

Leslie Langtry

MARSHMALLOW S'MORE MURDER

CHAPTER ONE

"Merry." Riley was breathing heavily—and not in the good way—through my cell phone. "Help me…"

The line went dead, and my world obediently exploded.

Twelve little girls started squealing instantaneously as if they were all rigged to the same C-4 charge and some idiot had pushed the big, red button.

"Girls!" I shouted in vain as I stared at my phone. But they ignored me because the First Lady was walking toward them.

Yeah, no way I could corral them now. Dammit. I hit the redial button and walked away from the scene of my troop surrounding the most important woman in the country. Oh well, the Secret Service agents could handle this. Maybe.

My heart was pounding as I listened to the endless ringing. Something was very wrong. Riley was in trouble, had asked for my help, and I was in no position to help him. In fact, why was he calling me? If my former handler was on assignment, why didn't he call the CIA?

"Ms. Wrath!" I heard shouting behind me and turned to see a Secret Service agent in his black suit, mirrored sunglasses, and earpiece, holding two of the Kaitlins apart. One of them had a bruise developing on her chin. The other had a smug look on her face.

We had four Kaitlins in the troop. Each one had the same last initial. All four had brown hair and brown eyes. And each girl spelled her name differently from the others. It was just easier to refer to them all as *The Kaitlins*. Easier mainly because sometimes I had trouble telling who was who. Of course, I was never going to admit something like that. Showing any sort of weakness around little girls was about as dangerous as poking a grizzly with a painful skin rash.

My Girl Scout troop was pretty large. Memorizing last names wasn't something I was good at. Kelly knew their last names and most of the parents—a task nearly impossible since the parents weren't really around much. Getting the first names down was enough for me because I was also in charge of making sure the girls didn't set fire to…well, anything. They really liked starting fires at camp and took up the task with the eagerness of pyromaniacs in a match factory made of wood.

I sighed, pulling the two aside so the First Lady could talk to the girls who *weren't* fighting. "What are you two doing?"

I was on my own here. My best friend and co-leader, Kelly, was back at home about to have a baby at any moment. Our troop had won a free trip to Washington DC for selling the most Girl Scout Cookies…*ever*. You can do that when you can blackmail a bunch of CIA agents. And trust me, I had lots of material to work with.

So, I had to bring the girls on this trip without backup. Well, technically that wasn't entirely true. I had a parent with me because the girl-to-adult ratio is very strict in Scouting. But Mrs. Evelyn Trout was once again AWOL—so I was handling things alone. An idea that was looking more like a bad one with every advancing second.

"She called me a stupid-head!" the smug Kaitlin snapped.

I looked at the bruised Kaitlin. "Why did you do that?"

The agent let go of the two and walked away, foolishly believing I had things under control now. He stormed over to help the other four agents contain the remaining ten girls, who were now mobbing the most important woman in the United States.

"She said the Secret Service carried Brownings, when *everyone* knows they carry Glocks!" Bruised Kaitlin folded her arms over her chest, and the smug look transferred from one to the other.

I threw my arms up in the air. "I don't care if they carry flamethrowers! You can't fight in front of the First Lady!"

A cry rose up from the group, and I turned to see five very panicked men backing up from an advancing horde of squealing children. The First Lady, Mrs. Benson, simply smiled and raised her hand, fingers in the quiet sign for Girl Scouts everywhere. Immediately, my girls stopped, raised their hands, and went silent. I tried not to laugh. I really did. An unarmed woman succeeded where five armed bodyguards had failed. Classic.

The Secret Service used to be made up of competent, professional men and women. And while I was sure there were still a handful of those dedicated agents out there, recent stories in the news had kind of tarnished that reputation. I could have wondered what happened to make it all go downhill, but that would have meant I had time to care about other federal agents. I didn't.

There wasn't a lot of love between the agencies. In fact, the annual softball tourney usually got a little out of hand. Especially that one time in the 1960s when Team CIA slathered the balls with LSD. I hadn't been born yet, but I wish I'd been there to see the FBI team running in terror from imaginary dragons in the outfield.

"You know, ladies…" the President's wife said to the girls who were now seated on the floor around her. "…I was a Girl Scout."

A chorus of "wow"s and "no way"s rose up around her before the silence settled in and the First Lady started telling them about her days as a Brownie.

"Were you ever in any shootouts?" Inez asked through missing front teeth.

"Why don't they have badges for throwing knives?" pretty, plump Hannah asked, her blonde hair in two ponytails.

The First Lady looked a little confused, "Um…no?"

"Girls!" I hissed. "Appropriate questions, please!"

Lauren, a tall, skinny kid with a long, red braid, stuck her chin out. I was a little worried. Lauren wasn't difficult at all. She just had a strange way of looking at things.

"Do you like dogs?" she asked finally.

Mrs. Benson laughed. "I do like dogs. That's one question I can answer. We have two golden retrievers here at the White House."

I relaxed a bit as the First Lady launched into a story about how she and the President had gotten their dogs. The girls were silent. They loved animals. Any animals. This would take little while.

My name is Merry Wrath, and I used to be an active CLA agent. And I know, if you saw me—with my short, unruly hair and slim frame—you probably wouldn't believe I could have been a field agent. I've heard that before. But it didn't take braw so much as brains and the ability to improvise to be a good agent.

At that time, my name was Finnoughla Merrygold Czrygy, and Riley, the man who'd just called begging for help, was my handler. I'd worked black ops all over the world for years until the previous Vice President outed me to a journalist to get back at my father, a US Senator, for a vote he didn't like. After several lengthy congressional hearings and some nasty finger-pointing, some random guy went to prison, and I was out of a job. The Agency paid me a very handsome severance package, and I was set for life. But still—I had to leave a job an lifestyle I loved because of political backstabbing.

Since that time, I've changed my name and appearance and moved back to Who's There, Iowa, where I lead a troop of twelve soon-to-be third grade Girl Scouts. Weirdly, my life is fa more dangerous now than when I was a spy, complete with the inconvenient appearance of dead terrorists in my house and being stalked by cat assassins. Go figure.

"Okay, girls!" I shouted as Mrs. Benson got to her feet. We were only allotted a few moments on her schedule, but no matter how long, I knew my troop would never forget this visit. "Let's thank the First Lady for her time! We need to get going!"

Being a former CIA agent and having a dad who's high up in political circles meant that I could give this trip some special side trips. Like meeting the First Lady in the White House. There were some perks from my forced early retirement after all.

But right now, my heart wasn't really in it because I was worried about Riley. There was no doubt it was Riley who called. I'd have known that voice anywhere. But why was he calling me? Riley was an active agent with the CIA. I stopped working for him two years ago. Calling me made no sense because if he'd called the Agency, they'd have entire teams trying to find him using every resource available. Which was about one hundred percent more resources than I had.

And I knew of only one place where I could find the answers—Langley, CIA Headquarters. The fact that I'd be dragging a bunch of eight-year-old girls along was simply a bonus. We left the White House and some very relieved Secret Service men and headed out.

The men with holstered guns at the main gate, however, were not amused.

"You're not on the visitor's list, Ms. Wrath," said the humorless man in the black suit, mirrored sunglasses, and earpiece. I swear—Feds are *so* unimaginative. Perhaps I could have Dad submit a congressional bill to make these guys dress like bananas or aardvarks. Nothing would confuse a would-be terrorist more than a banana toting an Uzi.

"Merry!" My old friend Maria Gomez waved as she walked toward us. "Knock it off, Smith, they're with me! Who do you think is responsible for those?" She pointed at the remains of at least a dozen boxes of Girl Scout Cookies littering the guard shack. I smiled as he winced.

Langley never knew what hit them. Apparently Girl Scouts would make very effective terrorists. Think about it—all they'd have to do would be show up in uniform with a little wagon full of cookies.

"Is that a dead *body*?" Ava cried with glee as she pointed to a gruesome photo on the wall.

"What kind of holster do you prefer—hip or shoulder?" Betty asked a horrified agent.

"Is this the NOC List?" Lauren asked as she punched a few keys on a computer. "Did Tom Cruise really come down from the ceiling in here and try to steal it? Can I do that?"

I ignored them as I filled Maria in on the call from Riley, handing her my cell in hopes she could trace it. Okay, okay, I didn't ignore them. The girls were always in my peripheral vision. Besides, they were only asking questions. These agents should have realized this was educational.

"Don't you have anyone helping you?" Maria asked as she eyed the girls running amok in her department.

I sighed. "Evelyn Trout—one of the parents—is supposed to be here. But she keeps running off before we leave in the morning." I shrugged. "I always find her in the bar at the end of the day. Besides, I can handle it," I totally lied.

Maria Gomez and I went through training together at The Farm. That was the secret CIA compound where they turned ordinary people into smart killing machines. There weren't very many women in our class, so Maria and I became close. She was funny and smart and fluent in every variation of the Spanish language on the planet. The woman was also a knockout with huge brown eyes, pouty lips, and waves of thick and glossy shoulder-length hair. It worked to her advantage every time.

One of the girls had found a way to access the speaker system through the phones and announced in a disguised voice, "Poopy Heads have infiltrated the building! I repeat, Poopy Heads have infiltrated the building!"

Maria looked back at me. "Yeah, I think you've got this. She turned to her computer and started typing. I'd tell you more than that, but it would be a breach of national security. While she worked, I shot my troop a glare that made them settle down a little. The only female agent in the room wisely showed up with pads of paper and colored markers, and the girls were cleverly distracted. At least for a little while. I made a mental note to send the assistant a case of cookies next year.

After a few minutes, Maria said, "I triangulated the call, and it seems to be coming from the DC metro area, but I can't get more specific." She squinted at the screen. "I think I can get it down to a six-block radius, but it will take a little time."

Damn. I didn't know how much time Riley had. But there wasn't much I could do. Everything depended on the technology we had, and the CIA was at the top of the list in that regard. At least he was in the country and in the same city. If he'd been in Bangkok, he'd have been on his own. For a moment

I pictured taking my troop to Thailand. The thought made me shudder.

I got to my feet and shook Maria's hand. "Thanks. Let me know. I'm going to take these kids to the hotel pool for the rest of the afternoon to burn off some energy." And hopefully do a little more thinking on this problem.

"No problem," Maria said. "It's the least we can do. I always felt bad about the way you were railroaded out of here."

"I know you can't tell me what Riley's been working on, but can you give me a hint? It might help narrow things down," I asked.

"I don't have that kind of clearance, Merry," she said. And she was right. I knew better than to ask.

I turned to the girls and announced, "Okay, ladies! Let's head back to the hotel for some pool time!"

The room exploded into cheers. That was one way to round up a bunch of kids. Promise them swimming. I'd have to remember that.

Maria laughed. "Where are you staying?"

"The Grand American Inn downtown," I said, my eyes on Ava, who had just hacked an absent agent's computer and was setting up a dummy database where everyone's name was *Fart Face.* Time to go.

Back at the hotel pool, I collapsed onto a chaise lounge while the girls drove the lifeguard crazy. He was cute, with long dark hair and a sweet smile. He was maybe sixteen—which meant he was in for it. My girls were a little boy crazy. I heard constant cries of "look at me" shouted in his general direction over and over. When he did glance at them, they swooned. Caterina, one of the quietest girls, actually pretended to drown. If I didn't know she was on a swim team, I'd have worried. These girls were good. If they didn't have a future in espionage, they definitely had one in acting.

Evelyn Trout had been soaking in the hot tub when we arrived but disappeared with a sour look on her face moments later. I was pretty sure she was one of the Kaitlins' moms. A short, plump woman with a poufy brown bob that resembled a hairy mushroom, Mrs. Trout had leaped at the chance to fill in on this trip when I sent the word out in my take-home newsletter.

She was the only mom who offered, which was one more volunteer than I thought I'd get.

But once we arrived at the airport she immediately upgraded to first class, leaving me to deal with the girls on my own in coach. Since we'd arrived, I rarely saw her. We had a suite, but I slept on the couch to keep the girls from sneaking out (which you'll be glad to know hadn't happened yet—mainly because it probably hadn't occurred to them). As a result, Mrs. Trout had a room to herself, and I only knew she was there by the messy bed and growing number of shopping bags that appeared each day.

I'd tried to talk to her and keep her up to date on our schedule, but she avoided me. Did she really think I wouldn't figure out that she was using this as a free *Me* trip? I *was* a spy. I was trained to notice these things. Of course, she didn't know I was a spy. No one in Who's There, Iowa did except for Kelly and my boyfriend, Rex.

I shouldn't have complained because it could've been worse. Juliette Dowd—my psycho Scout nemesis—had volunteered to go in a way I could only describe as obsessively eager, but once Evelyn offered, I was able to turn her down. Therefore, I didn't really mind an AWOL mom. Juliette Dowd, a low-level Council employee, hated me with a fury I could only compare to a pit bull with OCD, because I was dating Rex—her ex-boyfriend. It was totally ridiculous, mainly because we were adults. At least I was prepared. I'd fitted her car with a tracking device so I'd know where she was. It really came in useful in our small town. I never told Rex this, but she drives past his house at least twice a day. I'm thinking of adding explosives.

The noise in the pool area was skull-splitting between the screechy girls splashing around and the constant sound of the lifeguard's whistle. Poor kid. He had his hands full. I'd feel sorry for him, but I had other things to worry about. Once again, I had to wonder. Riley could've called the CIA for help.

Unless he'd been disavowed. You might have thought something like that would only happen on *Mission Impossible*—but it was real alright. Especially on black ops in a place we weren't supposed to be. I couldn't really tell stories out of school.

They made me sign a confidentiality clause when they "retired" me.

Alright...just one. We had this agent in India who got drunk and took notes of his meeting with his handler on a napkin that he inconveniently left on the bar table. He might've been okay, but in his blurred mind he miswrote instructions as, *blow up Prime Minister's dog.* And although that wasn't what he was asked to do at all (can't tell you but suffice it to say it was something more akin to say, *stow the logbook*), the Prime Minister, whose niece was working at said bar, wasn't amused. He had a security detail on his schipperke for a whole year after that. As for the agent—well, he now sells insurance in Topeka.

So why did Riley call me? The only thing I could think of was that it was personal. He'd gotten into something unrelated to work and didn't want his boss brought into it. If that was the case, what did he think *I* could do? I was here with twelve little girls. Was I supposed to drag them with me across DC, toting guns and looking for trouble? I mean, sure, they could totally handle it, but I wasn't going to do it. He'd have to get his own troop for that.

The only kind of problem Riley ever had was with women. If that was it, he could just figure it out himself. But in the phone call, he'd said, "Help me." Did that mean more than one woman? If so, he probably deserved whatever they were going to do to him. He made serial womanizers look like priests who were overly eager about celibacy.

I couldn't really say anything. I'd fallen for his charms once. I couldn't help it. Riley had this sexy, surfer vibe with longer-than-normal, wavy blond hair, a glowing tan that never seemed to fade, and a smile that not only lit up a room but also dissolved the underwear of any woman present. We dated very briefly, but it turned into a compatible working relationship until a year ago when he barged into my life and started to confuse me with random kisses.

An idea flashed into my mind. What if it had to do with the yakuza? Then it *was* my problem. Almost one year ago, yakuza leader Midori Ito had rudely shown up dead in my kitchen. At first, we thought it was related to the deaths of other baddies who also inconveniently inserted their corpses into my life. But it had turned out to be unrelated.

Riley and I had taken it upon ourselves to dump the body behind a Japanese supermarket in Chicago in order to disconnect ourselves from the murder (of which we weren't guilty). The CIA hadn't known about it. Ito's body had been found a few months ago—but as far as we'd seen, no one could trace it back to us.

Unless they had. A shiver went through me. Was Riley being held by the yakuza? That sucked. The Japanese mob was scary. They were a very stabby crew and had lots of very sharp swords. Dammit. Why didn't he call me back? Why didn't Maria call me back?

Who had Riley? And why?

CHAPTER TWO

———

"Ma'am?" I looked up to see the lifeguard standing over me. His right hand rested on Betty's shoulder. His left was on Inez. The other girls crowded around, their eyes as big as headlights. It was then that I noticed that the water in the pool was almost black. Its transparency was gone, and it looked like something you'd see in a moat filled with giant, incontinent squid.

"What were you thinking?" I scowled at the girls as I led them back up to our room. The lifeguard, who would probably have nightmares for the rest of his life, had told us we were now banned from the pool for the rest of our stay.

Betty and Inez shrugged. They'd refused to explain how they'd changed the water's color, and the lifeguard had no ideas. He said one minute the pool was clear. The next minute it was black. Maybe I should loan these girls out to the military.

"How many dye packs did you steal from Langley?" I asked once we were back in the room.

Betty sighed. "Seven. How did you know?"

Because I'd been a spy. Because I'd been trained in counter-terrorism measures. Because that was the only idea I had.

"I've got psychic powers," I told them.

"Whoa!" Inez said quietly.

"We didn't mean to do it," Betty added. "I just wanted to see if the canisters would float so we could play with them. I didn't know they'd explode."

I stared at them, trying to figure out if this was a lie. It was possible that they just thought they'd grabbed some sort of pool toy. At CIA headquarters. A place one didn't usually consider when searching for aquatic playthings.

On the other hand, eight-year-olds can read, and the canisters were clearly marked.

"Why were we at CIA HQ?" Inez asked.

Uh-oh. I'd hoped they wouldn't notice. My troop had no idea about my past.

"It was one of the stops on the visit," I assured them. "And I wanted to thank them, since they were our largest group of cookie buyers."

"Oh," Betty said. "Well, they really should keep things like that locked up. We *are* just kids."

I decided to give up. Interrogating children was much harder than interrogating adults, and I was pretty sure I wouldn't get much more out of them.

So I sent them to their rooms to change into dry clothes. Evelyn Trout came out of her room looking like she'd been napping. Apparently, we'd woken her up—something she seemed to be unhappy about.

"You have to be with us all the time now, Mrs. Trout," I said, pointing at her for effect. "We've been banned from the pool, and I can't handle twelve kids by myself."

Evelyn Trout looked at me as if a skunk had just sprayed her. "But I have a massage scheduled in ten minutes."

"Not anymore," I said with as much finality as I could muster. "You came along to help, and you are helping. No more disappearing. Got it?"

"But it's a Swedish massage. It's with this cute Swede named Gunnar. That's why it's a Swedish massage," she said, as if that was supposed to change my mind.

"No, that's not why it's called that. And unless you can change your appointment to later in the evening, it's not going to happen." I put my hands on my hips and gave her my best intimidating glare.

The woman stomped back to her room and slammed the door. I thought I could hear her talking to herself. She certainly wasn't on the phone to her husband. He'd hardly be sympathetic to the idea of Gunnar giving his wife a rubdown.

The girls started trickling out into the main room. They seemed to know they'd pushed things too far. I told them to sit quietly until everyone was there. To my complete surprise, they did.

Evelyn's door opened, and she emerged in shorts and a T-shirt. She sullenly stalked to a chair and dumped herself into it, arms crossed over her chest. She gave the appearance of a surly teenager—not a middle-aged mom. Well, this was going to be fun.

"Okay, ladies." I held up the sign for silence. "We've only been here two days, and already you've caused chaos with the Secret Service, the CIA, and the hotel. We've been banned from the pool area, and I'd guess each and every one of you now has a file with your name on it in a secret basement somewhere inside the beltway."

I thought I heard a few murmurs of, "Awesome!"

Mrs. Trout made no response. She probably wasn't even listening.

"This trip is an honor. It's a privilege," I continued. "The National Council has paid our way. Remember, this trip is a reward for selling more cookies than anyone else in the country. We can't cause international incidents while we are here. We are representing the Girl Scouts. And we will go back home first thing in the morning if you don't shape up!"

I waited for this to sink in. The girls grumbled a little, but it was Evelyn who looked the most shocked. Maybe this would convince her that I needed her assistance. If she helped, I'd cut her loose the last day or so. Maybe.

It was too bad I had to get tough with them, because the girls weren't normally like this. Sure, they were overly curious when it came to weapons and matches, but usually I had some semblance of control. But then I also had Kelly with me most of the time. She could silence them with her angry-nurse look.

The troop knew how to behave, and they were good girls. I guessed travel made them a little crazy. That made sense. They were out of their comfort zone and only had one adult chasing after them. Stupid Riley. Things had gone south since he'd called this morning. It was clearly all his fault.

"Tonight, we're going to order pizza and hang out here. I'll order up a movie on pay-per-view, and you can take turns showering. Then tomorrow, we'll start this again and do it right.

Okay?"

The girls nodded. I put Evelyn in charge of finding an appropriate movie and ordering the pizza. She didn't look too happy about it but didn't refuse, which I took as a total win.

I slipped into one of the bedrooms and dialed Maria.

"Any word?" I asked.

"How's it going?" Maria asked. "I heard your girls wrecked the pool."

"How did you know that?" I asked. Stupid CIA. They always knew everything.

"My cousin is the assistant manager." She laughed. "I smoothed things over, but you won't get to swim again until you last day. And when you do, you'll have to pay for four more lifeguards. My cousin said something about stun guns, but I think he was just joking."

I would bet her ten to one he wasn't.

"Fine. But what about Riley?"

"One of my guys heard some chatter about him at the Japanese Embassy, which was weird. Riley's not working on anything in the Asian theater of ops."

Damn! "Really?" I asked innocently. "Maybe he's just sleeping his way through the staff?" Alarm bells were clanging inside my skull. The thought that this involved the yakuza was now becoming more possible. I'd much rather have had him being held hostage by a group of pissed-off boyfriends. That I could handle. I wouldn't even need a gun.

"I don't think so," Maria said, more quietly now. I imagined others were listening. "Wrath, what's going on?"

"Why do you think anything's going on?" I asked. Something was going on, but what could I tell her? Involving Maria any further might cost her her job. She was my friend…and my most valuable cookie sales client. There was no way I was jeopardizing that.

"Meet me in the hotel's restaurant for dinner. In an hour." She hung up.

My stomach was doing flip-flops. By involving Langley in his disappearance, I'd put Riley's job at risk. Maria would keep things discreet—I had no doubt about that. But I didn't want to get her in trouble. She was a good friend, but she hadn't done fieldwork for years. Her desk job definitely came in handy for me now, but how long did we have before someone at the Agency spotted irregularities?

I filled Evelyn in on my dinner plans and fled the suite before she could refuse. And I didn't feel bad about it in the least.

Maria was already waiting for me. She'd ordered two glasses of wine and motioned for me to sit. I slumped into the chair.

"So here's your situation as I see it," Maria said before I could speak. "You and Riley were involved with Midori Ito's murder and disposed of the body without telling the CIA. And now you're in over your head with your Scouts, who we probably should begin recruiting now for future wet work." She took a sip from her wine.

"How did you know?"

My friend threw back her head and laughed. Her shoulder-length brown curls bounced attractively. She really was stunning. A desk job didn't do her justice.

"It doesn't take much to put it all together. I may have been out of commission for a while, but I still remember how these things work." She took a drink of wine.

"We didn't kill her, but stuff happened, and we were involved. What are you going to do?" Maria didn't owe us any allegiance. Why should she help us and risk her pension?

She shrugged. "I've decided to take a week off for vacation. Thought I'd help you out."

I stared. It felt like my eyes bulged out of my head. "You want in on this? Are you serious?"

"Sure. I miss the field. And besides, you look like you need help. I like your troop. They remind me of my nieces."

"This is your idea of a vacation? Are they still putting stuff in the employees' coffee for experimental purposes?" The CIA was supposed to stop doing that back in the '80s, but every now and then some unlucky intern or accountant would go berserk, strip off all his clothes, and hold the coffee machine at gunpoint. The last one actually garroted a stapler.

Maria shook her head. "Riley's my friend too. I'm completely bored sitting at a desk now. And I do well with kids. This is gonna be fun!"

I leaned in. "You and I have a very different idea of wha fun is."

She laughed again, and I relaxed as we ordered dinner. I was actually a huge relief having my old friend at my side. She'd aced manipulation in training, so maybe she'd have a positive effect on the girls. It made sense what she'd said about assignments. I also missed the action of the field. My career had been cut short, and I resented it. And I would've hated administration. Maria had earned her desk job, but it lacked the excitement of working undercover. I'd feel the same way if I wa her. I'd practically gift wrapped this opportunity without even realizing it.

My troop made me feel a little of the excitement I used to have. They were smart, funny kids who liked learning off-the grid stuff like knife throwing. They didn't have a badge for that, sadly. In fact, I was pretty sure the Council would frown upon such training, so I'd made the girls swear not to say a word. The agreed only if I'd teach them more stuff like that. I agreed, mostly because so far we never set a date for that kind of trainin to happen. I was starting to believe that I was living on borrowe time.

I filled Maria in on my troop's itinerary for the week. W were going to visit Capitol Hill, meet my dad (who the girls knew only as their state's senator), go to the zoo, see a show at the Kennedy Center, and visit the usual tourist sites. How we were going to fit in rescuing Riley was beyond me unless he wa being held inside Lincoln's head at the Lincoln Memorial.

You'd be surprised how many monuments are hollow inside. George Washington used to hide inside Revolutionary War monuments and jump out at people, toothless and giggling. And there are Cold War stories of how the CIA had built a huge statue of Stalin and placed it out on Red Square. When the Soviets dragged it inside KGB headquarters, two dwarves, spies who had infiltrated the Moscow Circus, had popped out and placed bugs everywhere. It would've been an effective Trojan horse too, except that they'd gotten caught and were summarily executed.

"Okay," Maria said as she finished her salad and pushed her plate aside, bringing me back to the present. "I think if whoever has Riley is watching you, I need to blend in."

"You could stay in our suite. I'm not using my bed," I offered. "And you can have the troop T-shirts Evelyn was supposed to wear." Each day of the trip we were in matching neon shirts with our troop number on them. This was so I could locate them quickly in a crowd. It helped in that I was usually able to identify the blur of an acid green shirt as it flew past me.

She nodded. "I'll move in tonight. I'll swing by the office after dinner and see if anything else has popped up before I come over."

"Thanks. I know I should dissuade you from getting involved, but it's obvious I could use your help." Our friendship was too good for me to lie to her.

"Merry, I don't want you to get your hopes up." Maria frowned. "Riley could already be dead." She said the last word quietly. It still made me wince.

"I know I should think that," I said. "But my gut tells me he's alive and that somehow I can help. I have to try."

Maria sighed. "As long as you know what you're getting yourself and possibly the troop into."

I nodded. "I'm not going to let anything happen to them. If it gets too dangerous, I'll back off."

"Okay," Maria agreed. "I'll hold you to that."

We finished dinner and chatted for a few moments more. In spite of the subject matter, I felt more relaxed. For the first time on this trip, I got to eat an entire meal without chasing girls around. I considered it a small victory.

Back in the room, I found twelve girls passed out on the floor in front of a James Bond movie. Mrs. Trout was awake and gave me a dirty look before stomping off to her room. I woke the girls up one at a time and helped them to bed. Moving sleepy kids was way easier than fully alert children. I was toying with doping the girls with Benadryl during the day when Maria knocked on the door.

I settled her in my room (thus irritating Evelyn because she would now have a roommate) but still thought I should sleep on the sofa in case the girls decided to wander in the night. And yes, I have reasons behind this suspicion. A few weeks ago, at a sleepover at my house, the girls put lipstick, eye shadow, and nail polish on my cat, Philby, and colored the kittens blue with sidewalk chalk. Philby ignored me for four whole days, especially after her tongue turned blue from cleaning her babies

I felt a small pang of regret at being away from my cat and her kittens. I'd never really had a pet before Philby showing up on my doorstep with suitcases and moving in. She looked rather unfortunately like Hitler and hissed loudly whenever she heard the name Bob, but other than that, she was a great kitty.

Rex was taking care of them for me. My neighbor and the town's hottie detective was a great guy. For reasons I couldn't understand, he adored me and liked my troop. It never bothered him that I was using Dora the Explorer sheets for living room curtains or that I thought Pizza Rolls were a food group. He was the perfect man.

As I drifted off, I felt a twinge of guilt. It had been almost twelve hours since Riley's call for help, and I hadn't gotten any closer to finding him. He just had to hang in there until I could manage a rescue. I forced him from my mind in an attempt to get some sleep. The last thing I remembered was the pay-per-view bill for fifty bucks that popped up on the television screen.

It was dark...raining. The bright lights of Tokyo melted on the pavement, running together like a damaged watercolor painting on black velvet. Yeesh. Where do I come up with these descriptions?

Obviously, I was dreaming. Why else would I be back in Japan? Was this a memory? Traffic tied up the street, so I stayed on the sidewalk. I had no idea where I was going, but hey, it was a dream. My feet just kept moving like they knew what was up.

Buildings blurred as I passed them. Where I was didn't seem as important as where I was going. I followed the sidewalk until I came to an alley and stepped into it. Really? A dark alley in a crowded city? Now there was a spy cliché if ever there was one.

I kept to the wall on my right, slipping in and out of the shadows until I found an unmarked door. Raising my fist, I gave a brief knock, and the door swung open. A man I'd never seen before nodded and stepped aside as I entered. Without giving him a second look, I made my way to the stairs and began to climb.

I kept my hand in my right coat pocket the whole time, curled around the cold steel of my Glock .45. I always liked the .45. It was invented to kill men the size of giants. I loved the slow drag after firing and the nice large hole it made in whatever I hit.

I stopped on the third floor and pulled my gun, gingerly opening the door. The hallway was dark, so I took no chances as I moved very slowly with my gun drawn. Noises at the end of the hall made me stop. I strained to hear in the murky dimness. Voices. Garbled. I slid closer.

"You know the drill," a man with a clipped British accent said.

"I do. Consider it done." I'd know Riley's voice anywhere.

What was I doing here? Was I spying on Riley? That didn't make sense. The doorman knew me. Why was I lurking creepily in the hall? Why didn't I make my presence known?

"Get her!" a woman cried as I made out a shadow standing in front of me. I began to run as if a rabid dog were chasing me...

I sat straight up on the couch, covered in sweat. My training kept me from calling out until I knew where I was. Oh right. DC. With my troop.

A glimmer of memory hung around the edges of my mind before fading. I'd had a dream. A dream the memory of which was slowly slipping away. I lay back down, wondering what the hell had just happened. Somewhere along the way, I fell back to sleep.

The Kaitlins woke me up first thing in the morning by screaming. As I scrambled to my feet into a defensive position, they jumped back, startled, before running out of the room. Oh well, it could've been worse. Much worse. Because they've snuck up on me before when I've slept, I no longer take peanut butter and cotton balls on camping trips.

I handed out breakfast bars and made a quick dodge through the shower before joining everyone in the main room. The girls were thrilled that Maria was going to hang out with us, and they swarmed her, peppering her with questions like: *Do you have a cat, and can I pet it?* and *Are you a supermodel?*

Evelyn's door was locked, and she wasn't answering. Maria said Mrs. Trout had come out, seen that Maria was wearing her troop shirt, and gone back into the room. My guess was the mom had decided she was off the hook. I decided that pursuing Evelyn's involvement any further wasn't worth the effort. At least not today.

After everyone had eaten, we discussed our plans. I'd decided to shake up the schedule a bit and do the zoo instead of Congress. It would give Maria and me a chance to talk and puzzle things out. From past experience I knew that there were too many ambitious and nosy interns on Capitol Hill. They were much more effective than any listening device the CIA had. You couldn't sneeze without the Speaker of the House finding out and asking if you had avian flu.

We needed a little more privacy. And people gave you that when they saw you coming through the turnstiles with a herd of kids wearing brightly colored, matching shirts.

"There was nothing on the radar last night when I checked in," Maria whispered as we watched the Giant Pandas sleepily tumble around their habitat. I was kind of jealous, truth be told. Well, that was only if I could put ranch dressing on the bamboo shoots they ate.

"Still no trace of the call?" I asked Maria.

She shook her head. "Riley either has turned off the phone, or its battery is dead, or whoever is threatening him has destroyed it."

The girls squealed as the female panda stretched and yawned. Wow. They were actually stunned into silence. I'd have to remember that. I wondered if the Chinese government would loan me a panda and if they got along with cats. I'd have to look into that.

"Do you think he'll call again?" Maria asked, giving the girls a huge grin. She was gorgeous, with dimples and perfect skin. The girls were totally smitten and basked in the glow of her smiles. I wondered if she knew hypnosis. That could really come in handy.

"No idea." I was worried. Really worried. Riley could be dead. Soon it would be twenty-four hours since he'd called. The odds weren't good, unless he was holding out on whatever information they wanted.

I'd been puzzling about how he'd gotten away from his captors long enough to call me. But the way he'd sounded made me realize he couldn't escape for some reason. Were they watching him? Were they having him call me so they could track my whereabouts?

Good thing I'd borrowed a few things from the CIA when I left. My SIM card was untraceable. By anyone. I wasn't too worried that the yakuza would show up at the zoo for a standoff. But then, what would I use for a weapon if they did? I made a mental note to check the map to see where the lions were held. I wondered when they fed them.

We made our way to the bird exhibit. The girls weren't as impressed as they'd been with the pandas. There were a lot of colorful birds in Iowa, from goldfinches to cardinals to redwing blackbirds. Maybe they didn't think these exotic fowl measured up. I was wrong.

"Look at that!" Ava cried, pointing at a weird-looking bird.

"It's a king vulture," Maria said, reading off the display plaque. "From Central and South Americas."

The large beast had a strange-looking, lumpy orange flap over its beak and googly eyes that looked like the pupils would wiggle if you shook the bird. He seemed bald on top with a bright reddish neck. He didn't look real. He looked like a mad scientist's experiment gone horribly, horribly wrong.

"I love him!" Hannah said enthusiastically.

The other girls agreed and piled around the glass to profess their undying love to the bird of prey. The vulture stuck his head out and walked over to the glass in a lurching manner. He studied each and every girl up close before clacking his beak loudly. His wings flew open, and he displayed his white-and-black plumage. Clearly, he enjoyed the female attention as he began strutting back and forth in front of the window.

"I wish we could have one!" one of the girls said.

"He could be our troop mascot!" another replied.

I couldn't take my eyes off him. He looked like an animated cartoon character. One that, if he could talk, would sound like Tigger and spew nonsense about cumulonimbus clouds or the color yellow. The vulture cocked his head to one side, and I could swear his eyes went in separate directions.

The bird strutted over to the middle of the window, his head low enough to be halfway down the length of his body. As he reached the glass, he rose up, spreading his wings, and did a weird little dance. Pacing back and forth in front of us while flapping his huge wings, he clacked his beak and, well, flirted. Was he performing a mating dance?

Each of the girls squealed and clapped, and the googly-eyed vulture then slammed his forehead against the glass and held it there for a few seconds. He kept repeating this ritual, as if he was convinced he'd find his true love in a group of eight-year old girls. It made me a little nervous, and I wondered if I'd need restraining order against the infatuated fowl. It was a good thing he was behind glass.

"It's got to be the yakuza who have Riley," I said to Maria, my eyes still on the bird. "It's too coincidental that Riley name would turn up in the chatter at the Japanese Embassy."

Emily, the usually shy girl in my troop, shouted, "Let's name him Mr. Fancy Pants!" The other girls giggled. I looked at the king vulture. He didn't look like a fancy pants. He looked like a turkey drawn and colored by an insane toddler with an LSD problem. But oh, well—Mr. Fancy Pants seemed the popular choice.

Maria's voice brought me back to our conversation. "You might be right. If that's the case, where do we start?"

I thought about this for a moment. "I think the girls should tour some of the embassies for a taste of foreign culture, don't you?" I took out my cell and called Dad.

CHAPTER THREE

———

My father was on the Senate Committee on Foreign Relations. He played golf with the Japanese Ambassador, who was only too happy to give a tour to Dad's constituents. In fact, he was so enthusiastic, he scheduled us for a tour the next day, first thing in the morning. That gave us a little time to plan.

We invaded the cafeteria at the National Zoo at noon, commandeering a lunchroom to ourselves. I'd like to think it was because they thought we were adorable, but I'm sure the staff had wisely worked with groups of kids before and wanted to separate us from the other guests.

My girls were great. I adored them. Yes, they were loud and obnoxious, and yes, they totally had it in them to cause problems, but they were just curious kids. My feelings were a little wounded when they stuck us in a room by ourselves. The girls were eating fairly quietly—maybe they knew what was going on. It was small moments like this that made me love them all the more.

Maria and I talked to them about the animals they'd seen so far and what they wanted to see next. There was a fair split between the pandas and Mr. Fancy Pants. I enjoyed this lunch more than I'd enjoyed anything else on this trip. True, the food was overpriced and tasteless, but give kids french fries and chocolate milk, and they think they're dining at a palace.

Of course, the main topic of discussion was Mr. Fancy Pants. They were fixated on the bird. Nothing could sway them into talking about any other animal we'd seen. I thought it was a minor victory for birds of prey. I was kind of hoping they'd have stuffed king vultures in the gift shop. Take *that*, cuddly pandas!

"Mr. Fancy Pants is way cooler than the pandas!"

Caterina shouted in a rare outburst.

Hannah shook her head. "The pandas were totes cray adorbs!"

I was just about to ask what that meant when Inez stood up. "Fancy Pants can fly! And he eats dead things!"

Hmmm… It looked like Inez was going to win this one on the gross-out factor—something kids found extremely important for some reason.

"Why can't they both be awesome?" Lauren asked. She had a point. I was about to agree when one of the Kaitlins got in her face.

"No! Only one gets to be the best." She folded her little arms over her chest. "And my vote is for Fancy Pants."

"Why are we even voting on this?" Maria asked me.

"No idea," I said, shoving a french fry in my mouth. "But you have to admit, it is entertaining."

In a rare moment of diplomacy, Betty got between the two sides. "I think both are great. You guys should quit fighting."

The girls slowly nodded and lapsed into a discussion over which animals were more likely to be eaten by vultures.

"I was kind of rooting for the pandas, myself," Maria said in a low whisper.

"The vulture was cool though," I said back.

We continued eating and then cleaned up. When all the tables were empty, I went over the rules again. You can never state the rules too often with little kids. For some strange reason they forgot them five minutes after they heard them.

I also told the girls about our change of plans for the next day and visiting the embassy. They seemed to like the idea. Or maybe they just liked that we were going to see the hippos next. It was hard to tell sometimes.

Maria and I firmed up our own plans for the Japanese Embassy as we wrangled the kids through the rest of the zoo.

"You're sure your dad won't slip and introduce you as h daughter?" Maria asked as the four Kaitlins aped the gorillas we were watching. They were doing a pretty credible job. Thank God there was glass between us. One of the gorillas had a shifty look about him.

I nodded. "Positive. Dad can keep a secret. We're just a troop visiting from his home state. Are you sure you're covered?"

"I never worked in Asia. My beat was South America. No one will know me," Maria replied as she pulled Betty down from the enclosure fence. She was fast. A few more seconds and she'd have made it into the enclosure where the hippo was happily playing with a huge bouncy ball. Maybe becoming Scout leaders is a natural progression for spies and Maria would join the ranks when she retired.

We were all set. It was a good plan for being spur of the moment. Infiltrate the Japanese Embassy, unleash twelve girls in an invasion that would mostly likely rival Pearl Harbor, and do some snooping while they had their hands full. Was it a perfect plan? Not really. But it was the only plan we had.

"Jenkins is sending me the floor plan later today," Maria whispered as the girls lined up for bathroom breaks. We had to send them in one at a time. More than one and the echo from the giggling would break the sound barrier. Seriously—why did they build bathrooms with the acoustics of a 1950s cement bomb shelter? It was as if someone thought: *Hey, this room is too quiet. Let's make it impossible to hear yourself think if a bunch of kids were in here.*

"He's discreet? You trust him?" I asked. Zeb Jenkins was a douchebag. No field experience, but you'd never have known that if you met him. One word of wisdom—if an agent had been in the field, he wouldn't talk about it. If he did talk about it, he was admin and had never left his desk. There was no exception to this rule.

Jenkins worked in the research department. He was more like a gopher—fetching info instead of digging for it. But his dream was to be out there, under fire, in some third-world country. I knew that if he ever got that dream, he'd be A) wishing like hell he was back at his desk and B) dead within a few hours of his plane hitting the tarmac.

"He's fine!" Maria waved me off. "He owes me. Big-time."

My eyebrows went up. "Owes you?"

Maria nodded. "I let him do a little field mission in Canada. It was nothing—he just had to pass some papers on. But

I sent a few guys I knew to shadow him and make it seem dangerous. Jenkins almost had a heart attack. He loved it."

I stood corrected.

"What did he deliver?" I had to ask.

"My mother's car insurance policy payment. It was due.

I whistled. "Must be some policy."

Maria laughed. "He thought he was delivering secrets to the Canadian Mounties. It was hilarious. I backed him up in a black van with all the bells and whistles. Totally priceless."

"I didn't know your mom lived in Canada."

"Toronto. My parents didn't like the heat in Florida, so they moved a few years ago," Maria said.

The girls blissfully ignored us as they ran from one exhibit to another. I barely saw anything because all my focus was on the planning. We paused for a brief rest at the American bison exhibit.

"Mrs. Wrath!" Lauren shouted. In spite of my best efforts, the girls referred to me as Mrs. Wrath. No matter how many times I explained that I wasn't married, they still did it. I figured that little kids only see two kinds of people—*Mr.* or *Mrs.* And while the feminist side of me wanted to scream, there wasn't anything I could do about it.

"It says that buffalo can jump six feet in the air!" Lauren continued.

Betty frowned. "These are American bison, not buffalo.

"What's the difference?" Lauren shrugged.

Both girls turned to me. I had no idea.

"I don't know. But there must be some difference," I said. You had to be careful as a leader. Kids assumed you knew everything. Depending on what you were doing, it could be either a benefit or a problem.

"Mrs. Wrath?" Ava asked, "Can you jump six feet in the air?"

Hannah squealed. "That would be so cool!" The girl then proceeded to attempt a six-foot vertical jump. She did maybe one foot. For some reason, that inspired all the girls to start jumping. I didn't stop them because I knew it would wear them out.

"They look like deranged kangaroos," I said to Maria.

One of the Kaitlins jumped too hard to the left and fell

on the ground. She was up in seconds and back to behaving like a Mexican jumping bean. The other girls tried even harder, but no one seemed to get higher than a foot and a half.

"I could probably do it," Maria mused.

"Seriously?" I was pretty sure I didn't believe that.

She nodded. "I played varsity basketball in high school and college."

"I didn't know that!" I said. "Has it ever come in useful?"

Maria thought about this. "Once I had to escape by leaping over a four-foot-high fence made of broken bottles."

I nodded. "I had to hurdle a goat herd once. Fell flat on my face."

"Mongolia?" Maria asked. "Three years ago, right?"

My mouth dropped open. "How did you know?" I never told anyone about that, mainly because while I'd cleared the first two goats, I fell flat on my face after the third. The rest of them head-butted me out of the way. Not my proudest moment, but I did score some decent intel.

She waved me off. "Everyone at work knows. A yak herder filmed it on his iPhone and uploaded it to YouTube. It went viral."

It kind of felt like a wall had fallen on me. "You're joking. Please say you're joking."

Maria handed me her cell, where she'd already pulled it up. I grimaced as I watched myself fall facedown into a mud puddle. The caption read: *Antics of a goat-jumping idiot.* Fantastic.

"Maybe I should show the girls." Maria took the phone back and walked over to Inez, who'd basically given up on jumping and was filming the other girls.

I pulled something out of my pocket and aimed it at her. "Don't you dare. I'll tase you!"

Maria laughed and shoved the cell into her pocket. "I give up. Please don't smear ChapStick on me."

Dammit. She called my bluff. But it worked, didn't it? Mental note: *Once we rescue Riley, have him make me a lip-balm Taser.*

A loud *snort* broke the silence, and we all turned to see the two bison standing as close to us as they could. The girls stopped jumping and swarmed the glass. One bison looked at the other and, without any warm up or trampoline, promptly jumped three feet up in the air. The other bison dropped the mic by pooping. The girls cheered enthusiastically as both animals walked away. I silently prayed that the girls wouldn't try that next because I was pretty sure we'd get thrown out for something like that.

After a few hours of running around, the girls still hadn't lost any steam, but I was exhausted. A few years ago I could've run a mile through the desert and still had energy to engage in hand-to-hand combat. Unfortunately, retirement had made me a bit soft. Maybe I'd join a gym when I got back home.

DC was a beast in the summer. Between the super-high humidity and the ginormous crowds of tourists, it was more like Hell instead of a relaxing vacation. I understood the allure of visiting the nation's capital. And to be honest, it was actually one of the cleanest, nicest capitals. Spend a week in Beirut or Lagos and you'd think DC is a mythical spa with sparkly unicorns.

I was wiped. We needed to cool off. I felt like someone had dumped a wet, wool blanket over my head in the middle of hay fever season. The hotel pool was out, so what were we left with?

"Thanks, Mom," I whispered as I released my troop into my parents' backyard and pool area.

"Girls! Let's thank Mrs. Czrygy for letting us use her pool!" I shouted, careful only to shake my mother's hand so as not to tip the kids off as to who this really was. They'd be meeting my father—their senator—in the morning. As far as they knew, I was just some boring adult who weirdly had awesome connections. I wanted to keep things that way.

I needn't have bothered. The girls started stripping as they ran, shouting their gratitude while leaving a trail of clothing across my parents' immaculate living room as they ran to the guestroom to change into swimsuits. They emerged seconds later and hit the French doors to the outdoor pool. I could already hear them splashing.

"I called the neighbor boy—the Irish Ambassador's son—to lifeguard," Mom said softly. "They're in good hands."

I looked toward the door. "It's not them I'm worried

about. How much do you like the Irish Ambassador?"

Maria winked and made her way to the pool to check things out. I let out an audible sigh.

"It's so good to see you, honey!" Mom wrapped her arms around me.

I hugged her back then pulled away, looking around to make sure no one had seen us. Judith Merrygold Wrath Czrygy was amazing. So amazing that I took my new name from her middle and maiden names. Mom was everything I wasn't. Where I was casual, she was formal. Even lounging around the house she was dressed up, wearing a sun dress with sandals. Her hair was perfect and her makeup flawless. She smelled lightly of lavender and roses. Had all of her life, really. Yet I'd never seen a perfume bottle in the house.

"Thanks for having us over." I slumped into a chair, and within seconds, she'd brought me a sweet tea.

"I heard about the unfortunate experience at the hotel," Mom said with a slight Southern accent. She'd never had that until they moved here. Mom just acclimated to any area very easily, adopting their culture, habits, and accents in a short period of time. Like her, I was also a mimic. It was probably what made me a good spy.

"How did you hear about that?" Between Maria and Mom I wondered if there'd been a story in *The Washington Post*: "Iowa Scouts Destroy Hotel Pool—25 Dead. Terrorists Suspected."

"It was all over the country club, darling!" She smiled, and I knew that she wasn't worried about the girls here. Just how good was the Irish Ambassador's son? Did he have crowd-control training? Riot gear?

"Your father told me about tomorrow," she said quietly. "Are you sure about this?"

I explained the whole story—about Riley's phone call and Maria's assistance. Mom nodded appropriately.

"I always liked Riley," she said when I finished. "I never trusted him, but I liked him."

"He's not dead, Mom. At least, I don't think he's dead." I was a little creeped out by her using past tense.

Mother straightened a lock of honey gold hair that wasn't

even out of place. I could never remember my mother in a state of distress or undress. Her thick, blonde hair was always silky shiny and perfect. Mine was curly, dull, and unruly. I'd have to ask her what she used. Maybe it wasn't bad genetics—just bad hair products.

"So tell me about Rex and Philby." She smiled.

Mom didn't know much about Rex, and she'd never met him. She seemed overly happy that I had a boyfriend in a way that made me itch. I couldn't remember ever bringing a boy home to meet the parents. I hadn't dated at all in high school and barely in college.

Of course, they'd met Riley on a few occasions. Everyone had been polite, but there had been an undercurrent I couldn't put my finger on until Mom mentioned it just now. I knew they'd like Rex. He was far more approachable and seemed like a regular guy. The two men also looked completely different. Rex's short, dark hair and quiet demeanor were a complete contrast to Riley's outgoing California style. Riley had worked hard to cultivate that look. Most people would have been shocked to know he grew up in a tiny town in Indiana.

Philby was my cat. She looked like Hitler. I mention that again because it's something that still surprises me every time I see her. Fortunately, it was just her appearance that matched— she showed no sign of megalomaniacal despotic tendencies. Well, not yet…

My cell rang. What weirdly unbelievable timing.

"Hi, Rex," I said as he grinned back at me on FaceTime. That man could really make me melt in all the right places.

"Hey, Merry." He held up a huge cat that looked dubiously at me. "Philby says hi."

Philby belched loudly then let out an annoyed *meooooooooow*. Rex set him down.

I introduced my boyfriend to Mom, and the two of them exchanged the usual small talk. It was a strange way to introduce Rex to my parents but oh well. When you were a spy, you took these opportunities as you got them. When I thought of the men I'd dated in the field, Rex was certainly an acceptable improvement.

Not that I'd dated a lot when on assignment. There were

fake dates and real ones. The fake dates were usually developed to infiltrate a state dinner or something like that. I'd dated Riley briefly. And there'd been one or two guys after that, but none of them took. Mostly because you move around a lot when you're an operative. You might spend a month in India then a couple of weeks in Spain. Trying to make a relationship work under those conditions is impossible.

So, I had the one or two nights out, complete with texting and phone calls. It always ended awkwardly with one of the two people leaving for somewhere else. I never took dating seriously then for that very reason. Well, except for Riley—but even that had a bad ending.

Dating Rex was completely different. It didn't help that our relationship started with lies about who I was. Fortunately, he accepted me once he knew the truth, and things had gotten kind of serious. Over time, I let my guard down and started to enjoy being with someone. Besides, he lived across the street, and we both owned our houses. Neither of us was going anywhere else anytime soon. Even though it took me a while to get used to, I liked that.

"Kittens!" Mom clapped her hands with glee as three little faces crowded onto the screen. Philby had had kittens recently—one white, one black, and one that looked like Elvis with little black sideburns on her white face. She was definitely the 1970s Elvis with her little potbelly.

"Oh, you have to let me have one," Mom pleaded.

"Really?" I asked. "Since when did you like cats?" We'd never had so much as a dust bunny when I was growing up. I had assumed Mom hated animals. I guessed I was wrong, unless she was going to sacrifice it to Satan. Hmmm… I should have probably had Maria run a background check.

"I've always loved cats. But your father doesn't. So I'll take one. Can I have the black one?"

What? Was there trouble between my parents? Why else would she want something that would drive Dad nuts? I'd have to interrogate her later.

"Okay. Once they're weaned you can have him," I said, taking the phone back. "Rex?"

The cat and her kittens disappeared, and my beyond-handsome-and-amazing boyfriend popped back on the screen. My stomach felt light, and I could feel my cheeks warming up. He really was incredible. I wished he were here with me. I didn' know if he could handle the girls, but he might have had some ideas on Riley. Or maybe he could just talk me out of dealing with it altogether. It would've been nice to have someone tell me to hand it over to the CIA and leave it alone.

"I've got to go. But I'll call you tonight, okay?" I hated cutting him off, but I had to check on the girls. In all likelihood, they were now holding Maria and the lifeguard captive.

"Alright," Rex said with a smile. "And you can fill me i then on how your troop got kicked out of the hotel pool." He hung up before I could ask him anything. Did everyone know about that? I'd have to check the internet later to see if one of th girls posted a video. Rex was a good detective, but I couldn't figure out how the intel got to Iowa so quickly.

In a way, I was lucky my boyfriend didn't give me a har time about it. He didn't have any qualms about my past—well, except for the inconvenience of having dead guys showing up o my doorstep. Somehow though, I knew he wouldn't be happy that Riley had asked me for help. Rex would consider that unprofessional. He'd be right, of course, but civilians didn't really understand how spies operated. We had few friends and were very loyal to our colleagues because in the field that's all we had.

I had very strong feelings for Rex too. We'd been datin for almost a year now, and it was going well, except that it was going slowly. Not that I'm in a hurry to take the step to the next level—we dated, and he was cat-sitting, but we maintained our separate residences, even if they were only across the street.

Something inside me wanted to take this further. Maybe it was because of years in the field, on the road, with relationships that lasted as long as Minute Rice. Maybe I was ready for a full-blown, serious commitment. Not marriage. I wasn't quite ready for that. And I didn't mean moving in together. There was no way I was ready for that.

Wait… So what did I mean exactly? We saw each other regularly and were monogamous. He sent me cards and flowers He even introduced me to the guys at work as his girlfriend. So why did I feel like something was missing? Kind of like we'd skipped a step in the *Relationship Handbook*. Was there a *Relationship Handbook*? That would come in handy. I'd have to look that up when I got home. I wished Kelly, my best friend and co-leader, were here. She'd know what to do.

I shook my head to clear it. Kelly wasn't here, and I needed to focus on the problems I was dealing with right now—from Riley going missing to a rogue Scout troop. I could figure it all out on my own, right? I made my way to Mom and Dad's pool, hoping it was still full of water.

The Irish Ambassador's son was named Liam. And he was handling things very well, mainly because he was extremely handsome, and the girls were locked in his thrall. The kid was maybe twenty and had that athletic lifeguard body. Dark auburn hair framed a pair of bright green eyes. His accent was soft…just enough of a brogue that you could still understand him. To be honest, I was kind of hypnotized too.

"What's going on here?" I whispered to Maria as I pulled up a chaise lounge. All twelve girls were sitting at the edge of the pool while the attractive young man spoke to them in a soft, lyrical voice.

"He's telling them some folklore story about the water fairies. The girls haven't moved since he started speaking." I noticed that Maria said all of this without taking her eyes off of Liam. He was good.

I listened for a moment. "Can he spend the rest of the trip with us?"

Maria's eyes glinted. "I wouldn't mind that at all. But I doubt it."

I decided to slip Liam a hundred bucks when this was over. Maybe two hundred. He was definitely worth it. I wondered if he knew hypnosis.

My cell buzzed just as Liam was getting to the good part. I looked at my phone and froze.

"Maria!" I whispered.

She looked irritated that she had to take her eyes off of our Irish storyteller. "What is it?"

I got up and motioned for her to join me. We stepped away from the girls before I told her.

"It's Riley. He's calling."

CHAPTER FOUR

––––––

"Riley?" I asked as Maria and I slipped into the house. I put the phone on speaker and set it to record the call.

"Wrath…" Riley's voice was choppy, and there was a lot of static. "Help me… can't… much longer…" It was a terrible connection for a local call, which didn't make much sense.

"Where are you?" I asked. "What do you want me to do?"

"Ito… Ito…" His voice faded in and out. "They know… Get help… Maria…" The call quality was as rough as if I'd been in the Amazon. How could that be?

Maria's eyes grew wide. "I'm here, Riley! How can we help you?"

"Maria? It's… I… You have to…" Riley asked as the call ended abruptly.

"Do you think they caught him calling?" I asked as I stared at the phone. If they did, they'd know it was me. Did they know I was in DC? Would they try to find me? Were the girls in danger?

"I know what you're thinking," Maria said.

Wow. Could she read my mind? Maybe I should have her start working on the girls…starting with Betty. I'd noticed her studying my parents' pool filter system. We'd have to keep an eye on her.

"Don't panic. I don't think they've made a connection to you or we'd have noticed being followed," Maria said.

"Maybe I should send the girls home," I replied. "I can't let anything happen to them."

She shook her head. "I'm sure they'll be fine."

"What are you talking about?" I asked. "We're using

them as cover tomorrow! We'll all be on Japanese soil. There's nothing we can do if they decide to hold us hostage."

Maria frowned. "And create an international incident? No, they wouldn't risk that."

"But you found chatter about Riley at the embassy." Sh was making sense, but in this business, you had to play devil's advocate to see both sides.

She shook her head. "Japan is an ally. If someone on th inside is responsible for taking Riley, they're working alone. I doubt they have the government's backing."

Maria was right. The Japanese government was no fan (the yakuza. And kidnapping a bunch of little girls wasn't exactl in its wheelhouse. Besides, holding my troop hostage would on be a nightmare for them in ways they could never imagine.

I sent the recording of the conversation to her cell. "Is there someone you know who can analyze this?"

Maria nodded. "I'll send it to Abdul."

"Cookie Abdul? Why would you send it to him?" Abdu Jones had bought tons of cookies from my troop last winter. He wasn't a very good spy. In fact, he was pretty awful at it. The man actually showed up in a disguise with a fake name to buy cookies. Who doesn't want anyone to know they like cookies?

"Because he'd do it for more cookies." Maria grinned. "And his sister works in IT. Could you get your hands on more peanut butter sandwich cookies?"

"I guess so," I mumbled. "Okay, send it off." Abdul had better not blow this.

"Pizza!" Mom announced as she walked into the room with six huge boxes. She plunked them down on the breakfast bar and opened them. My stomach rumbled. I never could resist pizza, especially pepperoni. If I could eat pizza for each meal, I would.

After swiping steaming, cheesy wedges from the box, Maria and I followed Mom out to the pool and set up the food a the girls played quietly in the water.

Wait, what? The girls were swimming and splashing bu calmly. Every few moments, they'd turn their heads toward Liar and giggle. He'd wave back, and they'd swoon. Oh yes. Two hundred dollars at least. I could afford it. My forced retirement brought me a very handsome payout. I wondered briefly if I could export Liam to Iowa for, like, forever.

"Cannonball!" A roar came from the French doors, and Senator Michael Czrygy, clad only in swim trunks, ran out onto the deck and jumped into the pool, causing a tsunami of water and squealing girls.

"Dad's home," Mom whispered. Did I detect a note of sarcasm? What was going on with my folks? Well, whatever it was would have to wait. I did not need one more problem on this trip.

"I think you're right," Dad said an hour later as Maria and I sat in his den. The girls were dried off, dressed, and watching a movie with Liam and Mom.

"The ambassador wouldn't have anything to do with organized crime. Someone else must be doing this without his knowledge. But I still don't think we should involve him. We'll just stick to the plan tomorrow."

Maria nodded. "I'll go check on the girls so you two can have a little time together." She smiled at Dad as she let herself out. "Nice to meet you, Senator."

I hugged my father. "Thanks for helping out, Dad. I really appreciate it."

"Well, kiddo, anything I can do to help, just let me know."

Michael Czrygy was every inch as handsome as his wife was beautiful. Sandy brown hair with green eyes, he was a force to be reckoned with politically. His demeanor was a bit different from Mom's. While he could terrify his enemies on Capitol Hill, he was really a big softie with a great sense of humor. They matched each other perfectly. If something was wrong, I couldn't for the life of me figure out what it was.

"I'm sorry to drag you into this," I said honestly.

"Nonsense. It'll be fun!" Dad slapped his hand on his desk, making me jump.

"Is everything alright with you and Mom?" I asked.

He frowned. "What do you mean?" I couldn't help noticing his eyes avoiding mine.

"That you didn't answer 'no' to that question." I folded my arms over my chest.

"Everything's fine. Don't worry about us." He gave me a look that I recognized as *this conversation is over.*

But he'd said, "Don't worry about us," which meant something was wrong between my parents.

"I hear Mom got to meet Rex and the cats," Dad said. "She likes him."

"And you're getting one of the kittens," I added, trying to bring the conversation back around to the issue of marital discontent.

Dad frowned. "So I hear. Oh, well. Your Mom spends a lot of time alone here in this big house. I don't blame her. I just wish she'd asked for a dog."

"There's still time left for you to change her mind. The kittens aren't weaned."

My father ran his hands through his hair as he thought about this. "No, that's okay. Let her have it."

I studied my dad. Throughout my life as an only child, I'd never seen my parents disagree, let alone argue. They always seemed happy. The perfect couple. My mother never said anything derogatory about Dad and vice versa. In fact, they were far more likely to team up on me instead of each other.

Dad wasn't a senator when I was a kid. He was an attorney who worked long hours but still found time to spend with Mom and me. My mother was the perfect stay-at-home parent—the envy of the PTA and adored by everyone who met her. We took the usual family vacations a few times a year and always had a good time.

Most only children would tell you they wished they'd had siblings to commiserate with, but I didn't. This didn't mean my parents spoiled me at all. I had to have a part-time job, get good grades, and behave responsibly. If I screwed up, I got in trouble, and if I did well, I was praised. I couldn't remember any time when I'd asked my parents for a sister or brother.

My parents didn't demand that I go to an Ivy League school or major in law or medicine. They thought it was great when I said I wanted to go to the University of Iowa and major in International Studies. When I was recruited by the CIA, they didn't mind that either. But that was probably because they'd moved to Des Moines and Dad was launching his political campaign.

Huh. I guess I had a pretty idyllic childhood. There was nothing I could complain about. Was I being too sensitive in thinking something was wrong here? That could be it. I didn't see my folks often—just on holidays. Could be I was looking for something that wasn't there. I decided to back down…for now. I had other problems—twelve who were sitting a few doors down the hall.

We chatted for about half an hour more about nothing really before Mom popped her head into the doorway to say the girls were falling asleep. I felt a little sad to be leaving. For a few hours I'd had other adults to help with the girls. Evelyn Trout came to mind. She hadn't joined us today since Maria was around. The woman was probably getting a two-hundred-dollar pedicure at one of the spas near the hotel. Let her have her fun. When I needed her, she'd better be there.

Liam helped Maria and me get the girls loaded into our van. I slipped him three hundred dollars and asked if he'd be available any other time this week. He said he would be and thanked me before walking back to the Irish Embassy just a couple of doors down.

Back at the room, Mrs. Trout appeared to help get the kids to bed. She didn't look too happy when I told her we'd need her the next morning for the tour of the Japanese Embassy, but she didn't complain (something that made me immediately suspicious). Maria and I had decided that we'd confuse the embassy officials with three adults. In their minds, when the tour started, they'd see two, and in the chaos that would no doubt ensue, wouldn't even realize there'd been three originally. Maria and Evelyn would stay with the girls while I slipped away to do a little snooping. Besides, I was the only one who could speak and read Japanese. That made me the main spy for this little trip.

As I climbed onto the couch and pulled up the blanket, I wondered if I was doing the right thing. Female spies are the worst at second-guessing themselves. Male spies never seemed to have that problem. Why was that? They just blustered through their assignments and blew off the mistakes. I'd have to ask Maria if she'd had the same experience. Most likely, her answer would be yes. I closed my eyes and quickly fell asleep.

I ran through the hall to the staircase, ignoring the shouts behind me. Maybe I should've identified myself. Chances were that running away was foolish. After all, Riley was my handler. I didn't know he had a British connection here, but I wasn't surprised. As a field operative, I was only told the details of my assignment. Handlers usually had two or three agents working for them at any one time.

I took the steps two at a time, landing hard on the ground floor. The man who'd let me in attempted to stop me, but I clotheslined him with my arm as he came at me, and he fell to the floor. I jumped over him and was in the alley in seconds.

Maybe the woman upstairs was another agent of Riley's. If so, I might have some explaining to do tomorrow. I raced into the street and into the first cab I found. Barking out an address close to my safe house (but not directly there—that would be stupid), I slid down in the seat so anyone following me wouldn't see.

Get a grip! What are you doing? The question stumbled around in my head, looking for purchase on my slippery brain. Why would I even think about following Riley?

Oh yeah, I'm paranoid. That's it. If you're a good spy, then you're properly paranoid. That sounded confusing, but it was a legit thing. Properly paranoid fell just between "whatever" and "oh my God, I'm gonna die."

It always bugged me how James Bond walked around, undisguised, dropping his real name everywhere he went. The man never even attempted a disguise. Real spies didn't do that. Real spies got killed for that. Maybe I should go around saying my name is James Bond.

The taxi swerved through traffic, and after several turns, I felt it was safe to sit up in my seat. My phone buzzed with a text message that read Finn, it's Riley. Can I come over?

Not a good time, *I texted back before stuffing my phone in my pocket. It wasn't unusual for him to request this—we'd actually started dating, and it was going well up until a week ago when I'd found him with another woman. The thought made me cringe. I shoved it aside.*

Was that why I was following him? Oh, for crying out loud! I was jealous! And when I got a text from a burner phone earlier this evening, giving me only the address I was just at and saying Riley would be there, I'd briefly thought it was someone tipping me off to the other woman.

Damn. I had it bad. I tried to tell myself I wasn't that into Riley. That it was just a fling. Agents often did that under threat of danger to release some steam. And I knew, going into this, that Riley had lots of women in his contacts list. I'd been hearing whispers around the Agency for years.

But Riley was hard to resist. When he looked at you with those blue eyes and smiled, it was like you were the only person in the room. He had charm by the boatload. Too much charm.

My cell buzzed, and I pulled it out.

Please? *Riley texted.*

No, *I replied as the taxi pulled up to the address I'd given. I slipped him a huge tip, putting my finger to my lips. The driver nodded and smiled before driving away. I walked the remaining five blocks to my rooms and leaned heavily against the door when I got inside.*

Flicking on the lights, I spotted something that made me pull my gun and go into overdrive. There, on the table, was a piece of stationary from the Tokyo Grand Hotel. Written on it was a phone number. And it hadn't been there when I left...

My eyes flew open. I'd forgotten all about that memory. Hazy fragments from my first dream were hard to remember, but this one was clear as day.

Of course I was dreaming about Riley. He was the biggest thing on my mind right now. I guess I'd forgotten how much our little fling had hurt me. I pulled the blanket up to my chin and closed my eyes. None of this mattered anymore. I'd resolve my personal issues with Riley when I found him. Obsessing about it wouldn't do any good. Slowly and uneasily, I willed myself back to sleep.

I got up early the next morning and ran out to get donuts because every secret mission should start with donuts. There is no exception to this rule.

An idea had sprouted once I'd gone back to sleep (as some of the best ideas in espionage do), and I'd decided the best way to go unnoticed was to start out as a member of my dad's staff. It would be easy for me to slip out under the pretense of taking or making phone calls, and in a suit, I wouldn't get notice walking the halls of the embassy. Mom still had a few of my suits, and I picked one up before heading back to the hotel—making it back to the girls with only a few donuts eaten. A personal best for me. Seriously—I loved donuts.

It had been a while since I'd worn heels. I borrowed a pair of Mom's kitten heels but still felt a little unsteady. At least the suit still fit—which surprised me, considering I'd developed serious Oreo addiction since my retirement. To complete the disguise, I'd bought a pair of thick-framed glasses with clear lenses and borrowed a suitable tote bag from Mom.

Maria helped me with makeup and hair—it had been a long time since I'd had to worry about that. As the dazed girls woke up and wandered into the main room, they stared at me.

"Why are you dressed like that, Mrs. Wrath?" Inez asked.

"We're going to play a little prank," I said. "We could only get tickets for two adults to go with you, so I'm going to pretend like I'm on the Senator's staff. Doesn't that sound fun?"

"That makes sense," Inez said with a nod.

"Make sure you keep a low profile," Betty advised.

"You don't want to blow your cover," Lauren added.

I grinned at Maria. My little girls were growing up and participating in missions with me. To say I was proud would be an understatement.

The girls nodded seriously. They seemed to like playing along, even though they really had no idea what we were doing. just had to make sure they kept our little secret to themselves.

Maria stuffed a notepad and pen into my bag, and Evelyn Trout just nodded in distracted agreement. She had a so disposition and told me she was blowing off a meeting with a personal life coach for this. What was a personal life coach? Maybe I needed one. As long as they didn't demand I change m eating habits, it was possible it might work out.

As for Evelyn, I'd already decided that if she caused a problem, I was taking her out. The jury was still out on whether meant *lethally* or not. Most likely I wouldn't kill her. It was nev a good idea to "off" one of your Girl Scouts' moms. That could come back to haunt me.

One by one, we all piled into the van and drove to my parents' house. They lived on Embassy Row, so we could walk to the Japanese Embassy from there. My father met us out front, and the girls gave him a group hug. His cannonball into the pool the day before had really won him some votes.

"The Senator is doing a great job," Maria whispered as we walked. I agreed. Dad was giving the girls the grand tour of the neighborhood, and they seemed to hang on his every word. My father managed to inform the girls while speaking on their level. How many men knew how little girls thought? Evelyn walked sulkily but kept up. That was something at least.

My heels were killing me before we even hit the gate to the Japanese Embassy. I needed to make this look good, or they'd see through it. No one would believe that a senator's aide wasn't accustomed to wearing painful shoes twenty-four seven. I'd just have to work through the pain. Like I did that one time, running through the streets of Sarajevo after a cocktail party exploded. And I was not exaggerating. The party literally exploded. Someone had rigged the furnace to blow.

"Senator Czrygy!" A tall, thin, Japanese man in a suit came toward us with his arms open.

"Mr. Ambassador!" Dad said, clasping the man's hand warmly. "Allow me to introduce Girl Scout Troop 0222, from my home state of Iowa!"

The girls curtseyed. Where had they learned that? They were all wearing neon yellow T-shirts with their troop number on them. All we needed to do if a girl got lost was turn out the lights, and they'd glow.

"These are their leaders, Ms. Santiago and Mrs. Trout." Dad indicated Maria's code name and Evelyn. "And this is my personal assistant, Ms. Mathers. I hope you don't mind me adding her, but she's dealing with some sensitive issues for me, and I need to have her nearby. I do apologize for the inconvenience."

The ambassador smiled warmly at me. "Not a problem, Mike. It is nice to meet all of you!"

"Thank you, Isas. Again, I appreciate this. Have to show off now and then for my constituency."

I liked Ambassador Isas Nakano instantly and felt more

than a little guilty for the deception. In my former line of work, was very good at summing up someone quickly. The ambassador struck me as sincere and open. I just hoped I could find the connection to Riley's distress call without disrupting things too much. With any luck, this place would be clean and clear of yakuza, and we wouldn't have to involve him again.

"Thank you," I said with a small bow.

I stifled a grin as my dad leaned toward the man and said softly, "She's actually a distant cousin. Not very bright, I'm afraid. But very good at organization."

The ambassador nodded knowingly. "I have two of my wife's nephews here. Idiots."

The idea was to make the embassy personnel think I was harmless, so if I wandered into the wrong area, they'd gently correct me like I was dim-witted. It was my dad's idea. It was just a little disturbing to see his lie come so easily to him.

The ambassador launched into welcoming the girls, charming them with a few jokes. Evelyn actually stopped grumbling long enough to smile. The people at the Japanese Embassy were known to be warm and amazing hosts. And the ambassador was no exception as he handed each girl a traditional, hand-painted fan.

He even had one for Maria and the now blushing and giggling Evelyn. I tried really hard not to roll my eyes. Was she…? Oh, my God. She was flirting with him. Yeesh. I wondered what Mr. Trout, whoever he was, would think about that.

The tour commenced, and as the girls followed their guide, Dad pulled me aside and said a bit loudly, "Mathers—can you call the office to let them know I'll be unavailable for the next hour? And see if there are any messages for me."

I nodded and fumbled for my phone, heading out of the main lobby area as Dad and the others went the other way.

"Allow me to show you to a private office?" A neatly dressed, severe young woman asked.

"Oh! Thank you!" I gushed. "That would be wonderful!" I gaped openly at the artwork, the décor, and everything else as I followed her down a hallway and into a small conference room. Acting as an idiot was no real reach for me.

"You have such a beautiful…um…embassy!" I held out my hand before she left me. "I'm Evelyn Mathers." I hoped it wouldn't get back to Evelyn Trout that I was using her name. Okay, so I kind of hoped it did.

The woman gave me a tight smile and a little bow. "I'm Ms. Ito, if you need anything more."

Ito? Now that was interesting. Not that it was an uncommon name, but I had to wonder what the odds were that she was connected somehow to Midori Ito, the dead yakuza leader who'd made an unfortunate appearance as a murdered body in my kitchen last year.

Ms. Ito closed the door behind her as she left, and I put my bag on the table and sat down. I noted a camera in the corner but couldn't tell if it was for teleconferencing or spying. There were no two-way mirrors or anything else remotely obvious. One thing about the Japanese government—they had the best tech ever. Chances were the stuff was all there—I just wouldn't be able to see it.

I had to be careful. Dad's reputation was on the line, and he could be brought up on charges of espionage, and I didn't want to blow that. I set my cell phone on the table in front of me and touched the screen. Maria had uploaded a top secret Agency app that would detect hidden surveillance systems. I'd worried that she could get in serious trouble if found out, but she insisted. According to the app, there weren't any secret cameras. Huh. I didn't expect that.

The Japanese Government had no tolerance for the yakuza—tackling them very much in the same way we go after the mafia in this country. However, it was possible that the Japanese version of the CIA, the Public Security Intelligence Agency, had an office in the embassy, and like our spy network, you never really knew what they were involved in. And it was also possible that there might be a rogue employee or two who had connections to the crime syndicate. That was what I was counting on. Riley's name came up here, so there must've been some connection.

I dialed my cell and listened. But instead of getting Dad's messages, I was listening on the frequency the CIA does when spying on embassies, cell lines, etc. Once again, I'd warned

Maria that me using this technology could get her fired. Once again, she'd insisted that I use it. Fortunately, the CIA had an app for that. There was the usual stuff: interoffice gossip, personal calls to family, business calls, but nothing stood out. I hung on the line for a few minutes more, pretending to take notes on a legal pad.

After a little longer, I put everything but the phone away and got to my feet. What did I expect, really? Did I think they'd just walk Riley over to me and say, "We give up. Here's your American. Sorry about that"? Time to do things the old-fashioned way. I opened the door and stepped out into the hallway, looking both ways in the pretense that I was lost.

While chewing on my fingernail, I pointed in the opposite direction that I'd come in, gave a quick nod to look like I'd made a decision, and trotted off down the hallway. The embassy had two buildings—the main center, where I was, and an auxiliary building that served as overflow offices as the embassy had expanded in the latter part of the last century.

There was no way I could explain finding myself accidentally in the other building, so I just had to deal with the main embassy. Under the pretense of staring at my phone, I hit another app that should locate Riley's cell phone, using the same technology Apple does for the Find My iPhone app. I had to be careful using the Agency's tech toys. I wasn't totally sure, but if they found out, I'd probably never be able to own a cell phone again.

To my surprise, no one was around. Nobody intercepted me. Maybe they bought the story that I was a moron. It seemed little suspicious, but for now, I just had to go with it. What choice did I have? Besides, I never turned down an opportunity. Yeah, it could've been a trap, but it was possible that the security guards were off that day…or the administrative assistant was too busy playing solitaire… Whatever the excuse was, I'd have to run with it.

I passed office after office, but no one looked up from his desk. It was eerie…odd. Maybe they were just very trusting, or maybe the security was lax. Whatever it was, I kept walking down hallway after hallway, pretending to look lost.

A blip showed up on my cell phone, and my heart

jumped. Was it Riley's phone? Maria had warned me that the app might not be one hundred percent accurate. Not that she had to. A lot of the technology developed by the Agency had a moderate success rate—usually because it was developed quickly to solve a problem and was needed in the field before anyone did enough testing.

I couldn't get my hopes up. Besides, it seemed too quiet for a place that could be holding hostages. There wasn't so much as a hint of sound. I could see people typing but heard no clicking. Maybe they were all ninjas. That would totally suck.

Granted, the floors were carpeted, and the atmosphere was subdued, but there should've been some noise, right? Maybe they were trying to achieve a peaceful atmosphere, but I was getting a little panicked by the complete lack of sounds. Something seemed really off. Maybe the people I saw in the offices were holograms. That would be cool. No, wait. That would also suck. It would mean the real people were somewhere else. Someplace I didn't know about, watching me.

I hit a dead end a few seconds later when the hallway ended. I'd have to go back. Had I cleared half of the first floor already? I looked at the phone. The blip was gone. I hit the app a couple of times, but it didn't reappear.

Maybe it wasn't really there to begin with. But I had to keep trying. This was our one chance to find Riley if he was in the building. It was highly unlikely that Dad, even with his skills, could arrange another meeting without raising suspicion.

The basement. There had to be a basement. My years of experience in the field and every spy movie ever made proved that each and every lair had a creepy, torture-y basement. That was where Riley would be.

Screw wandering around slowly. I ran to the end of the hall to the large *Exit* sign and studied the door for a second before quietly pushing it open. You couldn't be too careful. Door alarms made up for about sixty-five percent of spy captures. Seemed kind of like a stupid mistake, but when you were on the run from people with guns, you didn't necessarily stop to read warnings on exits.

I managed to get through unnoticed and slowly closed the door behind me. I was in a cinder block stairwell—your generic government building type. Some things really were universal. Without wasting a second, I headed down the staircas on the right. That's when my cell vibrated. The blip was back. Riley's phone was sending a signal, and I was back in business. was also running out of time. If she were worth her salt, Ms. Ito would certainly have noticed I wasn't where I was supposed to be. And she didn't seem to be the type I could bribe with Girl Scout Cookies.

Following the stairs down two more flights, I finally hit the dead end I was searching for. This door had no sign. Nothin to indicate where I was. Gingerly, I swept my fingers around th edges, trying to find a trigger for an alarm. Nothing. I turned the handle. Damn. It was locked. Of course it was. What did I expe from an evil lair?

I paused for a second to think. It was a keyhole lock, an that shouldn't be a problem—if I'd brought a lock pick kit with me. Which I hadn't. Because I didn't think I'd need it for anything on a fun trip with my Girl Scouts. I'd ignored the sacre spy mantra (which was, ironically, shared by the Girl Scouts) of "Be Prepared."

I looked over my suit. Nothing there. Even the *Visitor* badge had nothing—it was a magnet—which was kind of nice because it didn't put a hole in my suit—but then not so nice because last time I checked, you couldn't pick a lock with a round magnet.

Meanwhile, I was on the clock. I'd have to get back soo before they sent people out to find me. There was no way I was going to destroy Dad's career by getting caught. Dropping my bag to the floor, I tore through it, looking for anything I could use when it hit me.

My pen. I stripped it in seconds and pulled the coiled spring out, straightening the coils as best I could. Using the inkwell, I jabbed both items into the lock and began furiously twisting and turning.

It felt like I was in a black hole, underwater. Beads of sweat broke out on my forehead, but I ignored them. If I didn't get inside, I'd be forced to come back here in the middle of the night, and even though I could manage to get away while the girls were asleep, I wasn't certain I'd get past security. Spy-craft skills would get rusty if you didn't use them.

Click.

I pressed the handle as soon as I heard it, and the door opened. But now I had a different problem. It was pitch dark. I dropped my tote bag and used it as a door jam. I'd get a little light from there. Flicking my thumb across the surface of my cell turned it into a flashlight. Time was running out. I had to move forward now.

There was no musty smell. No smell of anything. It had to be the cleanest embassy/evil lair basement in the universe. In fact, there wasn't anything in there. No boxes of old records…no dusty filing cabinets, not even a chair. I crept forward, lighting the way as I went but found nothing. It was just a huge, dark, empty room.

Moving faster, I raced through to the other end. The room had to be about the half the length of a football field, and it took a few moments…moments I didn't have. Nothing. I started swinging my cell phone wider, casting a broader sweep, but the light wasn't powerful enough. In a few minutes, I'd have to get back upstairs, or we'd be busted for sure.

I took off my shoes and darted back and forth from one end of the room to the other in a zigzag manner, in a final attempt to find something…anything. And that's when I spotted it. A small, black pouch lying against the right sidewall. Without stopping, I swept it up and raced for the door. After closing it quietly behind me and grabbing my tote, I threw the pouch inside and took the stairs two at a time.

As I opened the door to the main floor and entered, I slipped back into my shoes and straightened my clothes, just managing to catch my breath before I heard a sound.

"You must be lost." The stern voice of Ms. Ito spoke behind me. I whirled around.

"Oh thank goodness someone found me!" I breathed. "It's so quiet here that I didn't want to knock on any office doors and bother anyone!"

The woman nodded, but her eyes were skeptical. "We maintain a simple, peaceful working environment here. Let me help you find your group."

My group! How was it possible that they were in the

same building with me? I should've been hearing them all along. Quiet was bad as far as they were concerned. I followed, hot on Ms. Ito's heels as we turned a myriad of corners.

I was sweating. All I could think was that everyone was dead, or they'd left...unleashed on the streets of DC. Terrorizing the city. Maybe they'd been irradiated and grew to be giants. I pictured twelve giant girls running around, stomping on memorials.

"They're in here," Ms. Ito opened a door to a dark room and stepped aside. I entered and felt the door shut behind me. That was it. I've been compromised. Now I was a prisoner on Japanese sovereign soil. Great.

I saw a dim light around a corner up ahead and found myself in a theater. The girls were watching a traditional Japanese puppet show. Every little face was fixated on the stage. How did they do that? There was no way I could pull off a puppet show. Not without puppeteers, at least.

My father was sitting with Ambassador Nakano in the front, so I took a seat next to Maria in the back.

"Anything?" Maria asked without taking her eyes off the stage.

"I don't know," I answered. "I'll show you when we get out of here."

The lights suddenly came up, and the silence was split by loud applause as my troop jumped to their feet, cheering loudly. *Wow. I should bring them here every day for the rest of the week.*

As the ambassador showed us out, he gave each girl a small, silk bag filled with Japanese candy. Okay, so maybe I didn't like him after all. All that sugar was going to give me a headache later, and I wasn't even eating it.

"Did you get what you needed?" Dad asked once we were outside.

I shook my head. "Not sure. What's your take on the ambassador?"

We entered the house, and I saw that Mom had put out two trays of giant cupcakes. Great. More sugar. Some sort of conspiracy against me was afoot.

"Go change," Dad said as he unwrapped a cupcake.

"Your mom doesn't let me have stuff like this."

As I struggled out of my suit and into my original yellow troop T-shirt and shorts, I thought about that. Mom was curtailing what Dad ate now? And he was defying her? Something really was going on with them.

Maybe Dad had health issues I was unaware of, and Mom was keeping him healthy. That could be it. And it made sense. If his cholesterol was bad or if he ran the risk of diabetes, she'd watch what he ate. Wouldn't she?

But it was unlike Mom to want to get a kitten. All of these years she'd gone without a pet because of Dad. So what changed? And her snarky comment by the pool? Health issues didn't explain that.

Maybe I should've been more involved in their lives these last two years. I called at least once a week to chat, but I rarely went to DC for a visit except for holidays. And most of the times they were back in Iowa, Dad was always touring the state on business.

If they'd grown apart, I hadn't seen it. And they were old. Old people didn't get divorced. Did they? This was the first time that I wished I'd had siblings. Someone else to carry the load. To commiserate with. But I didn't, and hoping wouldn't make it a reality. So I had to go it alone.

Where would I even start? I'd asked Dad, and he told me to leave it alone. Ugh! Why did everything happen at once? I wasn't sure I could handle this trip, Riley's kidnapping, and my parents' presumed marital crisis all at once. I was in way over my head here. I'd bet Mr. Fancy Pants never had problems like these.

I finished changing, but before I left the guest room, I transferred the black pouch to my purse. Checking it out here and now wasn't a good idea. Paranoid as it may have seemed, if it had a tracking device, I wasn't going to lead anyone to my parents. They seemed to have enough problems.

I joined the sugar assault already in process. The girls were bouncing off the walls, their lips colored by red and blue frosting. Maria was laughing as she watched them. Evelyn Trout was sullenly banging away on her cell phone. Sadly, Ambassador Nakano's charms didn't reach to the Czrygy household.

"Okay! Everyone thank the Senator for our great trip today!" I shouted.

The girls crushed my dad in a group hug, and he laughed. He didn't even seem to mind the frosting on his suit.

"You girls have fun!" Dad waved them off as Maria and I herded our troop outside and into the van. We were back at the hotel in ten minutes, and I sent the girls to clean themselves up. Evelyn flicked on the TV in the main room, giving me hopeful looks.

"Thank you, Evelyn," I said. "You can take the afternoon off if you want."

The woman was out the door before I finished my sentence. I had no idea where she was going, and I didn't care. I took my purse to the kitchenette counter.

"So what did you find that you didn't want Trout Face to see?" Maria asked with a wicked grin as she joined me.

I laughed. "That's the perfect nickname for her. Let's give her the code name TF. She's the mother of one of the Kaitlins."

Maria looked around cautiously. The girls hadn't come out of the bathroom yet. "Which one?"

I shrugged. "No idea." Whichever girl it was, she wasn't admitting it, and I kind of got that.

Gingerly pulling the pouch out of my bag, I set it on the table for Maria and me to examine. It was just a small, black, leather pouch with a zippered top. About the size of the bags used to make a bank deposit. It had felt as if there was something like a cell phone and some papers inside.

Touching it any more was out of the question until we knew a little more about it. Reaching into a drawer on the counter, I pulled out two forks and, using them as tongs, gently turned the bag over.

Maria studied the zipper. "It looks okay. I don't see any triggers."

I nodded and gently unzipped the bag. We waited for a second or two. You never knew what could happen when you opened a strange package. I've had everything from smoke in Cairo to screeching in Budapest and, in one unfortunate situation, snakes in Belfast. Bitey snakes. And they said St.

Patrick drove all the snakes out of Ireland. Yeah, right.

"We're clear." Maria nodded.

I dumped the contents of the bag on the table. A small, extraordinarily thin smartphone slid out along with a sheaf of folded papers.

"What's that?" Emily appeared next to me, her hands on the countertop.

"Nothing. It's nothing. Go watch TV for a little bit, please," I said quickly.

The girl shrugged and ran to the couch where she was joined by half of the girls. The TV mumbled in the distance as Maria and I turned our attention back to the counter.

"This is the newest Taki phone!" Maria whistled. "It's not supposed to come out for another year!"

She picked it up and ran her thumbs over the screen. I watched as she pressed a button on the top, and the lock screen came up.

"Not until next year?" I asked as I unfolded the paper bundle.

"Yup." She nodded, clearly enthralled with the phone. "I'm on a waiting list."

"Can you unlock it?" I asked.

"I don't know." She stared at the gadget. "I'll give it a shot."

I turned my attention to the bundle of papers. When it was unfolded, I could see that there were fifteen pages, all in Japanese. This would take a while. I was just starting to decipher the first paragraph when I heard the girls screaming.

"Mrs. Wrath!" Betty and Inez shouted in unison. "Look!"

My eyes followed their fingers to the TV screen. There was a picture of the king vulture we'd seen yesterday. That was weird. His face filled the screen. He looked like a cross between a circus clown and a deranged turkey.

A hush fell over the room as Maria and I moved closer to the TV.

An anchorman with disturbingly glossy hair said, "And in other news, the king vulture at the National Zoo has escaped his enclosure and disappeared."

"Mr. Fancy Pants is loose!" Hannah shouted.

CHAPTER FIVE

———

"What?" I asked the screen. It didn't respond. The anchor had moved on to a story about some weird mold found at the Washington Monument.

I whipped around and stared at the girls on the couch. They were strangely quiet.

"What did you do?" I asked.

The girls looked at each other and shrugged. By now, the initial screaming had brought all of the remaining girls into the living room.

"Ladies," I said, trying to control my rising panic, "tell me you didn't let that bird out."

All twelve girls shook their heads.

"How could we have done that?" Betty asked. "You were with us the whole time!"

She had a point. The other girls nodded furiously. They didn't act suspicious.

"She's right," Maria said. "We were with them. I didn't see them do anything."

I narrowed my eyes. I wasn't putting anything past these kids. They'd really liked the vulture. If they'd really wanted to, one of them could've slipped off and done something. But what

"We can't do anything about it anyway, Merry," Maria added before turning her attention back to the phone.

I looked at the papers in my hand. I needed a little time to translate them.

"I'm hungry!" Inez complained.

"Okay, lunchtime!" I shouted.

"Really? Now?" Maria asked.

I didn't answer, instead dialing the hotel restaurant. When in doubt...order out. That's what my dad used to say. I felt a little sick thinking about their marriage having problems. I pushed those thoughts aside. There was too much to do.

"Yes, I'd like to order takeout lunch for fourteen please," I said into the phone. "Yes, burger baskets are perfect. Thanks." I hung up.

Twenty minutes later, we were picnicking in the park across the street. Maria and I sat under a tree on a bench as the girls sat on the ground and ate. The minute they finished they were off to the playground—which had a weird American history theme. I watched the Kaitlins go one after the other on the George Washington cherry tree slide before I took out the Japanese documents and a pen. It would take me at least half an hour to get the gist of what was written here. I studied the pages, looking up every few minutes to check on the girls. Maria tackled the cell phone.

"It doesn't make sense," I said after I finished a cursory reading. "These are all maintenance documents for the Japanese Embassy. Warranties for the furnace, stuff like that." I shuffled the papers again. There wasn't anything written in the margins, no hastily scribbled coded message...nothing.

"Maybe they were just packed in there to hide the phone?" I mumbled as I turned the pages over in my hands. That had to be it. Why else would they be there? I'd gone over every word, and there was nothing covert there.

"I got in!" Maria whispered excitedly.

The phone's screen came up. It was a picture of cherry blossoms with a bunch of apps. Maria ran through them, but they seemed to be basic—the time, a calendar, a camera...

"Hit the photos," I said.

Maria's thumb hit the photo app, and Riley's face popped up on the screen. I winced. His normally handsome face was bruised and swollen. His left eye was black and closed. The normally golden blond hair was stringy and crusted with blood.

I sucked in a deep breath. "Oh, no."

It wasn't unusual to get beat up in our line of work. I'd actually had my nose broken twice. You couldn't tell. I knew a plastic surgeon in Paraguay who owed me a favor. But you're still never really prepared to see it when it happens to your friends.

"He's still alive," Maria said quietly. "That's something." But from the look on her face I could tell she was worried.

"Go to the album. See if there's anything more," I pleaded, mostly to get the image of Riley's battered face out of my head.

"There's a video," Maria said. "That's it." She hit play.

Riley's face filled the screen—this time he looked fine. He must've made the video before his beating.

"Wrath…" he said to the camera, "if you find this, and I hope you will, the yakuza found some connection between Midori's death and me." He paused to look around himself, before turning his attention back to the camera.

"I don't think they know about you. But they're closing in. If you find this, it means they've got me. No one else in the Agency knows about Ito. You need to get help."

A crash sounded in the background, and Riley turned to his left. "They're here—" Then the screen went black, and the video ended.

Dammit.

I leaned back on the bench, defeated. That was it? The packet just had a phone Riley had left for us so we'd know he was in trouble—something we already knew? I'd hoped the packet had detailed directions to where Riley was being held, complete with timetables as to when his captors would be breaking for dinner or the bathroom. Instead, it was just a video message that told us this was about Midori Ito.

I knew sometimes clues didn't pan out like you'd wanted them to. No matter what you had to do to get them. Like sneaking around the Japanese Embassy. And wanting the clue to be more wouldn't make it so. It was a hazard of the trade.

"So it is the yakuza," Maria said. "And they have him here." She swept the park with her arm. "Somewhere in the area."

"This is not good." I had a talent for stating the obvious. How could Maria and I take on the yakuza alone? They always travelled in large groups. There'd be a lot more than just two of them. And finding their safe house would make the classic idea of a needle in a haystack look like finding an atom on a planet. I wasn't in a good place to deal with this. I had twelve little girls with me, and I didn't work at the CIA anymore.

"This may be a lost cause, Merry," Maria said.

I shook my head. "No. I can't give up." I couldn't figure out how to manage it, but I couldn't quit. "Riley helped me twice in the last year. I can't abandon him now."

We sat there for about ten minutes sightlessly watching the girls play, our minds working on the puzzle. Both Maria and I were trained agents with field experience. That was an advantage. And we had a couple of resources still at Langley we could exploit. That was another advantage.

Riley was here, somewhere. We'd just missed him at the Japanese Embassy. That was something. Now we just needed to find him. But how?

"This isn't Riley's phone," I said, as if that would help. "All of Riley's calls were from his phone. We've tried calling him back, but that doesn't work. I don't even know how he's charging it."

Maria shook her head. "What should we do?"

I sighed. "We're going to have to find out who the new yakuza guys in town are."

To be honest, I knew this might come up. I just hoped it wouldn't.

"You have a contact here?" Maria asked.

"I have a contact. She's not here. She's in Virginia," I said, regretting each word as I spoke it.

Maria stood. "What are we waiting for?"

"A reason not to go," I said. There was no way this would be easy. It was a two-hour drive from the city, and I had no idea what to do with the girls. But if anyone knew which members of the yakuza were in the States, it would be this woman.

"Why not?" Maria asked. "I mean, aside from the girls."

"Because Elvinia Loretta Thigpen is a huge pain in the ass," I said as I stood to join her. "We can't take the girls."

Elvinia. Damn. That woman was what some in the South would call "eccentric," and those in the Deep South would call her "touched." She was completely mad and also meaner than a cornered Chechen terrorist. It didn't help that she lived in the middle of the Blue Ridge Mountains, running illegal moonshine. Getting to her would not be easy, and talking to her would be even harder.

Still, Elvinia had this weird connection to the yakuza. She'd been stationed in Okinawa back in the 1970s when she'd been in the army and for some strange reason made a lot of friends in the Japanese crime syndicate. In the eighties she'd married into the biggest yakuza family in the Okinawa branch and had a couple of kids before her husband "accidentally" fell on the wrong end of a samurai sword.

The woman was still in Japan when I was stationed there, and we had crossed paths more than once. For some reason, Elvinia took a liking to me. After her husband's unfortunate death, she had relocated to her family homestead in the middle of nowhere, hillbilly Virginia. Her sons stayed in Japan, keeping an eye on the family investments there. If crime bosses came to the States, Elvinia threw them an old-fashioned barbeque complete with blackened possum and her special recipe moonshine. It was considered an honor to be invited.

I'd been invited when I retired. And while it wasn't the media circus Valerie Plame had when she was outed, I still made the news. Elvinia had remembered me from our time in Japan and had invited me down to her homestead. At the time, I couldn't figure out why she'd asked me to visit, and I couldn't figure out a reason not to go.

It didn't take long to find out why she'd invited me. Elvinia tried to fix me up with one of her cousins who was also nephew and brother. That idiot clung to me all day into the night. Every time he got me a drink, I was afraid it had a date-rape drug in it. It was the single most terrifying night of my life. And I'd hoped I'd never have to go back.

I dialed my cell. "Mom, I know you just had them, but can you take the girls for the afternoon? See if Liam's available."

To my complete surprise, she said, "Yes."

A few hours later and a dozen girls shy, Maria and I were entering Amherst County, Virginia. We'd changed into jeans and boots. Armed with Glocks and bug spray, I thought we stood a 40/60 chance of survival. I didn't tell Maria because, as good spy, she already knew that. You'd have to be realistic, if not a bit pessimistic, in this job. It made you feel better when you get through something with no problems. I wish I could've said that was the norm.

I'd turned the pickup truck we'd rented off the main highway about twenty minutes earlier, and we had wound our way through crumbling concrete until I'd found the hidden gravel road that would take us most of the way there.

"What do you mean by most of the way?" Maria asked as she held on to the armrest. Had I said that out loud?

The road, if you could truly call it that, had gotten very bumpy. Deep ruts in the mud from recent rains and erosion made the driving treacherous. It was slow going. So slow that the mosquitos kind of flew alongside us, waiting for their dinner to stop and emerge from the vehicle.

"I hope your insurance is paid up," I said, wincing at another bone-jarring jolt.

"I think my intestines are no longer connected to anything inside me," Maria said grimly.

I stopped the truck. The road had vanished, crossed with a huge, felled tree that had been taken over by kudzu.

"We walk from here," I said, unbuckling my seat belt.

It was even hotter here than it was in DC. Turning the AC off and stepping outside caused my sunglasses to fog over. I threw them into the truck—the woods were so dark and thick I really didn't need them. Instead, I reached for the bug spray and coated myself in a fog of the sticky, smelly stuff. Bio-conscious sprays didn't work here. You needed the full strength only a DEET neurotoxin could supply. Maria winced as she sprayed herself head to toe. Sure, it smelled bad. But the alternative of turning into one human-sized mosquito bite was worse. Way worse.

The walk was straight uphill. I only knew we were heading in the right direction because Elvinia had planted poison ivy along the trail to what she called the "meeting place," where we'd be met by someone who'd take us to her. She had a great sense of humor, that woman. She'd figured only a crazy person would follow a trail of toxic plants. I was starting to think she was right.

"Leaves of three, let it be," I said to Maria.

She gave me a look. "That bug spray has made you crazy."

"That's what we say in Scouts to identify poisonous plants like poison ivy," I replied. "Avoid any plant that has three leaves, or between them and the mosquito bites, you'll want to kill yourself."

"Such a charming place." Maria smirked. "I wonder why more people don't build summer homes here." She swatted away a cloud of mosquitos that were apparently impervious to the toxic poison we'd used on ourselves.

"And watch for ticks too," I added. I probably should've briefed her before we got out of the truck.

"Wonderful." Maria's eyes began darting back and forth now, watching for any tiny bug approaching.

Ticks were bad here. Last time I was at Elvinia's I actually saw a whole herd of them crawling toward me through the grass. There weren't many spy weapons you could use against them. Well, none that worked anyway.

We started walking more slowly as the foliage got thicker. The trail was barely visible. We were almost there.

"Whatever you do, don't scream. And don't pull your pistol first," I said.

Maria gave me a look. "I'm kind of missing my desk job right now."

"Don't worry. We'll probably be okay," I said without a lot of hope.

"When do we find whatever it is we're looking for?" Maria asked.

"We don't. *It* is actually a *they,* and they find us. This is the trail to find them," I said, climbing and keeping my eyes open.

We didn't talk as we hiked the last few hundred feet, mostly because it was too hot and humid and we needed to save our lung capacity for making it up the mountainside. Sweat poured off of my face and found its way down my body, pooling in my clothes. My skin was crawling with what I hoped were imaginary bugs. I just kept thinking about Riley. And how much he was going to owe me after this.

"Yew can stop rightchere," a male voice snarled in front of us. The man was short, skinny, and wore camouflage that mostly hung in rags around his bony frame. Oh yeah, and he was carrying a twenty-gauge shotgun which was unfortunately aimed at us.

"Elvinia's expecting us," I said with my hands raised in the air.

"Well mebbe she is," the man growled, "and mebbe she ain't." He stood there, staring at us. A bird chirped. It was so quiet I swear I heard the ticks crawling toward me.

"So…" I said slowly. "Are you going to take us to her?"

"Mebbe I will, and mebbe I won't," the man said, not moving a muscle. Apparently he hadn't made his mind up yet. This was a hillbilly standoff. It's a little different than a Mexican standoff, where each person has a gun held on the other. In this case, only one guy had a gun, but he wasn't entirely sure what to do with it.

"Okay." I shrugged. "So what do we do now?"

The redneck (I decided to name him Clem since he didn't introduce himself) looked a little surprised by my question. Apparently, the word *mebbe* was the only one in his vocabulary.

"Well?" I pressed. I'd had to deal with his type before. It didn't matter if you were in backwoods Mississippi or the wilderness of Romania—there was always *this* guy.

Clem looked around himself. Maybe he thought he had others with him, or maybe he was afraid of a black bear sneaking up on him. It was a little unclear what he was thinking at this point. But time was running out. We had to get to Elvinia and back to my parent's house before the evening ended.

"Hey, Clem!" Another voice echoed through the trees. Really? His name really was Clem? Maybe the bug spray made it possible for me to read minds. It wasn't doing a good job because, outside of his name, I was drawing a blank.

"Whatchya doin?" The voice belonged to a giant of a man whose face was hidden by matted black hair. It might have been a bear for all I knew. This guy was about six-foot-five and probably three hundred fifty pounds. Long black hair hit his shoulders, and a grizzled beard hung down to his navel. The

beard was full of leaves, twigs, and unidentifiable matter that m
gag reflex really hoped was food.

"Hey, Earl," Clem said. "I wuz fixin ta shoot these uns."
He pointed the gun toward Maria. She didn't look intimidated.
She had one of the best poker faces in the business. That was,
until he spat a long, dark stream of tobacco juice onto the
ground. Her face expressed something that looked a little like a
cross between horror and disgust.

"Zat so?" Earl brushed hair from his eyes, with what
could only be described as a giant, hairy paw, and squinted at u

Clem shrugged. I felt a bit more nervous realizing that
Clem might just shoot us for no reason at all.

"Wut fer?" he finally asked. Earl scratched his beard,
and a pinecone fell out.

"Wuttuya mean, wut fer?" Clem countered.

And once again, we were at an impasse.

"If it's all the same to you"—I interjected this meeting
the minds—"we'd rather not get shot. For whatever reason.
We've actually come to see Elvinia."

Earl thoughtfully scratched his head. "Okay," he said at
last. "I reckon I can take ya to her."

As we walked up to him, Earl held out his hand. "I'll
need your shooters."

"We don't have any," I lied.

Earl nodded to Clem, who stepped up and felt the small
of my back. He pulled out the pistol, then took Maria's. I'd
figured they'd do something like this, but you really are limited
to where you can hide a gun when you're somewhat slender. An
no, I wasn't about to use any caliber smaller than a .45. If these
guys were on the 'shine, they wouldn't even feel a .22, .380 or
even 9mm.

"Can I shoot 'em for having guns?" Clem looked
hopeful.

"Nah." Earl wiped a hairy paw across his forehead.
"Let's go."

Maria and I followed him, trying not to make eye
contact with the now dejected Clem, who sadly hung his head a
we passed.

It was easy following Earl. Kind of like following a giant, sweaty bulldozer wearing overalls. He moved slowly, lumbering through the woods with a definite sense of purpose. I made sure to leave a trail of scratched bark and broken plants so we could find our way back just in case we didn't have our chaperone. Elvinia's homestead was well hidden in the Blue Ridge Mountains. If we were lucky, she'd have someone take us back, but we'd have to make sure we didn't piss her off.

Maria tapped me on the shoulder. "How far is it?"

"Not much longer," I said, even though I really didn't know. Earl was walking so slowly we were in constant danger of bumping into him. Even though he seemed fairly easy going, I didn't want to find out if I was wrong.

Eventually, we crested a hill to see a valley below, tucked in between three small mountains.

"That looks like a Colombian drug lair," Maria whispered.

I nodded. "You were thinking tar paper shack with an old-timey still, weren't you?" I waited for her to nod. She didn't. She was staring at a frog that had jumped out of Earl's beard. It hit the ground running and hopped away into some brush. Earl didn't even notice.

"Elvinia likes things a certain way," I said as we carefully picked our way down the steep hillside to the compound.

Elvinia had built a Spanish-style mansion, complete with tiled roof and fountains. Considering her background, you'd have thought she'd have a Japanese-type décor. But no, she was just crazy that way.

"Feeeeeyun!" a woman screamed from inside the house before stepping onto the front porch. Elvinia squealed when she saw me, then hurled her short but plump body at me. I braced myself for the impact.

"You have to call me Merry now," I croaked through a crushing hug.

Elvinia released me, and I staggered backwards, clutching my throat, "Nice to see you too!" Our host wore overalls that matched Earl's. Frizzy red hair stuck out of her head at all angles, and she smiled through missing teeth. You couldn't let her looks fool you. *Crazy* and *shrewd* were the only words you could accurately describe her with. It's funny how often those two things went together.

I motioned to Maria. "This is my friend and colleague, Maria." I watched with some amusement as Elvinia crushed her in an embrace.

"Well, come inside, y'all!" She held the door open for us and we went in.

I should've prepared Maria for the shock. Sure, the outside looked like a Spanish hacienda, but the inside was something entirely different.

"Are those real Picassos?" Maria gasped, pointing to a row of paintings. Inside the house, the décor was postmodern with white floors, walls, and ceilings and very little of anything else. The furniture was so eclectic you needed a manual to find out how to sit in it. Everything was brushed steel and white leather. It was unsettling to say the least.

"Yep! You've got a good eye!" Elvinia grinned. She looked like a backwards redneck in a European museum. Like someone who'd have been thrown out just for thinking about setting foot in there.

"I've met his former lover, Françoise Gilot." It was weird hearing a sharp, Southern accent speak a French name. Somehow, she pulled it off.

"Anyhoo, Françoise sold me some of Pablo's stuff. Ain't it pretty?" Elvinia looked very pleased with herself. I'm sure she couldn't talk art much with Earl and Clem. And even then it would probably be over Andy Capp or Li'l Abner cartoons.

"Elvinia," I started. "We need your help."

"Come on in for some sweet tea! Brewed it myself!" Our hostess waved me off before turning to head down the hall to the kitchen.

"Wow…" Maria said, eyes agog. "Just…wow."

"You'll get used to it," I replied, even though we weren't going to be there long enough to get used to anything.

The kitchen was modern and up to date with stainless steel appliances, quartz countertops, and every kind of pot and pan available to mankind. She even had a pasta arm between the sink and stove.

"Here ya go!" Elvinia pushed two glasses filled with tea toward us. She'd added a lemon and mint garnish to both. "Now I know you didn't come back here to see my cousin Knob again. Although I don't mind tellin' you, he was mighty interested."

I suppressed a shudder. "No, I'm not here to see Knob." I gave Maria a look that hopefully said "don't ask."

"Dammit," Elvinia said. "That boy needs to get married! Not many girls would take him, you know, due to his affliction." She turned her attention to Maria. "I don't suppose you're single?"

Maria shook her head and waved her hands in front of her. "I'm not really into guys," she lied. I smothered a grin.

"Don't that beat all?" Elvinia said with a surprised look. Her expression faded immediately, and she got down to business. "Oh well, whatchya want?"

I tried to make myself sound as casual as possible. "We need some info. On the yakuza."

Elvinia's face went from smiling and happy to dark and stormy. You never really knew with her what it would take to set her off. I knew she had a soft spot for the Japanese syndicate. Would it be enough that she'd take offense?

"Why do you ask?" A chill seeped into her voice, and I tried not to shiver under her piercing glare. It was possible I'd figured this all wrong. Maybe I should've said I *was* interested in Knob.

"It's Riley, my former handler," I started slowly. "He's missing, and we traced some intel back to the Japanese Embassy."

Elvinia put her hands on her hips. "And you figured it had to be the Ninkyo Dantai, right?"

"Ninkyo Dantai?" Maria asked.

"Chivalrous Organizations," I explained. "It's what the yakuza call themselves."

Elvinia's scowl deepened into a snarl. "It's what we are! We take care of family! We ain't no renegade criminals!"

I raised my hands. "Sorry. I'm sorry. I shouldn't have put it that way. It was insensitive of me."

Our host muttered, "It ain't our fault we get blamed for everything. Why do ya want information on the family?"

"I just want to know if you've heard anything. That's all I'm not asking you to turn Riley over or to negotiate his release, I lied hopefully. Because that would've been awesome.

She shook her head. "They'd only take 'im if they thought he had sumphin ta do with Midori's murder."

Please, please let me look completely normal.

"Oh?" I asked as innocently as possible. "Remember th I'm retired. I hadn't heard anything about a murder."

Elvinia studied me for a moment. I held firm on my poker face. Hopefully, she'd buy that.

Then she launched into the story.

"Midori's body was found in Chicago behind a Japanes grocery store a little ways back. She'd been murdered. No one knew she was even in the US. They just thought she'd gone to a spa for a real long time." Again, Elvinia glared at me to gauge my reaction.

"So she just disappeared, but no one thought anything was wrong?" I asked. We never did figure out how or why the yakuza boss had been in this country. Maybe Elvinia knew.

She shook her head. "Don't know. All I know is they didn't realize she'd gone missing until she turned up dead."

Oh, well. It was a long shot to think she'd know more than I did.

"If Riley had sumphin ta do with Midori's murder, I'm afraid that no one can help him," she said finally. "Maybe you had sumphin ta do with it too?" Her eyes narrowed.

Uh-oh. This was not good.

"I've been retired and living in Iowa for almost two yea now, Elvinia. I'm just as out of the loop as you are." I tried not t smile as I said this. Elvinia was notorious for wanting to be in the know on everything going on in the US as far as the yakuza went.

The woman's face turned bright red, matching her hair. She looked like a tomato that was about to explode. "I am *not* o of the loop on *anything*!"

Elvinia stomped out of the room, slamming the door to the kitchen as she left.

"Is that good or bad?" Maria whispered.

"I'm not really sure," I answered back. "I think it's safe to say we might be in trouble."

I looked around for any weapons, pulling open drawers in hopes of finding a hidden Uzi or bowie knife. But no such luck. Elvinia had played this game before and decided to hide all pointy things in case they'd be used against her. There wasn't so much as a corkscrew. The closest thing I could find was a cheese grater, and it would be pretty hard to kill someone with that. Oh, you could shave off some skin, and it would be painful, but that's about it.

"No knives," Maria said as she shuffled through drawers along with me. "Who ever heard of a kitchen with no knives?" She pulled out a meat tenderizer and considered it thoughtfully.

"Someone who's had those knives used on her," I grumbled as I tore through a drawer containing fifteen rubber spatulas. How many does one cook need?

"Who's Knob?" Maria asked.

"Someone I may have to marry if things go south," I said, carefully closing a cupboard.

"Why is he called Knob?"

I glared at her. "You don't want to know. You don't want me to tell you. Trust me on this."

"Maybe we should just run…" Maria said.

I shook my head. "We wouldn't get far. There are a lot more guys out there like Earl and Clem. And they all carry shotguns."

"Well then"—Maria cracked her fingers—"I think I can take her."

I shook my head. "Don't be too confident. That woman can fight. She was in the Army before she married into the syndicate."

My eyes scanned the kitchen one last time. Our only advantage, it seemed, would be to smack Elvinia's head on the countertops. There were two of us, so maybe we could pull it off.

The door flew open, and that's when I realized it was kind of weird that she had a door on the kitchen. What with most houses having open floor plans and all, it didn't make much sense. And why was I even thinking about that? Behind my back I gripped the cheese grater a little tighter.

"Here!" Elvinia slapped a thin file folder on the counter "There're some new guys in the area from the Tokyo family. See? I'm not out of the loop!"

I picked up the file before she realized that she'd actuall fallen for my trap. There were two photos inside. The first picture had two Japanese men in suits and dark sunglasses. One had an unnaturally tall, Elvis-y pompadour, and the other had a goatee. Both looked dangerous and also a little hipster.

The next photo had one man in it. He was older and bal but wasn't wearing sunglasses like the others. He wasn't the mo: important thing in that photo. The most important thing was the woman with him. It was Ms. Ito. From the Japanese consulate.

"What are they doing here?" I asked as I showed Maria the photos.

"Looking into Midori's murder." Elvinia pointed a fat finger at the woman in the picture, "She's Midori's daughter. Ar from what I understand, she's way deadlier than her mom."

Great.

"Why are you sharing this with us?" Maria asked, befor I could catch the words and stuff them back into her mouth.

Elvinia thrust out her chin. "I don't like the Tokyo branch."

Right now, I didn't like the Tokyo branch either.

CHAPTER SIX

———

Elvinia had Earl give us a ride back to the trail in a small tractor that went almost as slow as he walked. I clutched the file, worried that at any moment Clem would show up to shoot us— just because. And there was always the chance Elvinia would realize we'd taken the file. After she'd handed it to us, she ran off to get us a jar of moonshine. She didn't seem to miss it as she waved us off.

As he dropped us off, Earl handed back our guns. Maria and I thanked him over our shoulders as we raced to the car. I opened the jar of pure grain alcohol and was immediately overtaken by the fumes. Weirdly, the mosquitos dropped dead out of the sky when they came into contact with them.

"Why are you dumping that?" Maria asked.

"This stuff is so illegal you'd probably get the death penalty just for having it," I said. "I'm pouring it out first so Elvinia will think we drank it. She'd think it was rude to ditch a full jar."

As the liquid hit the poison ivy surrounding us, the plants immediately curled up and died. Maybe I shouldn't have poured it out. It could have proven to be a valuable weapon. Oh, well. That wasn't my mission. We were soon back on a road that had been paved. I gave silent thanks for concrete and rebar.

"So Ito's daughter was in the Japanese Embassy," Maria mused as she studied the photos while I drove.

"Yup. It's too much of a coincidence. She's got to be here to solve her mother's murder," I said. My heart was pounding. If Ito Jr. knew that Riley was involved in her mother's death…well, he wouldn't be around much longer.

"But Riley didn't kill Midori. So maybe he's safe?" Maria asked.

I shook my head. "I don't think that will make any difference. He helped me dump her body behind a Japanese grocery store. She won't take kindly to that."

Maria threw up her hands. "What were you supposed to do? Arrange a state funeral? She was on our No Fly list. The fact that she was in this country is a huge embarrassment. You did what you had to do."

I loved Maria for saying that.

"She won't see it that way," I said. "She'll just torture the hell out of Riley for fun." And she would. Baby Ito was smarter than her mother and took crazy risks just for fun. We were totally screwed if she had my former boss.

"What if she finds out you *were* involved and you're in the city?" Dammit. Maria said it. Out loud. I would've preferred she hadn't.

"That can't happen," I said through my teeth. "I can't let anything happen to the girls. They'd definitely be a target."

"Maybe you should take them home," Maria replied. She sounded disappointed.

I didn't know what the hell to do. Sure, I could take them home, but then the yakuza could show up there. They might still be in danger. This was a nightmare. I wondered if Ms. Ito had taken a good look at me in the embassy. Would she have recognized me? My hair, name, and, due to tinted contacts, even eye color were different. But I was with my father. If she knew about my connection to her mother's rather disrespectful burial, she might've figured it out.

On the other hand, Riley wouldn't give me up, no matter what they did. They might not even know I was involved. But how did they know he was? It was highly possible if they knew about him…they knew about me. Damn. I didn't know what to do. If we stayed here, I had the whole city to protect the girls and hide from the yakuza in. Our small-town police force back in Iowa wouldn't be prepared to deal with an international crime syndicate. Rex was a cop and could take care of himself, but he was my boyfriend and that made him another potential target.

My head was spinning.

"We've got to get back to my parents' house. If Ito connects me to Riley, she'll look there first. And the girls are there." I took out my cell and dialed.

"Merry?" Mom was good. She'd adapted to my new name easily. Things were finally getting to the point where people didn't call me Finn anymore. Although, if Ito the Younger killed me, it wouldn't matter what they called me.

"Mom," I said, trying to sound like I wasn't freaking out. "Is everyone okay?"

"Yes, of course! Liam's here, and the girls are making hoagie sandwiches. We're fine." She sounded so reassuring. Was there anything better than being reassured by your mother? I didn't think so.

"Put Dad on," I said.

My father got on the phone, and I gave him a rundown on what I knew.

"We'll be fine, but I'll have Congressional security come over for the night." He sounded like he wasn't worried at all. That was okay because I was panicked enough for the both of us. I thanked him and ended the call.

We were quiet for about ten minutes. Just watching the road as the sun slipped behind the trees that lined the highway.

When I'd first met Ms. Ito at the embassy, I wasn't sure if she was even related to Midori. But after seeing her in the photo, with full confirmation from Elvinia, I realized she had to be behind Riley's disappearance.

Ito Jr. was pretty young when I was stationed in Japan, and I'd never met her. But I'd heard some rumors after I'd moved on to another field assignment. Leiko Ito (her name meant *arrogant*—as if that was a surprise) was a capable murderer in her own right with a thirst and talent for vengeance that no fiction writer could have imagined.

There'd been many stories over the years, but the one that stuck with me involved a goat. When she was twelve, Leiko went to the zoo with her mother and their entourage. The little girl wanted to feed the tigers. The zookeepers refused because the last thing they wanted was to have the head of the yakuza watch her only child get eaten. Midori agreed that this was the right decision, and the group moved on.

The next night, the zookeepers discovered that the star attraction of the petting zoo, a goat named Flower (because she had a spot on her back the shape of a lotus), was missing. A week later, the director of the zoo received a pair of goatskin boots. The right boot had a spot shaped like a lotus.

Midori insisted that she had nothing to do with it, and the zoo backed down, fearing any reprisals. According to the story, Leiko stole the goat on her own, slaughtered it, and had her mother's special shoemaker work on the boots and deliver them.

Things kind of went downhill from there, and it even got to a point where Midori had to homeschool her daughter because no one wanted her in class. So naturally, Leiko started apprenticing with the yakuza and with Midori dead, probably headed up the Tokyo branch.

If she had Riley, she'd stop at nothing to get the information out of him. Nothing. The question was, would Riley sell me out if pushed too far? I'd sing like a bird if anyone threatened to make a pair of boots out of me.

"So…" Maria broke the silence. "What's up with this Knob guy that Elvinia tried to hook you up with?"

I shuddered but was happy to stop thinking about Ito's psycho daughter. "Why do you think a man would be called Knob?"

Maria laughed. "You want the clean answer or the dirty one?"

"Try bizarre," I said. "He has a weird deformity on his forehead shaped like a doorknob. And he loves it. Like, really really loves it. So he had it tattooed with metallic ink to look like an actual doorknob."

"You're joking…" Maria made a face.

"I'm not. I mean, I have no problem with…whatever you'd call that. It's not his fault. But what was his fault was the constant string of dirty jokes he directed at me."

"Well, maybe he was just trying to put a brave front on it?" Maria asked.

"How many times could you listen to *pull my knob*, and *have more than one way to satisfy a woman*?" I shuddered again. Knob had really turned out to be…well, a knob.

"Okay—that's awful. At least you gave him a chance," Maria said.

"I did. But the jokes only got more disgusting and suggestive. When I finally pried myself away, I realized he hadn't asked me one thing about myself." *I'm not vain, but come on! Shouldn't the other person at least ask your name?*

"That does sound bad." Maria was laughing now. "What did Elvinia say?"

"She said to just tune him out. Like that was even a possibility. He followed me everywhere," I muttered.

Elvinia had been pissed. She'd thought I hadn't given the guy a chance. I'd felt like I'd given him way too much. Did you know how many jokes there were for a guy like that? Turned out there were forty-three that a woman could swallow before it was time to go look for the cocktail wienies.

"What was his real name?" Maria asked.

I frowned. "Orville. Orville Door."

Wait for it…

"His name was Knob Door?" Maria collapsed in a fit of laughter. "Now you're joking. You have to be!"

"And he was born with the huge bump on his head. I didn't meet his parents, but I know what I'd ask if I did." I turned to her, annoyed. "Can we just talk about something else please? It's not like the guy stood a chance. I didn't even go on a date with him."

"Okay." She grinned. "How come you and Riley never got together?"

"We can talk about anything but that." My insides ground against each other as Maria said his name.

"It's either that or I start coming up with names for your and Knob's children…like Belle, Jam…the possibilities are endless," she said.

I sighed. "Riley and I had a thing…a brief thing…about six or seven years ago when we were stationed in Japan."

"What?" Maria screeched. "Why didn't you ever tell me about that?"

"When I say it was brief, I mean like, in minutes," I said.

"That's certainly enough time," she mused. "What happened?"

I didn't want to talk about this. "Look, Riley and I were over before we ever were a thing. It just didn't work out. We've been friends ever since."

Okay, so that wasn't entirely true. We had a fling that lasted about a week. It was nice. Very nice. Riley was very romantic when he was motivated. I actually thought it was going somewhere, even though dating your handler was considered a bad idea in the Agency. You never knew when you had to leave a man behind. And if you were involved, an entire operation could be at risk.

"He was sleeping around, wasn't he?" Maria probed.

I nodded. "I walked in on him with this bimbo from the German Embassy. And that was that."

I didn't mention that I'd been crushed. Or that I'd considered killing him. I probably could've gotten away with it too. But that was all water under the bridge. Okay, it was sort of under the bridge. In the past year Riley had confused me by kissing me on more than one occasion. And he'd seemed to be unnaturally interested in my welfare—even though I didn't work for him anymore.

"He spent a couple months with you back in Iowa last year," Maria said. "And he called you when he was in trouble this week. Why do you think that is?"

I shook my head. "The CIA was worried about what was happening then. And I think he just happened to know I was here in DC, where he's being held…somewhere."

"I don't know," Maria said. "I think he still has a thing for you."

"It doesn't matter because I'm seeing someone," I snapped as I pressed a little harder on the gas. Maybe I'd get home faster and not have to answer Maria's probing questions.

"Oh right, the hottie detective. What's his name?"

"Rex. And we're totally kind of serious," I said a little defensively. "He's watching my cat, Philby, and her kittens while I'm out here."

"A local police detective when you were investigated on murder charges…and your handler when on assignment," Maria said. "You can really pick them."

Now I was pissed. What did it matter who I was seeing? Maria's grilling was getting on my nerves. I didn't want to talk about Riley or Rex. Wait… Why wouldn't I want to talk about my boyfriend? Wasn't that what you did? Something seemed wrong about that. Was I feeling guilty because I was going to such lengths to find Riley?

I hadn't told Rex about it. He didn't know what I was doing. Shouldn't I have told him? Seems like honesty was important in any relationship. But then, I'd been a spy, and as a spy, I wasn't likely to share information until I knew what I was doing.

What was I doing? If I was smart, I'd just hand this all over to the Agency. And yet, I wasn't doing that. Was it because I didn't think they could do it? Was it because I still had feelings for Riley?

"Whoa! Look out!" Maria shouted as I corrected the truck, bringing it back onto the highway. I hadn't been paying attention and had driven off the road. Killing myself wouldn't help Riley or anyone else.

"Let's just keep the conversation focused on this investigation," I said.

Maria changed the subject. "Why do you think Elvinia gave us this information? Do you really think she was just mad that you insinuated she didn't know what was going on?"

I relaxed. Now this was better. I could talk about this sort of assignment without getting distracted. I shoved all the boyfriend talk out of my mind.

"I have no idea. It's not like her to fall for that." And it wasn't. Elvinia was smart. Folks usually underestimated her with the hayseed accent. But she was one clever lady. I was just as surprised as Maria was.

"Maybe she really isn't in the loop anymore," I started. "Maybe she's sensitive to that."

"Do you believe the intel?" Maria asked.

"Yes. But only because I recognized Ito Jr. in the photo." If I hadn't seen that same woman before, I'd have been more suspicious.

"So who did murder Midori?" Maria wondered.

"No clue."

"Doesn't that bother you?"

I nodded. "It drives me crazy. All we know is that she was found dead in my kitchen. And at the same time as some other terrorists started dropping dead around me. But we'd solve those murders. Just not hers."

"Are you sure it wasn't the same person?" Maria asked.

My thoughts scaled backward to a year ago. "I'm sure. So were Riley and Rex. Turns out it was just coincidence."

"Do you believe that?"

"I don't believe in coincidences as a rule. But in this case, it was. No one has ever figured out how Midori got here o why she was in Who's There, Iowa."

"Look out!" Maria pointed, and I slammed on the brakes.

There, in the middle of the road, was Mr. Fancy Pants, the escaped king vulture from the National Zoo. Looking at us with his googly eyes.

CHAPTER SEVEN

———

"Are you kidding me?" I asked. Almost killed by rednecks in the Virginia hills and now stalked by a zoo animal? I didn't have days this crazy as a spy. Oh wait, there was that panda who thought I was his mate and kept showing up at inconvenient moments to let me know. Like when I was being held at gunpoint by a couple of gun runners in the middle of a bamboo forest. Relax. I didn't use him as a shield or anything. The gunrunners were dead, but the panda now had a new lady love in the Beijing zoo. And she was an actual panda.

I got out of the car and walked to the front of the truck. Mr. Fancy Pants didn't move. Well, his eyes did. They rolled in opposite directions like lazy eyes on meth.

"What should we do?" Maria joined me. Her cell was out, and she was searching for the number of the National Zoo.

"Um…catch it?" I asked.

"How are you going to do that?" Maria stared at me.

"I have no idea." How did one actually catch a giant bird of prey? Was it dangerous? Docile? For all I knew, it could be a killer vulture. Hey! Maybe he was sent by the yakuza! That would be extra devious.

"Too bad we don't have a blanket in the truck we could throw over him," Maria said.

"Rental trucks rarely come with blankets," I murmured, studying the bird. "My question is, where do we put it once we catch it?" I pictured the vulture sitting between us in the truck as we drove it back to DC, staring at Maria with one crazy eye while staring at me with the other. It didn't seem like a good idea.

Maria found the number for the zoo and dialed. She

started talking quickly into the phone.

"Where are we, exactly?" she asked.

"About twenty miles north of Charlottesville on 250," I replied, my eyes still on Mr. Fancy Pants.

His body didn't move, but his eyes did. Why was he there? What did he want, and why did he think I had it?

"They said to be careful," Maria said as she put her cell away. "They're going to send animal services out from Charlottesville to try to catch him."

"So we have to stay here or go around it?" I asked.

Maria shrugged. "I guess so."

This was ridiculous—a sort of stare down between two spies and a vulture. I didn't want to stay here any longer than I had to—the girls needed me.

"Get back in the truck," I said softly. "We're going to backtrack to the last junction. I can't wait forever for this stupid bird."

"We can't just leave him here," Maria whispered.

"Why not? He's just going to fly off anyway. Maybe he follow us?"

Maria and I carefully got into the truck. I started it up, and we looked behind us as I threw it into reverse. A crash distracted us. When we turned around, Mr. Fancy Pants was standing on the hood of the truck, staring at us.

"Now what?" Maria asked out of the left side of her mouth—as if the bird could hear us.

"I'm starting to think Ito Jr. sent him…" I mumbled.

It was a good thing Earl, Clem, or Elvinia weren't with us or else this bird would be fricasseed for dinner.

Mr. Fancy Pants began to pace back and forth across th hood. Clearly, we weren't going anywhere. I sent a silent prayer to Charlottesville in hopes animal control would get a move on.

"Why is he doing that?" Maria asked.

"No idea," I replied. "But we're going nowhere fast witl him on the truck like that."

We were stuck. An important specimen of the Smithsonian's zoo was holding us hostage, and it seemed there was little we could do about it.

"Why us?" I asked. "Why is he stalking us?"

Maria shrugged. "Maybe he didn't like the name the girls gave him?"

The vulture stopped in mid-strut and walked right up to the windshield. He reared back and began pecking on the glass.

"I think he heard you," I said as I slowly rolled up the windows.

Mr. Fancy Pants stopped pecking and cocked his head to one side, studying us. I had an idea.

"Maybe he's hungry," I said as I fished around inside my backpack. I'd brought a pink backpack with me because it was a gift from the girls. And it held a lot more than a purse did. For instance, it held snacks for between meals. Snacks like the Girl Scout Cookies I'd packed just in case.

I pulled out a box of shortbread cookies and held it up to the windshield. Mr. Fancy Pants went nuts, pecking harder at the glass, as if that was the only direct path to the bright blue box in my hands.

"How does he know what Girl Scout Cookies are?" Maria marveled.

"No idea," I said. Now what? I had the cookies. And he wanted the cookies. But how to get them to him?

I lowered my window and opened the box. The vulture became very still before shivering in expectation. He looked like he was having some weird avian seizure. I tossed a couple of cookies onto the hood of the truck. Mr. Fancy Pants snatched them up, swallowing before he could even identify what they were. Then he started hopping up and down, excitedly.

"I'm not sure that things are better..." Maria said as I tossed two more cookies onto the hood.

"Well, at least we have a defense should we ever find ourselves surrounded by king vultures." I threw a couple more cookies at him, and he caught one in midair. The other was devoured seconds later.

Where were those animal control people? We didn't have all day. I wanted to get back to my troop.

Unfortunately, Mr. Fancy Pants was tired of waiting for the cookies and had now begun pecking hard at the windshield. I threw him a couple more cookies.

"I think you should quit feeding those things," Maria

said.

"You're going to get your wish in a minute. I'm almost out," I said.

The last few cookies went onto the hood of the truck and were immediately devoured. Mr. Fancy Pants looked right at us and then took flight, soaring up into the air. Now how do you think he knew we were out?

Just then, a truck pulled up beside us. On the side it said *City of Charlottesville.* Nice timing.

"You guys are a bit late," I said as they got out of the truck and walked toward us.

"Are you the ones who called?" the first guy asked. Both men were wearing white coveralls, and one was carrying a net.

"Yes—but the bird's gone now." Maria let out a long sigh. Had she been tense the whole time?

"Great," said the second guy. "Well, maybe we can still get it."

The man with the net nodded. "Should be just fine, as long as you didn't feed it."

Maria and I looked at each other as I dropped the empty cookie box to the floor of the truck, shoving it under the seat with my foot.

"Why should that make any difference?" I asked.

"Because that bird"—he stabbed at the sky with his index finger—"has a problem with processed, white flour. If he eats any, he kind of goes nuts."

"How did you know that?" Maria asked.

"The folks at the zoo told us. They said under no circumstances were we to feed it. And if it got hold of anything with flour in it, we were to avoid it at all costs. I guess he almost killed his handler one time when a troop of Girl Scouts accidentally dropped a box of cookies into his pen."

I started the truck. "Well, thanks for the heads up! We have to go now!" I floored the gas pedal and drove off in a cloud of dust.

Maria whistled under her breath. "Great. We just handed the equivalent of raw meat to a lion on the loose."

"How was I supposed to know that?" I asked, pushing harder on the gas pedal and racing down the highway.

"You couldn't," Maria said. "But it explains why he got excited when he saw us at the zoo and possibly why he escaped in the first place."

I didn't say a word. I'd been responsible for pissing off the yakuza and turning a bird of prey into a cookie-guzzling killing machine. And I had no idea which was worse.

We made it to the rental-car place in record time and turned in the truck in exchange for our van. Neither one of us had spoken for the duration of the trip. I didn't know what Maria's motivation was, but I felt like mine was a mixture of guilt and fear.

"Hello?" I called as we burst through my parents' front door fifteen minutes later.

A flying blur of neon pink came at me, tackling me in the entryway. The four Kaitlins had me in a group hug. I hugged them back, grateful that they were okay.

"Mrs. Wrath! Mrs. Gomez!" they squealed. The girls then all started talking at once as the remainder of the troop joined us.

"Hold on!" I held up my hand, making the Scout quiet sign. The hallway was immediately silent.

"Let's hit the kitchen, and you can tell us all about it," I said.

"Hey, ladies!" My dad stood at the kitchen island, handing out paper plates with chocolate cake. My troop was certainly not getting a balanced diet here. "You made it back, I see." Mom took his place and handed out the rest of the plates while Maria and I followed my father into his den.

"There," he said as he sat in his chair and closed his eyes. "Peace and quiet."

"Sorry, Dad," I apologized. "We had a couple of delays."

"It's alright, kiddo," Dad said. "In fact, I had fun. You have a great group of girls there."

"Really?" I asked. "I mean, I know that."

My father laughed. "Tell me what happened today."

I filled him in on our trip, ending with Mr. Fancy Pants but leaving out the part where I fed the animal its version of crack cocaine.

"So Midori Ito's daughter is at the embassy, eh?" he said,

leaning back in his chair. "I don't think I can get you back in there without raising suspicion."

He was right. There was no way we could ask for another tour without piquing the ambassador's interest. And if Baby Ito was on to me, it would be like serving me up on a plate to the yakuza. I pictured Mr. Fancy Pants sitting at that table, eating mint cookies, and fixing one of his eyes on me.

Maria shook her head. "I don't see how we can go there again without blowing Merry's cover."

"Well, at least we know a little more. And that helps." I shrugged. "I'll just have to find a way to do this on my own."

Dad pointed at me. "I know what you're thinking, and I don't like it. You shouldn't go back there."

"We don't even have evidence that Riley's there." Maria nodded.

"I know." The one person whose advice I needed on this was Riley. But he was the reason I needed help in the first place.

"Is it possible to solve Midori's murder?" Dad asked. "That would give you some leverage. Something to trade."

He was right. If we knew who'd killed Midori in the first place, we could use that to negotiate Riley's release. But that case had long gone cold. Almost a year cold. And Rex didn't even know about it. I'd never told him about finding Midori's body in my kitchen. There was no evidence. No trail.

And yet, Midori had somehow made it into this country, come to my hometown, and gotten herself murdered. That's where it happened. That's where the mystery was. The one place where I wasn't.

I'd need Rex's help. And to get that, I'd have to tell him everything. Which meant he'd be really pissed off I hadn't told him before. Which was the equivalent to lying to my boyfriend. Our relationship had started to get better. We were doing well. So how could I tell him about Midori and not ruin everything we had going for us?

I needed to talk to the one other person who'd been there when we found Midori's body. I needed to talk to Kelly.

CHAPTER EIGHT

———

"Merry!" Kelly squealed into the phone, and I immediately felt awful. My best friend and co-leader of the troop was about to have a baby any second, and I hadn't called her once since we'd arrived.

"I'm so sorry, Kelly! I should've called before now! How are you? What's the news on the baby?"

Kelly laughed into the phone. "Don't feel bad. I knew you'd have your hands full. I figured you'd call when you needed bail money."

I sighed with relief. She wasn't angry. That was good.

"The baby is late," Kelly continued. "It was due two days ago. I think it's refusing to come out."

I laughed. "Maybe it knows about the troop." The girls were extremely excited when they'd heard one of their leaders was about to have a baby, and they'd immediately named it an official mascot of Troop 0222. The kid was doomed.

"Well, it has no choice," I said. "It has to come out sometime. I've never heard of a woman who was pregnant forever." It sounded like something an evil villain would come up with. That would've been worse than torture, I'd think.

We were back at the hotel, and I was in Evelyn's room. Evelyn and Maria were wrangling girls through the showering process. I'd have some privacy for a while.

"You need to tell the baby that," Kelly said.

She sounded happy. Really happy. Kelly usually was more frustrated with me. Either the baby was mellowing her out, or she was happier because I wasn't there. I hated to think the latter was the case.

"Okay, put it on," I teased.

Kelly laughed. "I'm glad you called—I'm going stir crazy. The hospital made me start my maternity leave last week. This house is spotless. So's yours, by the way."

"You cleaned my house?" I kind of felt bad about that. Not that it was very messy to begin with.

"It's called nesting. I needed something to do. You have actual drapes in the living room now—you're welcome. And I organized your weapons in alphabetical order. I even cleaned them."

I groaned. "Tell me you didn't clean my guns!" Kelly knew nothing about guns…by choice.

I was also a little sad that the Dora the Explorer curtains were down. And while it was true I had to get real curtains sometime, those sheets were the first thing I bought after I got the house. They'd been on sale at the dollar store, and I liked them. Dora was kind of a kids' cartoon version of a CIA agent, I thought.

"No. But Rex did. He saw me waddling around and came over. He had Philby and the kittens with him. What's up with the one that looks like Elvis?"

"Isn't that better than having her look like Stalin? Or Pol Pot?" I adored the Elvis kitty. I hadn't named any of them yet. I wasn't sure why. Maybe because I was in denial about being the owner of enough cats that they could eat me if I died.

"Ooof!" Kelly grunted.

"Are you okay? Are you having the baby? Are you going to name it after me?" I fired off questions like a well-greased Uzi fired off bullets.

"Relax. The baby just kicked is all. It's been doing that a lot."

Kelly didn't know the sex of her baby. She and Robert wanted it to be a surprise. So she called the baby *it*. Which was weird. But maybe that was the pot calling the kettle black since I hadn't named my kittens.

"So why did you call?" Suspicion crept into her voice. Ah, that was the Kelly I knew.

I sighed. "Remember Midori's murder?"

"How could I forget?" Kelly snorted. "It's not every day I find a dead terrorist in your kitchen."

"You said you thought her neck had been broken with a blow from behind—something like a baseball bat. Right?" Maybe I should get the details straight before I told Rex.

"That's what I thought," Kelly said. "But we didn't exactly do a detailed autopsy, now did we?"

My best friend had been really mad at me when we found Midori. I understood that. She was a nurse. Her job was to save lives, and instead, I'd involved her in covering up an international murder. Even pinkie swears couldn't help that blow to a friendship.

"We have a problem…" I told her about Riley's kidnapping. About Baby Ito, my trip to the Japanese Embassy, and my trek into the Virginia Blue Ridge Mountains. To her credit, Kelly just listened. As I spoke, I realized I felt better. Well, a little better. But still. I left out the part about the vulture. She didn't need any more blackmail material. The woman had plenty of that.

"Riley's missing?" Kelly had a soft spot for Riley, and they had first met over Midori's body. I wouldn't say the two of them were BFFs, but they had each other on speed dial.

"I'm trying to find him," I answered, but it came out a little weak.

"Merry,"—Kelly's tone was measured—"you can't put the troop in danger. It sounds like that's what's happening."

I shook my head, even though she couldn't see it. "I'm not. At least I'm trying not to." And that was the truth. Wasn't it?

"Riley is the CIA's concern—not yours." Her voice was what I'd have called urgent, with a dash of fury. "You shouldn't deal with this."

"The CIA still doesn't know about Riley and me hiding Midori's body. He'd lose his job and be part of a federal investigation—maybe even go to prison," I protested.

"You know I adore Riley," Kelly said. "But he knew the consequences. You, on the other hand, have the lives of twelve little girls in your hands. They are your first priority." I'd bet she was shaking her finger at the phone. I could picture the disapproval on her face. It made me a little homesick.

"I know that, but Riley did what he did to save me. To keep me from being the target of a foreign crime syndicate. It will all come out if I turn what I know over to the Agency."

"The girls come first," Kelly growled. "You can't get involved in this." Now she was probably shaking her head at me. I wondered if the baby would inherit her ability to project disappointment. Maybe it was shaking its little fist at me inside her.

"You're absolutely right," I said, flinching. "I didn't want to interrupt their trip. So far, they're safe, but I need to think of what happens should everything go south."

"I understand," Kelly replied. "And maybe you can do both. But you have to promise me if it gets bad, you'll send the girls home."

"My parents seem to want them here. I'm not worried when the girls are with them. Dad has access to security service. And the police would respond instantly to a senator's call."

"Merry," Kelly said. "I know you want to help Riley. And I have to admit, if I was there, I'd probably do the same thing. But you can't multitask this. You aren't Super Spy."

"Right," I said, a little wounded. Who didn't want to be Super Spy? "I said I'd promise to send the girls home if it gets bad. But that's not why I called. I called because I need some detective work done."

"And you thought a woman who is more than nine months pregnant could do that? Are you nuts?"

I deflated. What did I expect her to do? Midori's body had already been found. There was nothing she could do to help.

"No. I just wanted to go over some details with you and ask you how I should break the news to Rex."

"What? You're going to tell your boyfriend now? And you won't tell the CIA? You really are crazy!" Kelly was reaching a point of agitation that couldn't possibly be good for the baby.

"Rex can do some detecting," I insisted. "It's his job. Besides, he might be able to find out a little more on what happened to Midori's body once it was found."

"I don't know, Merry." I could sense my best friend rolling her eyes at me. "If you tell him, you risk losing him. He won't take too kindly to you covering up a murder across the street from his house. Not to mention the fact that you never tol him about it in the year you've been going out."

I slumped. "I've thought about all that."

"Is Riley worth it?" Kelly asked.

And there it was. Out in the open. Was Riley worth it? On the one hand, he'd saved my ass with helping cover up Midori's murder. But on the other hand, he was my former boss and still employed with the CIA.

"His life is. He's my friend," I mumbled.

"I didn't mean it that way," Kelly said after a moment. "I meant shouldn't you think about yourself for once? You're not on missions anymore. You're no longer a secret agent. You're a Girl Scout leader, girlfriend, owner of multiple, weird-looking cats, and someone's best friend. Riley needs to face the consequences."

"So you don't think I should involve Rex at all?" I asked, maybe a little too hopefully.

"I guess I don't know. You should definitely tell him about it at some point. But do you want to do that over the phone? Do you want him to dump you from one thousand miles away?"

Of course I didn't want that. My feelings for Rex were very real. I was starting to envision a future with him. That was something spies rarely did. We didn't think past tomorrow. The future was too unpredictable. But now, I was beginning to imagine what it would be like to spend the rest of our lives together. This kind of permanency was new to me. The longest relationship I'd had before Rex was with Riley—and that was only as partners at work and now...friends.

"Thanks, Kelly," I said. "You've given me a lot to think about."

"Just call me before you do something stupid, okay?" I could tell she was worried.

"Okay. Make sure your husband lets me know if the baby comes while I'm out here."

Kelly agreed, and we hung up.

This was hard. A week ago I would've thought the hardest thing about this trip would be that the girls would get lost. Now things were a lot worse.

Maybe Kelly was right. I should turn this over to Maria.

Of course, then she'd leave me, and I'd be stuck with Evelyn Trout—the surly mother of one of the Kaitlins. Whichever Kaitlin it was probably liked Maria more than her mother. None of them claimed her.

If I turned this over to Maria, she'd have the whole Agency behind her. All the resources they had would be targeted toward finding rogue agent Riley. And Riley should know that. He had to know that he was putting me and my troop in danger. He knew we were coming to DC.

Now I felt a little angry. How could he put us in this position? It was selfish. Well, that was Riley. It had always kind of been about him. From his bevy of blondes to his perfect tan and body. Riley was very much into himself.

Except that he hadn't been. Not really. He'd come back last year to help me when I had dead terrorists popping up all around me. He'd helped me hide Midori to keep me out of the limelight and away from the prying eyes of the yakuza and the Agency. Riley had been there every time I'd been in trouble. He looked out for me.

And he'd kissed me. More than once too. Riley had confused me with his attentions. More than once I'd wondered if he was into me. All that changed when I chose Rex. I'd made the right decision. Hadn't I?

Oh, wow. I was rehashing this all over again. Didn't I just do that in the truck before we were attacked by Mr. Fancy Pants? I needed to make a decision about Riley's situation before we all ended up dead...or worse.

I needed to keep my head clear now. I'd do whatever I could to keep the girls' trip going without putting them in danger. I'd have to remember what my priorities were. If I could help Riley and allow the girls to stay on and finish their tour of DC, I'd keep going. But when things got bad...

"Wow." Maria interrupted me from the doorway. "You're doing some intense thinking."

She closed the door and sat on the bed opposite me. "The girls are asleep. Want to talk?"

"Where's Evelyn?" I asked in an attempt to stall.

Maria waved her hand in the air. "Sloshing around the kitchen. I think she hit the bar after a major shopping spree. You should see all the bags in her room! It's as if she'd never seen a Macy's or Nordstrom before."

I shook my head. "We don't have those stores back home. You have to drive five hours to either Chicago or Minneapolis to find something like that."

"Well, she's making up for lost time. I spotted a bill for spa services on the kitchen counter. She owes the hotel a lot of money. Make sure she pays her share before you check out." Maria stretched and crossed her legs.

"What would happen if I just turned the hunt for Riley over to you and the Agency?" I blurted out.

"Ah. So that's what's been on your mind. Well, I'm pretty sure we'd find Riley. But he'd probably be drummed out of the CIA and possibly do some jail time. On the other hand, we'd be able to protect him from the yakuza."

"Is there any way you could find out if anyone did an autopsy on Midori after she was found?" I asked.

Maria frowned. "If the Japanese government ordered one, I could. But if the yakuza took control of her remains, I doubt it. Why?"

"Just wondering," I said. "At the time, we found her in a puddle of blood on my kitchen floor. Her neck was broken from a blow to the base of her skull with a blunt object. But maybe there was more to it."

"You're thinking if you solved the murder, you could get them to release Riley, aren't you?" Maria asked.

I threw my hands up. "Well, why not? It could happen. Then we'd get the yakuza off our backs and free Riley."

She studied me for a moment. "I appreciate what you're doing. I really do. You don't want to get me or Riley in trouble. But how can you solve a murder that happened a year ago, halfway across the country, while you are here?"

"Can you get the intel or not?" I asked.

"Sure. I'll try. I'll head to the black box tonight and see what I can find out." She pointed at me. "But you need to get some sleep. You look like hell."

"I haven't slept very well since this whole thing started," I admitted.

"Take my bed. I'll crash on the couch tonight. That's not

a suggestion—it's an order."

She was probably right. I felt like I'd been hit by a semitruck with a king vulture hood ornament. I agreed and lay down on the bed, fully dressed. I was out in seconds.

I cleared the apartment and found nothing. There wasn't even any evidence of a break-in. Stuffing the note with the phone number into my pocket, I dialed Riley.

"My safe house has been compromised," was all I said.

"Meet me at the office," was all he said. I packed a small duffle with everything I had and left.

Once again, I found myself out in the drizzly Tokyo night. I couldn't really take a cab from one safe house to another, so I walked. Walking at night didn't bother me. I could handle myself. Besides, it gave me time to think.

Who had broken into my apartment and left the number? Probably the same person who texted me the address earlier. I thought about the woman Riley had an affair with. A tall, voluptuous blonde from the German Embassy. She was beyond beautiful. And she had assets that I didn't have.

But how would she know where I lived? And how did she get in? All the windows had been locked from the inside, and the door hadn't been forced.

My head was pounding. I wasn't going to get anywhere with this until I had time to call that number. First things first— get to the office. Then find a place to crash. Nothing was going to happen until I had a moment to myself.

I pulled my coat tighter around me in the damp chill. That's when I heard a sound behind me.

The street was empty. Dammit. I hadn't checked to make sure I wasn't followed. I was letting this business with Riley trip me up. Stupid, stupid, stupid. Emotions could compromise a mission. I wondered how James Bond was able to do it—what with falling in love with every woman he met.

I turned a corner and quickly flattened myself into a recessed doorway. Seconds ticked by in time with my beating heart. Any moment now, whoever was following me would appear. Then maybe I'd have a few answers. I wasn't greedy—I'd take one. Was this the person who'd been contacting me tonight?

Seconds turned into minutes, and no one showed up. I

couldn't wait here all night, especially if it had been a false alarm. After a few moments, I stepped from the shadows and cautiously looked around the corner. Nothing.

Still, I took no chances, keeping to the shadows and making several false turns until I got to HQ. If someone had followed me, they'd either given up or mastered invisibility. And if it was the latter, I was screwed anyway.

"Anyone follow you?" Riley said when I finally came through the door. He was all business when it came to one of his agents in trouble.

I shook my head. No point in telling him I'd freaked out over nothing.

Riley led me to a room in the back. Our headquarters had a small, one-room apartment in the back.

"Need any company?" Riley asked with a seductive smile.

"No thanks," was all I said as I shoved him out the door and locked it behind me.

I waited until Riley left before taking out my secret phone. It was a smartphone with a Wi-Fi connection that I kept hidden from the Agency and my boss. It was just a precaution, but now it came in handy.

As I dialed the mysterious number, I kept an eye on the door. Just in case Riley decided to double back.

"Hello?" a woman with an American accent answered.

"You left me your number," I said.

"Meet me tomorrow at noon." She went on to give me the address before hanging up.

I got ready for bed, wondering what on Earth I'd gotten myself into.

CHAPTER NINE

———

Clink...

"Philby!" I shouted with my eyes closed. That stupid cat got into *everything*. My eyes were so heavy I couldn't open them. Exhaustion formed a haze around the edges of my brain, and I started to drift back to sleep.

A grating sound, like ceramic sliding over a counter, made me groan. What was that cat up to? Hopefully she wouldn't knock my favorite *Spies Love Wet Work* mug over. She liked pushing things off countertops to watch them smash onto the floor below. It was a sort of hobby with her.

Wait. I'm not at home. I'm somewhere else. Forcing my eyes open, I saw a room unfamiliar to me. A woman on another bed snored like a buzz saw. Huh. I dragged my sleepy brain into the present. Oh, right. I'm in Washington DC with my Scout troop. I was in Evelyn and Maria's room. *Man—I must really be out of it to forget that.*

I grabbed my cell phone and saw that it was three in the morning. The noise on the other side of the door was probably Maria getting a glass of water. I slid back down onto the bed and began to doze off.

Crash...

I sat straight up. I wasn't going to get any sleep until I confirmed that Maria was moving around out there. Hey, I was still dressed. That was convenient. I slipped into my shoes and, using my phone as a flashlight, made my way across the room and gently turned the doorknob. I wasn't going to go out there noisily. Years of spy experience taught me that.

The living room and kitchen area were pitch black. That was weird. Even spies don't usually move around in total darkness. Turning off my phone, I stood in the doorway until my eyes adjusted to the dimness.

The couch was empty. Was Maria out there? I stepped into the main room and looked toward that area. There was a small glow from a light over the microwave, and a figure stood there, going through the cabinet. It was too big to be one of the girls.

"Hello? Maria?" I called out.

The figure reached out and snapped off the small light, plunging the area into darkness. Nope, not Maria. Adrenaline raced through my veins, and I grabbed my pink backpack off a nearby chair.

A shape came hurtling toward me in the darkness, and I swung the bag at it with all my strength. It connected with the figure's head, and he or she went down with a loud *oomf*.

Before it could get to its feet, I attacked with a kick to the neck. I was met with a satisfying gagging sound, but the intruder grabbed my foot and drove it upward, knocking me to the floor.

I lashed out with my other foot, connecting with whomever it was, but he got up and ran to the main door. I heard it slam shut just as I made it across the room. Flinging open the door and diving into the brightly lit hallway, I looked both ways, but the intruder was gone. My eyes were struggling to adjust to the blazing lights, and I went back into my room, dead-bolting the door behind me.

Very carefully, I checked each bedroom and counted the girls sleeping there. Everyone was present and accounted for. I turned to search the main area. But nothing seemed out of place. I texted Maria to bring a bug detector from the office. If the intruder had planted a listening device, I wanted to find it before whoever it was could discover my plans.

Maria texted back that she would and she'd check with the hotel manager to find out if there was any CCTV footage from the hallway. She was a good agent. Do what you're told without asking a lot of questions. Besides, she knew she'd get the answers when she got back here.

Someone had broken in, and I was pretty sure they weren't looking for Girl Scout Cookies. This was bad. I didn't like the idea that someone out there knew where I was. Where my girls were. That struck a nerve. Maybe it was time to call it a trip and send the girls home. I could stay here and keep the baddies' attention focused on me while I tried to find Riley.

I guess I'd made up my mind to finish this. Okay. Then was going to do it without my girls. Putting them in danger was not going to work for me. They'd be disappointed and upset to cut their trip short, but I wasn't going to put them in harm's way.

I was still searching the kitchenette when Maria gave the special knock at the door. I didn't use peepholes. Too many of my colleagues had had their brain matter rearranged by looking through that tiny window. We called it a *lobotomy hole* in the business.

Maria didn't say a word. She just nodded and pulled the bug locater from her purse and turned it on. The device was the newest model, and it looked like a smartphone. It kind of operated on the same principle of many locator apps. She silently waved it around, working in one-foot by one-foot square increments as she made her way around the room. I sat on the couch and watched her work. We wouldn't be talking until her scan of the area was complete.

It took a while. The work was slow going, but that's what you did if you were serious about the craft. Too often, young and impatient spies let valuable intel slip because they were too impatient to use the equipment properly. Maria and I knew better. And knowing better had saved me in the field many times over.

An hour later, she turned off the device and slipped it into her pocket.

"All clean," Maria said as she flopped down on the couch next to me. She looked tired. It was almost five a.m., and she'd had no sleep. I didn't want to tell her that we had another full day of visiting monuments ahead of us.

I filled her in on the intruder. She didn't like the news.

"So, they found you," Maria said quietly. "Not good."

"What did the manager say about CCTV?" I asked. If we had a good image, we'd know for sure who we were dealing with.

Maria shook her head. "The camera on this floor was tampered with last night. Whoever broke in was smart about it."

"The only reason they got in is because I didn't deadbolt the door, knowing you'd be coming back here," I mused.

"Could we find another hotel?" Maria offered.

I shook my head. "No, it's obvious they're watching us. Besides, it's a little difficult to run around with a bunch of kids dressed in neon colors and not stand out." Maybe I should dress them in city camouflage suits. Or little ninja costumes. That would be cool.

"Why plant a listening device? Why not just take you if that's what they're after?" Maria asked.

That was an excellent question.

"I think this means they don't have any proof about my involvement in Midori's murder. If I was here alone, they'd definitely take me and not worry about if I'd be missed— innocent or not. But we're here in a high-visibility capacity. There was some publicity about the National Council awarding the troop with this trip. If I was to go missing now, word would get out, and it would be investigated. Even the yakuza wouldn't risk that."

Maria nodded. "That's a good point. And good news. It means that Riley is, in all likelihood, still alive."

"I hope so."

I jumped out of my chair and ran to the pink backpack, ripping open the zippers and searching through it.

"What is it?" Maria had joined me.

"The phone!" I said as I tossed the bag aside in disgust. "It's gone."

CHAPTER TEN

———

"So that's what they wanted." Maria whistled.

"Yeah, and I gave it to them." I frowned. I should've kept the backpack with me in my room. It was spy-craft 101, and I'd flunked.

Maria arched her left brow. "What do you mean?"

"They were looking for the packet I took but hadn't found it when I'd interrupted them. It must've fallen out of the backpack when I used it as a weapon." I slunk down in the chair the backpack had been on.

"Big deal," Maria said. "We know what was on the phone, and the papers revealed nothing."

"I hope so. I really do." But I wasn't quite convinced. "It does point the finger at Ito Jr. though. She caught me running loose in the embassy where I'd found it."

"Maybe Elvinia tipped them off after our little visit?" Maria asked.

I shook my head. "That doesn't really fit Elvinia's style. She's crazy, but she's not the type to rat us out. Besides, that would only draw attention to the fact that she'd given us the photos and info that yakuza were in the US. She wouldn't want their attention on her."

"So, what do we do now?" Maria asked. The sun was up, which meant the girls would be up any minute. I watched as she made coffee. I wanted to hug her. Maria wasn't giving up on our day.

"Now," I said as Betty, Lauren, and Hannah came into the room, rubbing their eyes. "Now we get ready to do some sightseeing."

Maria groaned but didn't complain as she poured hersel

a cup of coffee. I was really lucky to have her with me. I certainly couldn't talk to Mrs. Trout.

My cell rang, and I ran into the bedroom to answer it. When I saw who it was, I closed the door.

"Rex!" I said as he appeared on my screen in FaceTime. I heard Philby meow loudly behind him, and my stomach dropped. I missed home. And with trained Japanese killers on the loose, I wished I was there.

"Hey, honey," he said, and I melted. It was very early in the morning back in Iowa, but he looked like he'd been up and ready to go to work. His dark, short hair was perfectly combed, and he had shaved. I watched as he lifted Philby up to the camera.

My cat was a dead ringer for Hitler. She looked at me and started to lick the camera, probably hoping it was edible. I couldn't help but smile.

"What's up?" I asked. Was this just an I-miss-my-girlfriend call? I could have used one of those.

"I just wanted to let you know that Kelly is in the hospital. I think she's having the baby today."

I felt a stab in my heart. My best friend was having her first child, and I wasn't there for her. Granted, I'd had no choice when the Scout office informed me of the non-negotiable dates for this trip. But still—I'd hoped the kid would at least hold out until I was home.

"Robert called you?" I asked. I thought Kelly's husband would've called me, but I wasn't hurt. He was probably out of his mind with worry and excitement.

"Yeah." My boyfriend gave me a charming smile. "He put me on speed dial because he thought he might need to have a police escort to the hospital."

I laughed out loud. "Aww, that's sweet."

"Anyway, I'll let you know when I hear more. I sent flowers to her room from us. I hope that's okay?" he asked.

"Okay? It's perfect. You are the best boyfriend ever." Seriously! What man would think to do that? I had a winner on my hands. This was not the right time to tell him about Midori and Riley.

"Oh, and someone wants to talk to you," he said as he

leaned down away from the camera. Rex plopped three kittens on the table, and they all looked at me on the screen and meowed.

"I miss you guys!" I said in a baby voice. Elvis kitten made a *fffffft* sound before her face filled up the camera.

"I have to go," I said sadly. "But please let me know the minute that baby is born!"

Rex promised before he hung up.

For a moment, I got to ignore the danger here in DC and get excited for Kelly and Robert. They'd refused to tell anyone—even me—the names they'd picked out. I turned the volume on my phone all the way up and joined everyone else in the main area, where a donut fest was taking place.

I held up my hand in the symbol for the quiet sign, and every girl turned toward me silently.

"Kelly has gone to the hospital. She's having her baby!" I squealed.

The girls screamed and clapped, every bit as excited as was. I couldn't help but get caught up in their enthusiasm. This baby meant a lot to them too.

"Okay, okay, let's quiet down," I said. "We've got a big day ahead of us and lots to do. So let's finish eating and get dressed and cleaned up. We leave here in thirty minutes!"

My announcement created a mad dash, only rivaled in cartoons, as girls and donuts went flying everywhere. Evelyn Trout made an appearance and frowned, but she didn't go back into her room. She even wore the electric pink T-shirt we'd designated for today. Was she going with us? One more bit of good news. Maybe things were looking up.

Maria and I changed, brushed our teeth, and joined the group jumping up and down in the living room. Evelyn stood on the outskirts of the fray, eating a donut. She was still frowning. wondered if I should explain that the Washington, Lincoln, and Jefferson Memorials wouldn't have shopping malls or spas in them. But she was an adult and had access to Google. I was tire of kowtowing to her. Besides, it would be nice to have another adult today, just in case I got kidnapped.

It took a while for us to clean up and go. Maria pulled the van around, and I herded everyone in. Maria seemed to like driving us, and I let her. She knew this city better than I did. Besides, it gave me a chance to watch for anyone tailing us. *Paranoia is a spy's best friend.*

Maria and I had decided we'd hit the Jefferson Memorial first, saving the Washington Memorial for last. That way, we could hit the Smithsonian museums if we had extra time. For a moment, I pictured my troop turned loose on a bunch of museums with priceless artifacts. Well, it would be the museum's fault if the Hope diamond was used as a football. *They should have better security.*

The sky was a bright blue, without a single cloud. The perfect day for exploring. Well, except for the stifling humidity. But the girls didn't seem to notice. In fact, they were excited. A full day of running around outside might even wear them out. *Might.*

The good thing about hitting the monuments today was that there'd be crowds of tourists...witnesses, should anyone decide to get all kidnappy with me. I hoped that nothing would happen, but you could never really be sure in my line of work. The Girl Scout motto was "Be Prepared." It made me wonder if Girl Scouts founded the CIA with that in mind. I'd have to let them know I had twelve good recruits for them in ten years.

"Okay, ladies," I said sternly as Maria parked the van. "You have to be good. You are representing the Girl Scouts and the state of Iowa today. So I want you on your best behavior. Got it?"

Twelve little girls nodded solemnly as I got out of the van and opened their doors. They bounced out of the car with excitement and raced toward the memorial. Cars and tour buses were beginning to fill up the parking lot. *Bring on the crowds—the more the merrier.*

Evelyn followed the girls up the marble steps of the portico as Maria and I hung back a little. If someone was looking to get me, I wanted to be as far from my girls as possible. And if they approached me, I'd go. No point in getting anyone hurt on my behalf. Maria and I had decided that if something did happen to me, she would get the kids to my parents' house. My folks would make sure the troop got home safely.

I'd called my parents this morning to let them know that.

Mom and Dad seemed a little alarmed that I thought something could possibly happen to me, but they agreed. I told Mom she could have my cats if I suddenly wasn't around anymore. Was it me, or did she sound a little excited to hear that?

A rather handsome park ranger who looked a little like Rex had gotten the girls' attention, and they huddled around him. Smart guy, I thought. Defuse the first threat you see with charm. Evelyn stood there with the girls, flirting with the ranger, grinning like a clown, and gushing over everything he said. Yeesh. What was with this woman? Actually, I hoped we'd never become close enough for me to find out. I watched as Maria joined them. She looked back at me and nodded.

My goal for the rest of the day was to keep a bit of distance between me and the girls and scope out the crowds to see if my suspicions were correct and I was being followed. I took up position against the wall and scanned the tourists.

A group of middle-aged tourists with huge cameras caught my eye when they seemed very interested in my girls. So did a couple of Japanese hipsters in suits and sunglasses. Expensive suits. One guy had a slick, Elvis-like pompadour—like the guy in one of Elvinia's photos. My heart skipped a beat as I studied them. It was hard to tell. The other guy with him didn't resemble the other men in the photos. I couldn't be sure enough to act.

They looked completely out of place though. But like the group of tourists, they made no eye contact with me. They didn't keep an eye on the exits or shoot suspicious looks around them. They simply focused on what the ranger was saying about Thomas Jefferson.

I didn't like it. Because if I was yakuza and didn't want to stand out—I'd do the exact same thing. These two were the only Asians in the whole crowd. I squinted at the big group. They were still staring at the girls. I could understand if they were eyeing the troop with fear or adoration. But a whole group watching them? That seemed a bit shady.

If you asked who I suspected more, it would be hard to say. Because of the photo, the two suits stood out as if they'd been naked and dipped in blaze-orange paint. They didn't have the right shoes or clothes for sightseeing, and they didn't look a refined as traditional Japanese businessmen.

On the other hand, the tourists with cameras would be the perfect cover. No one would suspect them, and an assassin could slip in there easily. With their large number, none of the other tourists would've called a stranger out for piggybacking with them. It was the perfect disguise.

Still, I had to wait for them to tip their hand, and it looked like they were prepared to wait. I was fine with that. It was way too early to deal with an attack. I needed a little more time to wake up. Getting up at three in the morning and staying up was not a good thing for me. I really needed a good, solid eight hours of sleep.

During our training at The Farm, the CIA was big on challenging us under the effects of sleep deprivation. It had been my only weak point, and I had barely squeaked through. I was hoping the three cups of Earl Grey I'd had before we left would help. Right now, though, not so much. Too bad Betty's ADD medication was back at the hotel. Those usually contained amphetamines, which would perk me up. I'd have to check that later. Great. Now I was considering stealing drugs from my kids. I was in danger of losing out on Role Model of the Year.

I moved around the memorial, reading the inscriptions on the walls, trying to blend in. No one followed me or even studied my actions. It could be that no one was there to watch me. Or it could be that they were just biding their time. Or I might get lucky, and no one was watching at all. But that was a risk I was not prepared to take.

The ranger finished his spiel, and the girls wandered away as the adult tourists stepped up to ask questions. We'd warned the girls in the van to stay in groups of four, and so far, they were following our advice. Maria and even Evelyn seemed to be paying attention to their every move. For once, Mrs. Trout seemed to be acting like a mom. Maybe I was being too hard on her. Maybe I should cut her a little slack.

The two Japanese businessmen asked a couple of questions before walking over to read the walls. The tourist group was polite and had shifted their attention from the troop to the memorial. Nothing seemed out of the ordinary. I relaxed. A little.

My cell rang out, echoing off the walls, and I slipped outside. I guessed that turning up the volume hadn't been the be idea. I'd given anyone looking the excuse to notice me. That wasn't good.

"Yeah?" I asked without checking the screen. My eyes were on anyone who might be following me. Would it be Kelly Riley? A butt dial from my cat?

"How's it going, kiddo?" Dad's voice made me sigh wit relief.

"So far, so good," I answered.

"Glad to hear it. I thought I'd check in and let you know that I got a strange call from the Japanese Ambassador just now

My ears perked up, and I focused all my attention on th phone. "Oh?"

"He asked about my assistant who'd wandered off at the embassy. One of his protégés, a Ms. Ito, had complained that you'd looked suspicious."

"Terrific." I sighed. I'd hoped she'd think I was incompetent. But then, if you looked for trouble, you'd find it. And my guess was baby Ito was on high alert.

"I think it's alright," Dad said. "I told him you were not very smart and most likely just got lost."

"Did it work?" I asked. "Did he buy it?"

"I think so. He laughed it off anyway. But I thought I should let you know," Dad said.

"Thanks for the heads up," I said as other tourists bega to pour out around me. "I'll give you a call later."

Hmmm… That meant that Ito Jr. was more connected the Japanese Embassy than I thought. They had to know who s was. You didn't hire the daughter of a crime boss without doin background check. It was a government job, for crying out lou

But was the Japanese Ambassador involved? If so, it seemed like it would be career suicide. Still, I couldn't rule it o I'd have to talk to Maria about this. Where was she?

The memorial had emptied out, and I didn't see the gir or the adults anywhere. That couldn't be good—unleashing a troop of sugared-up little girls on DC might qualify as a terrori attack.

I turned and ran outside, stood at the top of the steps, a

stared down into the parking lot. Okay—the van was still there. That was a good sign. At least they didn't leave me. I started the trek out to the vehicle to see if anyone was inside.

I heard the squealing before I was two hundred yards away. Yep. That was my troop. Waves of relief washed over me as I finally pulled open the passenger door. Of course, the screaming significantly increased once the door was open.

"What took you so long?" Evelyn barked at me from the front passenger seat. No shotgun for me, I guessed. Maria gave me a sympathetic look that told me all I needed to know. The Trout was there and going to stay there.

"Look!" Lauren squealed, and the girls started screaming again. I followed the line of her tiny finger to the top of the memorial. Where, perched as if he were an American bald eagle in clown face, was Mr. Fancy Pants.

I climbed in the van and closed the door. Maria hit the gas, and all we could see behind us was a strange looking bird taking off in flight. Did I pack any cookies for today's snack? I rummaged through the pink backpack but found only pretzels and crackers. That was either a great or terrible thing—I wasn't sure. So I called the zoo and reported the sighting, and they agreed to send some people out. I'd done my civic duty, and it was up to them to find the bird. I had other priorities.

As we climbed out of the van at the Lincoln Memorial, I grabbed Maria's elbow and pulled her aside.

"Go ahead and take them inside, Evelyn," I ordered. The woman gave me a glare that would've broken mirrors but led the girls toward the memorial.

"I thought you'd been kidnapped," I said softly to Maria as we kept a short distance behind the troop.

"No. I just managed to get them to the van. I may…or may not…have mentioned ice cream." Maria grinned sheepishly.

Great. Donuts for breakfast, ice cream for lunch. What could go wrong?

"You were worried about the two guys, right?" Maria asked. "They might be safe. Wouldn't they have tried something if they were yakuza? We don't even know that they're Japanese."

I shrugged. "You know how it is—every coincidence is fraught with suspicion."

"Right," Maria said. "You're walking a fine line between paranoia and racism."

The girls were starting up the tall steps with Evelyn grouchily egging them to keep moving. I'd really learned my lesson on this trip. Taking parents was a bad idea. At least taking Evelyn was. Kelly would just have to strap that baby to her back and come with us next time.

When we reached the top of the stairs, I sent Maria inside while I scanned the parking lot. Sure enough, the large group of tourists was following us. Okay, so maybe they were just having a memorial visit day too. It would make sense for them to follow our same plan, with the Lincoln and Washington Memorials opposite each other. Maria was right. I needed to calm down. No point in seeing danger that wasn't there.

Except…that had been my training. To see what wasn't there. It was the CIA's fault I saw kidnappers around every turn. On the other hand, it didn't hurt to be careful. It made me look kind of stupid, but better safe than sorry, right?

I joined the girls inside, where another park ranger had taken it upon himself to act as tour guide. Okay, so the girls were safe here. That made me feel a little better. I went back to being paranoid.

The Lincoln Memorial had always been my favorite. There was something comforting about the statue of him, sitting and watching over us. It was pretty inspirational that someone who grew up in the middle of nowhere, had no formal education and even taught himself to read, was able to guide the country through its toughest crisis. I wish he could help me with mine. I think he would've made an awesome spy.

Something crashed to the ground behind me, and I whirled around to see an elderly woman retrieving her dropped cane. If it worried her that I was facing her in a full-on defensive position, she didn't say so.

I had to calm down. My nerves were shot. I was overly caffeinated and had no sleep—a lethal combination in the past. Would I even make it through the day being so jumpy? The tourist group was happily listening to the Park Ranger who was still talking to the girls.

If only I could just enjoy this trip. Enjoy the time I was

spending with my troop. That's what most people did. But I was so busy looking for crazed revenge killers around every corner and shoving the kids off to my parents' pool—I wasn't having fun.

When would I finally relax? When Riley was found? When my friends at the CIA retired? It wasn't when I retired, that's for sure. For the past year and a half, I'd had to look over my shoulder constantly. And instead of just me, I also had to look out for my best friend, twelve little girls, my boyfriend, and even my cats. Was this what parenthood was like? If so, I'd never survive it.

Midori Ito's murder had put a target on my back. It seemed a little unfair, since I had nothing to do with her death. And here was Riley being blamed for it too. With everything else that happened during that time, it was obvious I was targeted somehow. But who really did it?

My experience with the bloodthirsty yakuza boss had been spotty at best. When I did fieldwork in Japan, I never ran into her. The yakuza weren't even in my sights. I was working on a Russian project.

There wasn't any reason for Midori's body to be in my kitchen or even in the United States. No matter how many times I wrapped my brain around it, I still came up with nothing. Zip. *Nada.*

This was ridiculous. I was moving in circles. I had no new information to prove motive or method in Ito's death. Of course, that would be cold comfort to Ito Jr. at the embassy. I briefly toyed with going in there and just marching up to her, asking her where Riley was, and insisting we had nothing to do with her mother's assassination.

"You aren't seriously considering that," Maria whispered moments later after I told her about this new option.

"Why not? Riley and I were completely innocent in that situation. It wasn't our fault."

"That is the most ridiculous plan I've ever heard." Maria shook her head. "You'd be outing her to the embassy and yourself to her."

I nodded. "That's true, but I think she already knows who I am. Baby Ito's as sharp as her mom was. Dad said she's already suspicious."

"I still think it's a terrible idea," Maria said. "Why blow your cover like that? And why walk straight into her hands?"

"Chances are she wouldn't do anything at the embassy with so many people around. And it would totally catch her by surprise," I insisted.

And it would. In fact, I wasn't sure that anyone in the entire history of espionage had ever done anything so bold. Maybe I'd finally get into the CIA's secret *Who's Who in American Espionage*!

"The risk factor is way too high," Maria responded as she swatted a fly away. "What if she just grabs you right then and there?"

"I've thought about that," I answered. "At least then I'd have an excellent chance of being imprisoned where Riley was. could wear a wire, and you could alert the cavalry and rescue us."

Maybe it was the lack of sleep talking, but this idea wa sounding better all the time. As long as I introduced some shadow of a doubt that Riley and I were innocent, maybe Ito's daughter wouldn't kill me on the spot.

"She'll shoot you on the spot," Maria said.

"She hasn't killed Riley."

"We don't know that. When was the last time you hear from him? They could be sending you recordings, and Riley could have been dead for days now."

I stared at her, stunned. Was it possible? Was Riley already dead? That would mean all of this was just a trap to lur me in and kill me.

"In a way," I said slowly as realization dawned, "you might be right. But then that means they've had my cell numbe to send me fake calls all along. Why not just kill me outright? Why toy with me?"

The girls, having finished with the park ranger, started reading the inscriptions on the memorial walls. They were so quiet and well-behaved, I suspiciously wondered if someone h slipped them Xanax.

Evelyn stood with the girls, and to my amazement, she was just as engrossed in Lincoln's quotes on peace, war, and th rights of all men. Did she have a normal side? I hadn't made any effort to get to know her on this trip. I kind of felt bad about that. On any other trip, I would've tried to bond with her. Granted, she made no effort to be friendly with me or even to stick with us earlier in the trip. But I was in charge here. It was my responsibility to make sure everyone had a good time.

Instead, everyone was on edge. Was I making everyone crazy over this mess? If so, then walking into Ito's trap would be worth it. I should just send the girls home early and do it. No one but me and Baby Ito. No one else at risk.

Besides, I couldn't take this home with me. I couldn't let the people hunting me follow me there. Too many people and animals to hold against me. And Kelly was about to have a baby.

As if on cue, my cell began ringing. I slid it out of my pocket and looked at the screen. It was Robert—Kelly's husband.

"Is everything okay?" I asked. "Is Kelly alright? Is the baby here?"

Robert laughed on the other end. "Yes. Everything is fine. False alarm. They're sending us home. Kelly just didn't want you to worry."

I thanked him and hung up. False labor. That would piss Kelly off. I could imagine her screaming at the doctor. She wanted this over and done. And the baby was late already. I didn't envy the doctor facing her wrath right now.

"Mrs. Wrath?" Inez was tugging on my T-shirt. "Where's the ice cream? I thought there'd be ice cream."

I looked around to see twelve little faces staring up at me. For now, I'd have to take care of them. They deserved it, Troop Leader Merry Wrath. I owed them at least that.

"Okay!" I shouted so they'd all hear me. "Let's go get some ice cream!"

A cheer went up, and we stepped outside, where I scanned the mall area for a vendor. I found one about halfway down the reflecting pool. A little old man with an ice cream cart.

He'd never know what hit him.

CHAPTER ELEVEN

———

We found a hot dog stand just a few feet from the ice cream vendor, so we made a completely balanced lunch out of it. Totally healthy. Evelyn managed to not frown as she found a picnic spot for us while Maria scored the hot dogs and I grabbed the ice cream and several thousand napkins.

"Okay, ladies!" I said as I passed out the food. "Remember that we have to collect up our garbage when we're done."

"We know." Betty rolled her eyes. "Take only pictures, leave only footprints. We got it."

Wow. They actually remembered the Scouting mottos we'd drummed into their heads for a year. I thought they'd just been ignoring us. The girls sat in a semicircle around me, and I decided this was the perfect opportunity for some quality time with them. After all, I could be killed as soon as later on today. Might as well give the troop happy memories to remember me by.

"Is everyone having fun on this trip?" I asked. I was pretty sure the answer was yes but a little prepared in case I was wrong.

"I love Washington DC!" the four Kaitlins said in unison.

"How come there aren't any playgrounds?" Ava asked.

"It's hot here," Inez said, ketchup running down her chin. "But that means we get ice cream!"

I wiped her chin and said to Ava, "We're not here to play in parks. We're here to learn about our nation's history. This is the seat of government." As soon as I said that, I realized my mistake.

"The government has a seat here?" Betty said as she chewed her second hot dog. "Can we sit on it?"

I'd made the mistake of not being clear. These girls took things literally.

"I said that wrong," I spoke up. "What I meant is that DC is the headquarters of our government. You've been to the White House and met a senator. This is where laws are made."

"We were at the White House?" The usually silent Caterina shrieked.

Hannah nodded. "When we met the First Lady, doofus."

Caterina looked at her. "We met the First Lady?"

I made a mental note to stop giving her sugar. The girls explained to her that we had met the First Lady earlier in the trip. Caterina didn't say any more, but her eyes bulged in their sockets. Yup, definitely cut her off.

"Mr. Czrygy is a senator…" Lauren said slowly as if that would make her believe it. "Does he carry a gun?"

"What kind does he carry?" Betty asked.

I shook my head. "A senator is an elected official." That might be too difficult. "Your parents voted for him to go to DC and represent them."

"Why?" Lauren asked.

"I didn't vote for him," Inez grumbled.

Maria giggled. "You have to be eighteen years old to vote for someone. And each state—including Iowa—picks people to go to DC to vote on laws for them."

The girls looked at each other dubiously. A civics lesson was probably premature at this point.

"What about ambassadors?" Hannah asked. "Do we vote for them too?"

"I liked that Japan place," Betty said. She'd eaten her hot dog and the remains of a couple of other hot dogs and was starting in on the ice cream.

"Ambassadors are chosen by the government of their country to represent them here. The Japanese Embassy is where Ambassador Nakano works."

"What about the CIA?" Lauren asked, staring directly at me. "Do we elect them too, or do other countries do that for us?"

Maria was in danger of bursting out laughing. I couldn't

blame her. Imagine Russia picking our CIA agents? They'd go for lobotomized goldfish if they could get away with it.

"No, the CIA employees are hired. The director is appointed by the president." I wasn't sure where this was going.

"You work there, Maria." Inez squinted at the woman who was desperately trying to keep a straight face. "Are you a spy?"

Before I could deflect that question, Hannah jumped to her feet and asked, "How many people have you killed?"

"Is it true you have a cyanide pill to swallow if you're caught?" Betty asked. "And can we see it?"

Maria looked at me. Time to change the subject.

"Which memorial did you like best so far today?" I asked before digging into my lunch. I loved hot dogs. Hot dogs were my favorite. Hopefully with my mouth full, they'd wait to ask any more questions. And no, we didn't have cyanide pills. That was so 1947.

"I liked Mr. Fancy Pants," one of the Kaitlins cried. The others agreed with shouts and screams.

"No." I was not giving that damn bird any more of our time. "I asked about the memorials. Lincoln or Jefferson. Which one did you like better?"

"Mr. Fancy Pants!" Hannah and one of the other Kaitlins squealed.

"Girls!" I shouted, a little frustrated. "I want to know what you think of the memorials we saw today. Answer the question."

"No! It's Mr. Fancy Pants!" Hannah shouted as she pointed to a grassy area just a few feet away. Sure enough, there was the king vulture. Standing on the ground and staring at us and monopolizing our whole trip. Stupid bird.

"Do you think he's dangerous?" Evelyn looked at me nervously.

I knew the answer but wasn't going to tell her to hide a cookies. That would just make the girls hunt for a box to give him. The last thing I needed right now was a bloodbath.

The vulture wasn't moving. But he wasn't flying away either. The girls were wound tight, and I was afraid that at any moment they might rush him. Where were the zookeepers? An we were right near the Smithsonian for crying out loud!

"Can we keep him?" asked one of the Kaitlins. The other three nodded vigorously.

"No," I said, my cell out as I dialed 9-1-1. "He has to go back to the zoo."

"9-1-1, what's your emergency?" a woman asked through my phone.

"I want to report a vulture," I said, keeping my eyes focused on the bird. I couldn't tell if he was staring at me or the girls.

"Technically," the voice droned on, "vultures aren't illegal. Is it threatening you?"

The girls were coiled like twelve little snakes, ready to spring on their prey.

"No. He's not. But he's looking at us," I said absently, watching the girls prepare to pounce.

"Ma'am," the voice said a little impatiently. "This number is for emergency use only. You can face fines and prison time for misusing it."

"No!" I shouted a little too loudly. "I mean, it isn't just any vulture. It's Mr. Fancy Pants." The girls were slowly edging closer to the vulture. He just stood still, waiting. Dammit.

The voice sighed. "Ma'am, I'm going to disconnect. And fortunately for you, I'm not in the mood to report this offense…"

The girls were slowly moving now. The vulture did nothing. He was so still I think his eyes were frozen in place.

"Sorry. Let me start over. This is the escaped king vulture from the National Zoo! He's here on the mall with us and surrounded by children. I don't know if he's dangerous." I gave the coordinates of where we were. The dispatcher sounded a little skeptical but agreed to send the info to the zoo and animal control.

"Wait!" I called out to the girls as I shoved my cell back into my pocket.

It was like I was moving in slow motion. The girls started running as a group toward the googly-eyed bird who stood there as if he faced down a Scout troop every day.

I was running after them, grabbing girl after girl as I went along. But it felt like everything I was doing was underwater. Silently, I was willing the vulture to take off into the air, but he showed no signs of doing that. Maria came out of nowhere on my left and threw herself between the bird and the girls.

They ran over her like a kid-shaped steamroller. Mr. Fancy Pants watched but made no effort to move. The girls surrounded him and then just stopped. They stood in a circle, with the vulture in the middle.

"Girls!" I said when I caught up. "Don't touch him! We don't know if he's dangerous!"

That wasn't really on my mind though. I was more worried that touching this vulture was the equivalent of touching a painting in the National Gallery of Art or Dorothy's ruby slippers in the Smithsonian. This bird was an exhibit piece. It was probably a federal offense of some sort to mess with him.

Lauren stepped forward, as if she were the girls' ambassador to the bird. For all I knew, they could've elected her to that very position, because the others didn't move. She held out her hand, and I saw slivers of her ice cream sugar cone in her upturned palm. Oh, no!

Mr. Fancy Pants looked at her for a moment before stepping forward and gently retrieving a piece. As he tasted it, he looked like some of the food connoisseurs on cooking shows. His left eye went up as his right eye went down. Then he scooped up the remaining shards of sugar cone and gobbled it down.

I had to do something before Mr. Fancy Pants decided that the girls might *also* be made out of cookies.

"Girls," I said in a steady voice. "I want you to step back slowly and head back to the picnic area. Do you understand?"

They looked at me in unison, then, with a collective sigh, began to back off. That was a surprise. I waited until they were several feet away before I turned back to the bird.

But he wasn't there. He'd flown off. Just as an animal control van pulled up. Nice timing. A couple of guys carrying nets got out of the vehicle and came toward me.

"Ma'am," one of them said. "Are you the one who called about the vulture?"

Lauren stepped forward again, as if silently elected by

the others. "We don't know what you're talking about. What vulture?" The other eleven kids all nodded in agreement.

The men squinted at me.

I glared at Lauren. "He was here. But he's gone now. Sorry."

"Don't listen to her," Betty shouted. "She's hallucinating."

Inez nodded. "Heat exhaustion."

"So there was no vulture…" One of the men said slowly. "And you called it in to 9-1-1? Do you think this is a joke?"

Maria decided this might be a good time to step up. "The girls are teasing you. Of course the bird was here. We all saw it."

I took the opportunity to wave the girls off to Evelyn. "The kids like the vulture. They're afraid that capturing it is a bad thing… You know, *Free Willy* and all that?" I was babbling like an idiot.

The men looked at each other then at me. "You are certain that it was the king vulture?"

I described the bird to them, and they nodded. I relaxed a little.

"Yup. Sounds like him," the first guy said.

"He's been following us," I added. "He shows up wherever we are." I didn't want to tip my hand and incriminate myself for having given him cookies. There was no way I was going to admit to vulture tampering.

The second guy squinted at my troop. The girls were sitting with Evelyn, eating their ice cream. One of the Kaitlins waved.

"Are you part of a Girl Scout troop?" he asked.

I nodded. "That's right. We're from Iowa. We saw Mr. Fancy Pants at the zoo the other day, just before he escaped." I explained the encounter in Virginia and at the Jefferson Memorial.

"Mr. Fancy Pants?" The first guy's eyebrows wiggled.

"Uh, that's kind of our nickname for him," I said.

"Well, this is bad," the second guy said. "That vulture has been known to follow groups of little girls around."

"So I heard." I nodded. "Animal control in Charlottesville just missed him too. They told us about his fetish."

"Then you know that this is serious, ma'am. He's a protected animal and property of the Smithsonian."

I shrugged. "I didn't ask him to follow us. What do you expect us to do?"

The second guy asked for my contact information in case the zoo had more questions. I gave it willingly. This bird was stalking us and had to stop. I watched as the men got into their van and drove away.

Maria and Evelyn were organizing the girls as they cleaned up the area. I decided not to yell at the girls over their little charade. There wasn't any point. These girls got attached t animals. We'd had a similar problem with a horse at summer camp. It went beyond obsessive.

Maria really was a natural with kids. I made a mental note to ask if she'd be willing to move to Iowa when she retired But by then, my girls would probably be all grown up. Did I want to start another troop when these girls were gone? At this particular moment, I would say no. But tomorrow might be different.

The girls were keyed up by the sugar and appearance o Mr. Fancy Pants. They skipped along the length of the reflectin pool, giggling and squealing. I was glad I'd dropped the whole *why did you lie to animal control* thing. I wanted to get back to the fun we were having earlier.

The sky was still clear and bright blue, and in spite of the suffocating heat, we were all in a pretty good mood. As we walked, Maria pointed out various landmarks and gave the girl fun facts about Washington DC. They listened to her because they loved her. I really was lucky to have her helping out.

Evelyn was listening too. She'd actually been useful at times on this trip. Maybe I should lighten up with her. It was possible that she'd never been here before and was dazzled by the shopping possibilities. I wasn't much of a shopper myself— just didn't see the allure. Most of my shopping consisted of buying Oreos and Pizza Rolls.

I decided to cut the mom some slack. Sure, she was grumpy, and we had to tell her what to do, but I didn't need on more thing on my plate. Between Kelly's baby refusing to com out, a possible problem with my parents' marriage, and Riley's kidnapping, I didn't need to worry about anything else. I made up my mind in the future to try to get to know her better if I could. With Kelly on maternity leave when we got back, it would be nice to have another adult to wrangle the troop.

We spent the rest of the day around the Washington Monument. Unlike the other memorials, this one had a line to get in, and it already wrapped around the base of the monolith twice. Which meant entertaining the girls until we could get inside—no easy feat for anyone.

Fortunately, I had a few tricks up my sleeves. We played the alphabet I Spy game, shouting out things they could actually see that began with consecutive letters of the alphabet. We had to disqualify a few suggestions, you really couldn't see farts or x-rays (and I was pretty sure *quizballs* wasn't a real word), but I had to admit, they were creative.

None of the other tourists from the Jefferson or Lincoln memorials had joined us, and that made me breathe easier. Paranoia was a tough thing for spies to control. I personally have been shot at by a sweet-looking little old lady in Peru, followed several times—including by a child on horseback in Mongolia—and compromised by a devious pigeon in Madrid. Watching for the unpredictable wasn't easy. Especially with the pigeon.

But with every assignment you'd start looking for danger everywhere, and retirement was no exception. I wondered if that would ever fade with time. It had to. I couldn't imagine that life following me around in retirement. In fact, I'd never heard of that happening in the Agency before. Was I the first?

I was just about to lead the troop in a rousing game of Telephone, when Maria nudged me. I had one of the Kaitlins take over, and we stepped away from the group.

"I just got the autopsy information on Midori," Maria said quietly. "Ahmed knows a guy on the Tokyo police force."

"She was killed by blunt force," I said hopefully. "What we thought was right, right?"

She shook her head. "Not exactly. I mean, yes, someone hit her pretty hard, but that's not what killed her."

"That's impossible!" I said a little too loudly. "I mean"—people were staring at me—"we've had those reservations at that restaurant for months!" Folks looked away, probably hoping it was their spot for dinner that had bumped us.

I leaned in closer to Maria. "So what do they think happened?"

"The coroner thinks she was already dead when she was struck on the back of the head. What really killed her was a thin blade inserted into her brain through her ear."

I thought about that. It was a nasty way to go. And difficult. The only reason to attempt it was to hide how the victim was murdered. And whoever killed her clearly wanted to do that.

"Do they have any idea how long it was between the stabbing and the bludgeoning?"

Maria shook her head. "Hours, maybe? Her body was in pretty bad shape."

That was on me. Riley and I had dumped the body, and it took many months before she was discovered. We'd inadvertently screwed up the evidence we hadn't known we'd need a year later. Didn't that just figure?

"So someone killed her then beat her to hide the real murder. Why would anyone do that?"

"I don't know." Maria shrugged. "Maybe the murderer wanted it to look more brutal?"

"Then why not just do that in the first place? What's the point of the cover-up?" I asked.

Maria frowned. Even frowning, she was gorgeous. I wasn't. When I frowned I just looked constipated.

"Maybe her death was accidental?" she suggested.

"How do you accidentally fall ear-first onto a long, thin blade?" I shook my head. "It had to be something else."

"What if they wanted it to look like she'd been mugged?"

"Not in my small town. I don't think anyone has ever been mugged in Who's There, Iowa. That's the reason the murders I've been involved with were so sensational."

"Mrs. Wrath!" Inez shouted. "It's our turn to go inside!"

Maria and I hurried over to the group. They were getting instructions for their ride to the top of the obelisk.

"I don't want to go." Hannah backed up. "I'm scared of heights."

Maria nodded. "Evelyn and I will take them up. You stay here with her."

I led Hannah over to a spot in the grass, and we sat down, watching the other girls go. I had a rule in my troop: no one makes anyone else do something she doesn't want to do. I didn't see the point in pushing a terrified kid off the zip line. There were other parts of Scouting they could get excited about.

I chose my field knowing full well all the risks I was taking when I signed on to be a spy. Hannah knew that this would be too much for her.

"You're sure?" I asked.

She nodded, her brown ponytail bobbing. "Heights are scary."

"They can be," I agreed. "How do you like the trip so far?"

This gave me a chance to have a little one-on-one. I couldn't remember being alone with just one girl before. Usually I was surrounded by a herd all screaming at once.

Hannah grinned. "I love it! It's so cool! I want to live here someday!"

I laughed at her enthusiasm. "What did you like best out of all we've done so far?"

The child looked thoughtful for a moment. "Spending time with you! We don't get to do that too much."

My heart sank. I'd barely spent any time with the girls since I got that call from Riley. I'd spent all my time pawning them off on other people. But Hannah didn't think that. I wondered why. I gave her a huge hug.

"And the zoo. I really liked the zoo. Especially Mr. Fancy Pants—and how he follows us everywhere." She nodded for emphasis.

"He's not exactly following us," I lied. "It's just coincidence that he's here."

"Oh." Hanna frowned. "Then why have we seen him so much today?"

I shrugged. "I don't know. But we're in DC, and he's in DC, so it makes sense we might see him." There was no way I was going to tell the girls that this deranged bird had a thing for Girl Scout Cookies. They'd probably leave a trail for him leading back to our hotel.

"Do you really think he isn't following us?" she asked.

"I really think he isn't following us," I lied again. This was getting to be a habit with me.

"Then why is he standing right behind you?" Hanna asked, pointing over my right shoulder.

I slowly turned around and found myself nose to beak with the king vulture. I thought he'd heard me. And I didn't think he liked what I'd said.

CHAPTER TWELVE

———

"Um, Hannah?" I said quietly as the large bird cocked his head. "You should probably go to the entrance of the monument."

"But..."

"Right now. Please," I said as calmly as possible.

"I can't pet him?" she asked. Hannah was closer to me now. I could feel her breath on the back of my neck.

"No, you can't. Now please do as I say." I wanted to get her away from this raptor in case he attacked.

"What if we bought him a hat and T-shirt—like a disguise? He could hang out with us all day!"

While this sounded like a great idea (and I was pretty sure the bird would go along with it), the chance that he'd murder us in our sleep for shortbread cookies was a bit off-putting. I shook my head and pointed to the monument.

"Fine. We never get to do anything fun!" the girl grumbled as she stomped away from me. There went my meaningful one-on-one. Stupid bird.

Mr. Fancy Pants started to walk around me. He was actually going to make a run for the kid.

I stuck my arm out to cut him off, and he opened his wings in preparation for taking off. I had no choice as I tackled the vulture and wrestled him to the ground. The giant bird struggled against me, protesting loudly with furious squawking. But I held firm. This only inflamed him more, and he began attacking me with his beak. Somehow, I got my arm up and around his neck as I rolled over and pinned him to the ground.

A sea of cell phones surrounded me, all taking video of my fight with the bird. I heard someone calling 9-1-1 in the distance. Great, now the zoo could take him back, and he'd leave my troop alone.

My arms ached as I tried to hold the vulture firmly enough to take the fight out of him but lightly enough so as not to crush him. If I lessened my grip a fraction of an inch, he would strain against me to break free. I prayed that animal control would come quickly.

Mr. Fancy Pants stopped struggling, and I breathed a small sigh of relief (and hoped I hadn't killed him). I could hear cameras going off and looked to the side to see that group of tourists off to my left, snapping away. That wasn't necessarily a good thing, but I couldn't let the bird go. He was too valuable for one thing and one more problem I didn't need for the other. I tried to ignore the attention and focus on the animal that was facedown beneath me.

His head turned to the side, even with my arm on the back of his neck. One googly eye gave me the once over as if he were sizing me up for an epic escape. That wasn't going to happen.

Where were those damned zookeepers? I was worn out trying to hold the bird down. If they didn't show up soon, maybe someone in the crowd that surrounded me had something I could tie him up with—like a camera strap or something. I doubted anyone brought a collapsible cage. I could never be that lucky.

"Let us through, folks!" A man's voice rang out behind me, and I relaxed a little.

Two strong arms roughly lifted me off the bird as a net dropped over Mr. Fancy Pants.

"Thanks!" I said as I landed on my feet. "I was really getting worried…" My voice trailed off as I felt handcuffs being clamped onto my wrists.

"Hey!" I protested. "Hey, I was just helping you!"

A masculine voice spoke. "You are under arrest for the kidnapping of Smithsonian property and for molesting an endangered species."

"What?" Molesting? I turned around to face the man. He was a Fed. I wasn't fond of the FBI. "You've got it all wrong!"

My troop started filing out onto the grass around me, their tour of the monument obviously over. Maria rushed over me. Evelyn smirked. The girls, seeing Fancy Pants straining against the net, began to cry. Loudly.

"What's happening here?" Maria flashed her badge at the Fed, who scrutinized it before looking a bit confused.

"We are arresting this woman as a domestic terrorist," he said simply, still wondering why a CIA agent was involved.

"She's a Girl Scout troop leader!" Maria said. "That vulture has been stalking us! She was probably trying to catch him for you!"

"Well, yes…that…" I said. "And he was going after one of my girls. This bird has a record for chasing groups of little girls."

The Fed looked at me curiously. He seemed to be weighing his options and probably thought I was crazy to boot. And the crowd around us was growing. It was getting out of hand.

"Sorry, ma'am. I've got to take you in to straighten this all out."

"But you don't know the whole story!" I protested as he gripped my arm and propelled me through the crowd that now parted to make way.

"We can sort it out downtown," he said, not looking at me.

"Look…Agent…" I stammered.

"Grayson," he replied.

"Okay, Agent Grayson," I continued as we kept walking. "This really is a mistake. I was trying to protect a child from a giant raptor!"

Grayson said nothing as we approached a black Lincoln Town Car. I rolled my eyes. It was always a black Town Car. He opened the door and carefully pushed me into the backseat. The door slammed shut and locked before he got in and started the engine.

I'd been bound and locked in a car before. I knew how to get out of this situation, but I didn't move a muscle. I wasn't going to have resisting arrest thrown at me too. It would be best to just do what the man said for now. Hopefully, Maria was on the case and taking care of things.

We arrived at FBI headquarters, and for the first time, it

hit me that this wasn't an ordinary cop. What did the FBI have to do with any of this? Wait… He'd called me a terrorist. Was that what I'd be charged with? That was overkill.

Agent Grayson led me to a cell, unfastened my handcuffs, and locked the door behind him. As I rubbed my bruised wrists, I realized something. After all my years of espionage, I finally got arrested. And it wasn't in a Turkish prison for spying…it was in DC for kidnapping a vulture. I had to admit—I never saw that coming. Not in a million years.

I was there for hours. No one came to read me my rights or process me. With my luck, I was heading to Guantanamo. Normally in this situation, Riley would have been here to get me out. But Riley was missing.

I was in no hurry to have my prints taken and run through the system. When I left the field, I changed my name and appearance. But fingerprints were different. I couldn't change them. Well, I could have, but it would've been more painful than it was worth. My cover would have been blown, and all the anonymity I'd worked for would be lost.

I was alone here. It seemed as though hours had gone by and no one even checked on me. The least they could do was bring me a bottle of water and maybe a little food. Okay, fine. I use this time to think about something else.

My mind wandered to the dreams I'd been having. I hadn't thought about my time in Japan for a while. In fact, I'd forgotten all about it. While that wasn't necessarily a great trait a spy, it had seemed necessary. Not to make room for more valuable information but to avoid thinking of the relationship Riley and I had then.

I felt a twinge in my stomach that could either have been emotional pain or hunger. I'd never really dealt with that mess. Maybe that was why Riley flirted with me, even to this day. He thought he had a chance. That was stupid. I had Rex now. Riley probably couldn't have imagined failure where women were concerned.

There were no clocks anywhere. No windows to tell me how much time had passed. I had no idea how long I'd been there. I lay down on the wooden bench against the wall and stared at the ceiling. The bench was brutally uncomfortable, but

I'd had worse. One time in Tibet I had to sleep on a rock. A rough rock that was ice cold. My pillow had been…you guessed it…a rock. It took weeks to get the kinks out of my back.

Where was everyone? Surely Maria could've brought in the CIA's big guns to get me released. Or my dad could have used his influence to do something. Or that stupid zoo could just have told the Feds the whole story. They knew I was telling the truth, and they knew that Mr. Fancy Pants had stalked groups of girl before.

And yet, here I remained, having to pass the time productively. It was all I could do. Save my energy for any fights ahead. Closing my eyes, I tried to meditate and succeeded only in falling asleep.

I arrived at the appointed place a little early. Skirting the park to surveil the area, I spotted a person in a fedora, dark sunglasses, and a trench coat sitting on a bench near where I was told to be.

The sky was gray and drizzly. Clearly, this was my contact because who else would wear sunglasses on such a dreary day? And how stupid to dress in a way that screamed espionage? I, myself, was in a stocking cap and black wool coat. After satisfying myself there was no one else around, I joined the contact on the bench.

"Thank you for coming," a voice with a slight German accent said.

"Oh, my God! You're that bimbo from the German Embassy!" I said. "What the hell do you want with me?" My first thought was that she was trying to drive me away from Riley, and if that was the case, she could have him.

The woman took off her sunglasses and glared at me. I was right. Bimbo.

"My name is Chlotilde," she snarled. "And I'm Interpol. I'm just undercover at the embassy."

I stood up to leave. "Look, if this is about Riley…you can have him!"

She looked startled—like I'd just told her aliens had landed. "Is that what you think?" She scoffed. "You spies always think you know everything. This has nothing to do with Riley."

I sat back down and waited for her to say more. I wasn't

going to speak until I knew what was going on. Spies often got into trouble by talking too much. It was human nature to babble on to fill uncomfortable gaps in conversation, and many a mission has been lost because of it.

Chlotilde waved me off. "Like I said, this has nothing to do with him, Finn Czrygy."

Okay. Didn't expect that. "Well, by sleeping with my boyfriend, you certainly achieved that goal."

She didn't even have the grace to look chastened. In fact she got that weird, confused look again. "Look, I need some information..."

"Forget it. You're not going to turn me into one of your stooges. Go find someone else," I said as I got to my feet again. was the one who recruited. I wasn't going to be recruited as a double agent and certainly not for those rubes at Interpol.

"Sit down!" the German hissed. "This is more important than either of us! There's a British mole trying to pass off information to the Americans."

I sat. Not because she told me to but because I was kind of curious as to what she had to say.

"I'll give you three minutes," I said. "Not one second more."

A twig snapped behind us, and we both looked over our shoulders. Nothing was there, but I knew better. Someone was watching us.

Chlotilde began to sweat. "Here." She shoved a packet of papers into my hands, along with a burner phone. "Look this over. I'll be in touch." And with that, she stood and strode off quickly.

I carefully stuffed the packet into my coat and began to walk in the other direction.

"Merry?" A man's voice shook me out of the dream. Riley had obviously come to get me out of here.

"Ma'am?" the voice said again, and I looked up. It was Agent Grayson, not Riley. Riley was still missing.

"Ms. Wrath," Grayson said as he inserted a key into the cell. "You are free to go. Your handler explained everything. I apologize for arresting you. I didn't realize you were with the CIA."

I sat up, and with as much dignity as a woman with messy hair and drool on her chin could have, rose to my feet and walked out of the cell.

"If you'll follow me this way, I'll take you to your handler and release you."

I said nothing, just stared at Grayson as he spoke. Now that he was my new BFF, I saw that he was a very attractive man. Thick, brown hair topped smiling, brown eyes. He was built like an athlete. If I didn't have Rex, well, maybe I'd have another option.

Holy crap! What was I thinking? I shook my head to clear it.

Maria stood waiting for me in the lobby. She smiled as I walked up to her and led me out the door. It was night. How long had I been in there?

We climbed into the van, which was filled with twelve little girls who stared at me without speaking. Evelyn frowned. Why was everyone so quiet?

"Okay, ladies," Maria said as she started the van. "Who wants dinner?"

Hands shot up, but the girls still didn't speak. What had Maria done to them? And did she have more of it? We were all silent as she drove to a historic tavern in Georgetown called the Wig and Pen. The maître d' showed us upstairs to a private room with several tables of four.

The filter came off, and the girls squealed, anxious to have tables to themselves. Maria murmured to Evelyn, who nodded, albeit with the usual frown fixed on her face. If she weren't careful, she was going to have frown lines. I watched as Mrs. Trout pulled a chair up to the Kaitlins' table. Which girl was she the mother of? Never mind—I'd find out when we got home.

Food came in family-style—Yankee pot roast, potatoes, baskets of bread, and corn on the cob. The girls dug in, and that was when I finally said something to Maria.

"Thanks for getting me out of there," I said quietly. I left out *what took you so long*. That didn't seem appropriate.

"It took forever. I called your father who called in a few favors at the Agency. I have no idea who he talked to, but they released you once whoever it was called. Sorry I can't tell you more than that."

I sighed. "It doesn't matter. I'm sure Dad will tell me later." Sure, I wanted to know what had happened, but it could wait.

Maria looked at me funny and then started to giggle. The giggle grew into laughter, and it wasn't long before tears were pouring down her face.

"It's not that funny," I said, a little wounded.

She nodded. "Oh yes, it is!" Maria held out her phone to show me a video of me wrestling Mr. Fancy Pants. "It's all over the net. It's viral!" She broke into fits of laughter again.

I took a bite of pot roast so I wouldn't stab her with my fork. That was the one good thing about getting out of espionage—everyone could film you and post it online. I got out before that became a problem to me.

Maria had done a great job of picking a restaurant. I had to hand it to her—the food was amazing. The meat just fell apart in my mouth, and the au jus was to die for. This might've been the best dinner we'd had so far on this trip.

I had just finished buttering an ear of corn when my cell went off. My buttery fingers fumbled the phone. Could it be Riley? Did Kelly have her baby?

"Merry!" Rex's incredibly handsome face filled the screen. "So, how was prison? Any different than it is back here?" He grinned and looked too adorable for me to be angry with him.

"You saw the video, I take it," I said, a little frostily.

"Everyone saw the video," Rex said. "One of my sergeants showed it to me. Then some of the guys blew up a still of you manhandling a national treasure and left it on my desk."

I rolled my eyes and groaned. "Great. I'm sure the whole town knows now."

He nodded. "They didn't say your name, but you might want to wear a baseball cap or something for a while when you get back." Again, he flashed me a mind-numbing grin.

"Well, thanks for calling and rubbing it in," I said.

"No problem." He laughed. "What are boyfriends for?"

My stomach did a little flip-flop when he said that. Even though we'd been dating a little while, I never tired of hearing

"I'll let you go. Looks like you have your hands full. Ju

wanted to tell you you're my favorite jailbird." And with that, he hung up.

I was just buttering a roll when my cell rang again. This time it was Kelly. If she wasn't pregnant and having a baby any day now, I probably wouldn't have answered.

"Hey, hero!" My friend said into the phone. "Saw some of your handiwork. Nice."

"I'll have you know," I said grumpily, "that I saved our girls from that monster. He had giant talons and a razor-sharp beak that—"

"I'm sure you did." Kelly laughed as she cut me off. "And I must say, I prefer this threat over some of the other threats the troop has faced in the last year."

"So are you having that baby or what?" I changed the subject.

"No. Not yet," My best friend's tone changed from laughter to fury. "If it doesn't make an appearance soon, I'm going to make it eat vegetables every day of its life."

"Well, since you're on the phone, I have some people who want to talk to you." Before she could protest, I handed the phone to the first table and announced that Kelly wanted to talk to each and every one of them.

"You're kind of evil," Maria said as she scooped up some potatoes.

"You have no idea...." I said with a wink before shoving more pot roast into my mouth.

CHAPTER THIRTEEN

My phone was still making the rounds when the pie wa served. Apple à la mode. The warm, flaky crust melted the ice cream in a heavenly puddle of goodness. I'd finished my desser when Inez handed me back my phone. Kelly wasn't there. Probably too angry to talk to me further. Maybe I'd done her a solid. I'd heard that intensity of any kind could stimulate labor.

Maria pushed herself away from the table. "Man! That was terrific. It's almost like we're just here as tourists."

She didn't have to say it, but I understood her meaning. For one meal, we weren't talking about Riley or the yakuza. Of course, we were talking about one of the most humiliating moments in my life—but that was beside the point.

"No word from Riley?" Maria asked finally. I guess she had to bring him up at some point.

I shook my head. "I'm thinking maybe I'll turn this over to the Agency."

Her eyes went wide. "Really?" I couldn't tell if she like this idea or not.

"Really. I'm supposed to be here for *them*." I nodded toward my troop. "And I don't work for the CIA anymore. I wa to spend our last few days having fun with the girls. I don't war their memories to be about the fact I'm never around."

Maria grinned. "I don't think that will be first and foremost in their memories."

"Well, I did take down a significant threat for them. W knows what might've happened if Mr. Fancy Pants had gotten hold of Hannah?"

We laughed for a moment, and it felt good. I hadn't see Maria in so long. It was nice spending time with someone who had a past similar to mine. If she wanted to stay with us, we could have some fun before we left for Iowa.

"This won't affect your job, will it?" I asked. "If I turn what I know over to Langley?"

Maria looked thoughtful. "I don't think so. Remember, I'm on vacation. It's just a coincidence I was helping you when you got these weird phone calls."

"You're sure you are okay with it?" Hurting her career was not a risk I wanted to take.

"Yes, it'll be fine. Plus, I'll get to hang out with you and the kids. They really are fun." Maria smiled and looked at her watch. "Uh-oh. It's getting late. We need to head back to the hotel. We can call the Agency tomorrow."

As we corralled the girls into the van and headed to the hotel, I felt relieved. Letting this go and letting the professionals handle it would work. They had more resources and a lot less to lose. Yes, there was the pinch of guilt here and there for not helping Riley myself. But what did I really owe him?

Okay—so he helped me with a couple of cases recently. He didn't have to do that. But then, the CIA had a vested interest because it involved terrorists. I was a civilian now. Running around after the yakuza wasn't something I wanted to do anymore.

Maria and I discussed the details once Evelyn and the girls were in bed. I'd call Riley's boss and explain what had been going on. And that would be that. They would find my old handler, and I'd finish up the last two days of our trip on a high note.

To be perfectly honest, my conversation with Hannah had hit a nerve. Her favorite thing about the trip was spending time with me. Except for the fact that they hadn't spent much time with me. I'd been brushing them off to chase nonexistent clues that had led nowhere.

In the past, when I'd been an agent, I'd worked with less. But now I shouldn't have had to. Unless the Japanese crime syndicate was going to send me the details on where Riley was and promise not to hurt my troop, I wasn't going any further with this. Riley was on his own.

Ouch. I didn't mean that. But come tomorrow, he'd have

every resource the Agency had put toward finding him. I had nothing to go on. The only clues I'd found—the cell phone and the weird documents in Japanese—did nothing to further the case. I was a civilian and needed to start acting like it.

Maria said good night and went into her room. I was alone. After brushing my teeth and changing into jammies, I stretched out on the couch. For the first time on this trip, I drifted to sleep without any concerns.

Riley set me up in another safe house once I got back from my meeting with Chlotilde. I toyed with mentioning my meeting with her—partly because I'd have loved to see my handler's face when he found out he'd slept with an Interpol agent. For some reason, though, I decided not to. I wasn't going to spy for the German woman, no matter what she did.

It wasn't that unusual in our field to get propositioned like that. Every nation's spy agency tried to do the same thing. It was just part of the game. Turning people to your own advantage was like filling a sales quota.

I found the new apartment easily enough. It was in a crowded residential district, so having a cab let me off there wasn't going to tip anyone off. I waited until the cabbie was out of sight before entering the building. The elevator took me to the seventh floor, and I found the place easy enough. In minutes, I was already running a nice hot bath.

As I stepped into the steaming water, I thought about Chlotilde. If she wasn't actually interested in Riley, why sleep with him? Seemed a bit unnecessary. I could understand it a little. Riley could charm the panties off most women. It had even worked for me, briefly. But she could've exercised a little restraint.

I toyed with these thoughts until the water turned tepid and I got out. Slipping into yoga pants and a sweatshirt, I settled on the generic couch and pulled out the packet the German had given me. Inside a blank envelope, I found ten thousand Euros and some newspaper clippings. Disgusted, I shoved the money back into the envelope. They couldn't buy me. That was the oldest trick in the book.

The newspaper clippings were from the last few days. The first article was about an investigation into Midori Ito's dealings with some sort of bank fraud. What did that have to do with me? The yakuza was on my radar here—that was true. But my main assignment dealt with tracing an arms dealer from Russia to Japan. I hadn't found anything that linked the yakuza to the Russians.

The second clipping was an editorial about the US Embassy in Tokyo. There was some concern that the Americans were getting involved in Japanese politics. There was some hinting that the British might be involved. I thought about overhearing Riley talking to someone with a British accent the other night. Again—nothing that related to me. If Riley was involved with the UK, that was his business. I wasn't supposed to get involved in anything outside my assignment.

I rubbed my eyes and read both articles again but could find nothing that had anything to do with me. Interpol was known to chase down international bank fraud. But what did they care if the Americans were schmoozing with Japanese politicians? And what else did they think we were doing here? Holding a chess tournament? Embassies were set up for interaction between nations.

This was ridiculous and obviously a case of mistaken identity. I shoved the papers back into the envelope with the money and got ready for bed. Tomorrow, I'd send the envelope by courier to Chlotilde, rejecting whatever the offer was. Seriously, these Interpol agents didn't do their homework, and I wasn't about to do it for them. I slipped into bed as the whole thing slipped from my mind.

I woke with a start. It was only one in the morning. The dream had kind of gotten to me, but I wasn't sure why. All of this had happened years ago. And it had been a nonevent as far as I'd been concerned. So why was I remembering it all now?

It didn't make sense, really. I'd messengered the envelope back to Chlotilde and never heard from her again. Oh sure, I kept an eye out for a while. You never knew when information you thought was useless could turn out to be something important. But it hadn't. Nothing ever came of it as far as I knew. I'd never mentioned the whole, weird thing to Riley and couldn't find a connection worth exploring.

This was probably my guilt coming out through dreams.

And yet…why were the dreams coming in chronological order like this? I hadn't thought about this since I'd left Japan. What was the point of thinking about it now?

It had to be the fact that I was dealing with Riley and the yakuza. My dreams reflected the only other time those two things were even remotely together. That had to be it.

My assignment in Japan had hit a dead end. The CIA had decided that there was no connection in the case, and a few weeks later, I'd been transferred to another country and another case. I'd thought about Chlotilde. She'd never contacted me after that. I remembered thinking at the time that maybe she had just been trying to get back at Riley for seducing her. And I'd never thought of it again before now.

I fell back asleep after tossing these thoughts around for a few more minutes. I'd learned to let go of a case that went nowhere. It happened a lot more than you might have thought. Sometimes a case turned out not to be a case after all. You dropped it and moved on. And that's what I was going to do.

CHAPTER FOURTEEN

———

The girls woke me up the next morning, jumping around like the little balls of energy they were. More than one showed me the video of me wrestling the vulture to the ground. It always ended with them laughing hysterically and me wishing I knew a black-hat hacker who could remove it from YouTube.

We decided to take them to a pancake restaurant for breakfast, and they were beyond excited. I couldn't remember the last time I'd been so excited about breakfast. I couldn't help but smile as they danced around us, singing songs they made up about waffles—Mr. Fancy Pants suddenly forgotten. This time, I was going to enjoy a meal with them instead of worrying about my old boss or anything else.

Maria and Evelyn emerged from their room, both smiling. Well, I think Evelyn was smiling. It was hard to tell. It might have been more like a disgruntled smirk. But I didn't care. We only had two days left in this city, and dammit, we were going to enjoy them.

"When are you going to call it in?" Maria murmured as we climbed into the van.

"After breakfast," I answered. No point in calling out the troops on an empty stomach. That was never a good idea. Breakfast was the most important meal of the day, and they weren't kidding. Some of the biggest mistakes in judgment I ever made were when I was hungry. In fact, that should be in the training. Maybe I'd throw that at them after I handed Riley's case over.

The waitresses were fun. They teased the girls and brought them crayons and paper to color with. The girls were having a great time, and for once, the Kaitlins mixed it up and didn't sit together. Now that was huge.

"What's on the agenda today?" Evelyn startled me by speaking. She was sitting with Maria and me for the first time on this trip. It was kind of weird.

"The Spy Museum," I said with a wink to Maria.

Maria shot me a look. "Seriously? The Spy Museum?"

I shrugged. "Why not? I've wanted to check it out since it opened. You can't tell me you aren't curious."

"Yeah, sure. I guess I was afraid it'd be corny," she said. "But what the hell? Let's go."

The girls erupted into screams when we told them. And the screaming didn't abate until we pulled up and parked. Have you ever been in a vehicle with a bunch of squealing little girls? I thought we should have considered weaponizing them.

After we paid admission and dragged the girls out of the gift shop, we headed in. I was getting excited. It was the one place in DC I'd never been to, and I couldn't wait to see what they had. I'd just have to be careful and not tip my hand to the girls. They didn't know I'd been a spy, and I didn't want that to change.

The first thing we had to do was go into a room with placards on the walls every foot or so. We were told to line up in front of the cards and memorize what was on them. That would be our cover story and assignment.

"Who designed this?" I asked with a giggle.

Maria shushed me. "I'm trying to memorize my cover."

I looked at mine. Okay, I'd play. Usually I did this for real, so how hard could it be? My card said that I was a sixty-five-year-old male Italian fishmonger who was in the US visiting his son who lived in Alexandria, Virginia.

Damn. I'd never been to Italy. I would've loved an assignment there but never got one. It would've been a far cushier job than the one I had in Bulgaria. That was for sure. You really didn't appreciate electricity and fresh water until you didn't have it.

And an old man who sold fish? I didn't even like fish. Oooh, maybe I could build that in—I sold fish because I didn't like it and therefore was not likely to "get high on my own supply!" I had a good memory but still went over and over the placard to burn Guiseppe Tutti's life into my head. I'd never had to be a different age, let alone sex, before. This was going to be interesting.

"Time's up!" A woman in a docent uniform announced. She told us that we had to check in on computers throughout the exhibit for assignments and leads. At the end of our tour, we'd be tested by a computer program to see if we'd survived. I was grinning like an idiot. This would be so easy. How cool was it that I got to pretend to be something I already was?

"Who are you?" I asked Lauren.

She scowled. "I'm just an insurance salesman from Buffalo. Why?" Her eyes slid sideways, checking for threats. Good girl.

"Just asking," I said.

"Would you be interested in buying a life insurance policy?" Lauren asked. "You know, you're not getting any younger."

Evelyn began laughing. It was the first time I'd heard her do anything but complain, and I jumped about two feet in the air. Not as good as an American bison, but I thought it was impressive.

So Evelyn Trout wasn't an angry robot after all. I wondered what her cover story was.

"I'm good," I answered Lauren. "Selling fish in Italy isn't very dangerous."

Lauren shook her head. "You never know. You could accidentally slice open a major artery with a boning knife. Or you could fall into the sea and drown. What would your loved ones do if that happened?"

I tried to recall if Lauren's parents were in insurance or regularly used a boning knife or if she was just really, really good at this. The girl shrugged and ran off to look at a collection of weapons made from everyday household items. When I spotted the camera built into a pack of cigarettes, it was all I could do not to blow my cover. I had that camera once. In Libya. It was eaten by a camel.

The lipstick gun also looked promising…until you had to use it to prove it wasn't a gun. There was no real pigment in it. It was fake. And I put on one hell of an act in Austria once just trying to prove it was real makeup. A helpful tip—you could color your lips and skin by pinching or biting it. Of course, this effect didn't last long, and I almost shot my lip off, but that was just splitting hairs.

"I hate to admit it," Maria said. "But this is kind of awesome. I've seen some of this stuff in action before."

"*Buongiorno*, do you speak Italian?" I asked her, deciding to keep to my cover. I could pull off the accent, but the language was hopeless. Maybe if I'd studied Italian I could've been sent to the Riviera. Of course, this was the United States government we were talking about. I had a few friends in the Foreign Service. Todd was fluent in Mandarin and Farsi. They sent him to Spain. And Amelia spoke Russian and Czech. She'd never been assigned to either place. She was doing a lovely stint in Bali though. The rule of thumb seemed to be if you spoke it and were completely solid with the culture, we'd send you to a place where it was completely useless.

She answered without missing a beat. "No, I'm just a college student here on break." Maria tossed her glossy curls arrogantly. "Do you know where the best club for any action is? I've got an awesome fake ID."

Inez came over and joined us. "Mrs. Wrath? Do you think they'll sell belt-buckle derringers in the gift shop?" No matter how many times I'd told the girls I wasn't married, they always called me "Mrs." I figured it was a kid thing.

I shook my head. "I don't think so, Inez." At least, I hoped not.

"I'm not Inez," the girl said. "My name is Angela, and I'm a puppeteer from Idaho."

Now why didn't I get that? I could pull off a puppeteer and I'd been to Idaho. Well, not at the same time, but I thought could have pulled it off better than an eight-year-old girl.

The kids were having a great time, and I had to admit that I was too. Even Evelyn was checking the computer in each room for updates to her assignment. The Kaitlins ran from exhibit to exhibit, oohing and aahing over things that had been the tricks of my trade for years.

"Did you talk to Langley?" Maria asked.

"Oh crap." I smacked my forehead. "I totally forgot. I'

do it when we get outside." I was starting to have fun for the first time on this trip and didn't want to spoil it by getting yelled at by the CIA.

Maria nodded and went back to browsing. This really was a cool place. There was a lot of history—some I didn't even know about. My favorite spy stories were of George Washington during the Revolutionary War. He was the first spymaster in this country and had an elaborate network of ordinary people feeding him information on British movements.

It was interesting to note that espionage was really frowned on back then. Spies were outranked by dysentery and rats. The museum had a letter from Washington himself. That was so cool. How did they get this stuff? It wasn't like the CIA willingly gave stuff up. I knew agents who'd received the highest honors you could get, only to have them confiscated moments later and locked up for decades until they were declassified. This wasn't the business to be in if you wanted fame and recognition.

I browsed the weapons. The nineteenth-century ring gun was beyond cool, and I went all fangirl over the courier shoes and Enigma machine. The technology was impressive for its time. There was nothing from this decade and probably wouldn't be for another forty years. I thought about that. What would be in the museum then? Things I couldn't even imagine…exploding breath mints? Cell phones that turned into jet packs? Laptops that were bulletproof and purified water? Poisonous breath so you could kill your enemies with halitosis?

I shuddered at the sight of the rectal tool kit. The little knives lay next to the capsule they were supposed to hide in. I had to draw the line at rectal knives. Sure, it seemed like a good idea, until you had to *use* them. And how exactly did you get them out in a fight? If anyone at the CIA had ever used them, they never said anything. I wouldn't have either.

Oh, my God. They had the one weapon I'd always wanted to see—the umbrella that injected its victim with a tiny capsule of poison! In 1978, the assassin, code name *Piccadilly,* came up behind a Bulgarian author named Georgi Markov at a bus stop in London and injected him with the ricin capsule, using the infamous umbrella. The murder was orchestrated by the Bulgarian government with a little help from the KGB. Markov died a few days later. This terrible event was legendary in the history of espionage—and here I was, standing next to it! Squee!

Looking around, I didn't see any of the girls, so I allowed myself a little end-zone dance. *I mean, come on!* This was a huge piece of the history of spy activity during the Cold War! It was comparable to seeing Michael Jackson's white, studded glove or Hitler's bunker!

This place was amazing. I found myself getting lost in the exhibits, reading absolutely every plaque on every item. For the first time on this trip, I was really enjoying myself. When I caught up with them, the four Kaitlins plus Inez were peppering Maria with questions about spies. It made me a smidge wistful. They knew she'd worked at the CIA. Wouldn't they think I was cool if they knew my past? Oh, well. It wasn't meant to be. I'd have to live with that.

I took the opportunity of being alone to log in to a computer myself. I selected my cover and hit enter.

You are being followed and are in great danger. Keep your eyes open!

I couldn't help but smile. It was just the kind of vague alert I expected. As I stopped to read a list of the Moscow Rules from the Cold War, I made a point to look around. No point in breaking character.

And that's when I spotted her.

Leiko Ito was standing a few feet to my left, pretending to be fascinated by a diorama of the Berlin Wall.

My blood ran cold. There was no reason for her to be here. I couldn't imagine someone like her being interested in spy culture. The yakuza were a little too *in your face* for covert activities.

Maria, Evelyn, and the girls were leaving the room, and I scrambled to join them.

"Stay with a crowd," I whispered as I caught up to Maria. I told her about Baby Ito in the next room. She nodded, concern played out on her face. Very gingerly, she reached out and squeezed my elbow. Then she herded the girls and moved them along. In any other situation, I'd have had her take the girls and get out of here. But my guess was that Ito had guys in the gift shop waiting for us. In which case, we were trapped.

No. Way. I spotted something I thought would be useful and made for it. Overhead was a large duct system inviting me to crawl through it to spy on other people in the museum. I ran up the stairs and dove in, following the ductwork to the room where I'd seen Ito. How convenient for them to have this here! Who knew the International Spy Museum would actually be a location for real spy activities?

Baby Ito was still in the last room, but her eyes were trained on the doorway my troop had just gone through. She was dressed casually in capri pants, a black T-shirt, and ballet flats. But it was her alright. I didn't doubt it for a moment.

Things were escalating if she was personally involved. And that wasn't good. Not good at all. We might've been beyond the point of no return, making it too late to alert the Agency. If she was doing the actual legwork, she was getting ready to strike.

Two men in business suits joined her, and I gasped. They were the two men at the Jefferson and Lincoln memorials yesterday. I'd been right about them. I leaned closer to the vent to hear what she was telling them, but she was too quiet.

The men nodded and headed back toward the entrance to the museum. They were going to catch us in the gift shop at the end. Damn. If I ever found Riley and he was still alive, I was going to kill him. Now my girls really were caught up in an international incident. I crawled back to the beginning of the duct and rejoined my group as Ito entered the room.

"Two guys," I said softly to Maria. "Waiting for us in the gift shop."

"What do you want to do?" she asked, scanning the room. Her eyes stopped when they landed on Ito Jr., and she quickly looked away before being detected.

"You and Evelyn stay with the girls. Try to slow them down. I'm going straight to the end. If they want me, they can have me. Then they should leave you and the girls alone."

"That sounds a bit suicidal to me," Maria said.

I nodded. "Who has more fun than me?" I pretended to take out my cell to check for messages and activated the *Find Your Phone* app, tuning it in to Maria in the contacts list. She watched me and nodded. I knew she'd take good care of the girls.

I was just about to return the phone to my pocket when it rang. Perfect. That would be my excuse to leave.

"I've got to take this," I said a little loudly. "I'll double back later."

Maria nodded as I put the phone to my ear and exited the hall.

"Merry?" Rex's voice made me feel a little better.

"Hey," I said as I kept walking steadily toward the exit.

"Is everything alright?" he asked.

Uh-oh. Did he know?

"Why do you ask?" I said, never breaking my stride. I couldn't risk looking behind me to see if Ito was following me. That would be too obvious.

"Robert called. Kelly's in labor, and in between cursing she called you a few names for putting the girls in danger."

On the one hand, I was flattered that my best friend even mentioned me during what had to be the most painful moment of her life. On the other hand, now my boyfriend knew something was wrong.

I passed through another room, this one displaying the art of disguise. I could use that right now. What should I tell Rex? He was halfway across the country. He'd feel helpless. However, if I was kidnapped and never saw him again, I didn't want my last words to be a lie. Oh sure, I was really good at it, and it would certainly be useful in this situation, but I still didn't want to lie to him.

The beginning of our relationship had been based on a lie when he was investigating me and didn't know I was a former spy. I'd been trying to make that up to him ever since. If I lied now, it could be the end of our relationship. I really didn't want that to happen.

"Merry," Rex said again. "Are you in trouble?"

"Right now, actually," I said in a normal voice. "It's a problem, but the company is working on it."

Okay—that was a lie. I'd intended to call the CIA this morning, and if I had, maybe I wouldn't be in this situation, but was pretty sure Maria was on the phone to them now. So they would soon be involved. Hopefully that wasn't a big lie.

"I can be there in three hours," Rex's voice hardened.

Awww! He wanted to ride to my rescue!

"It's okay." It wasn't. "Don't worry about me." He totally should've.

The main exit was coming up. A couple of tourists ahead of me opened the door to the gift shop, and I spotted the two suits standing there, waiting. Okay, so I kind of got the idea of rectal knives now.

"I'm not going to stay here and wait to hear that something horrible has happened to you!" Rex sounded angry.

"Just sit tight. I'm heading to the gift shop in the International Spy Museum. I'll meet them there. Call my Dad." I hung up but kept the phone to my ear. Rex was smart. He'd figure out what I was trying to tell him and call my father. I'd left their number in case of emergencies. Hopefully, between Maria tracking me and calling in the CIA and Rex letting Dad know that I was about to be kidnapped, someone would come to my rescue.

The cell vibrated against my face, but I ignored it as I opened the door to the gift shop.

"Thanks for checking. I owe you one. Bye." I pretended to hang up and marched straight up to the first suit.

"So what happens now?" I asked him in Japanese as he struggled to keep a blank expression.

I felt something hard pressing into the small of my back.

"Now," the clipped voice of Leiko Ito said behind me, "you go for a little ride with us."

CHAPTER FIFTEEN

———

It felt like a gun in my back, but I wasn't sure. No point in taking unnecessary chances. For now, I'd pretend it was.

"Okay," I said, turning to face her. She was, after all, th boss. If I was going to talk to anyone, it would be her. I looked down. Yup. A gun. I hated being right.

"On one condition or you'll have to kill me here," I saic folding my arms over my chest.

Her face hardened. "You are not in a position to negotiate anything."

"Yes, I am. I will go with you three quietly as long as you leave my troop alone. They know nothing about any of thi: Only me. Deal?" I wore my best all-business face. This had better work.

Ito considered it for a moment. "What about your frien in there? The Latina? She works for your Agency."

I shook my head. "Just a desk jockey. She's just a frien who took vacation time to help me with the kids. She knows nothing and has never been in the field."

The door opened behind Leiko, and two tourists came into the shop. I heard my girls talking in the distance. I had to this deal done before they showed up.

"You are sure she knows nothing?" Ito looked skeptic: but I could see her weighing the merits of me leaving quietly with her and her goons.

"Nothing. Do we have a deal? Or do you gun me dow in public without getting the information you want?" My heart was pounding in spite of my cool demeanor.

I looked down at the gun again. It was a small .22 cali pistol. At this extremely close range it would rip into my stomach and intestines. It wouldn't make sense for Ito to shoot me here. It would cause too much of a scene, and they'd have to run off before the ambulance showed up.

But I was sick of all this cat and mouse crap. It needed to end, and it needed to end now. Hopefully, they'd take me to Riley, and somehow we could convince them that we knew nothing about Midori's murder. They'd probably still kill us. The Japanese syndicate wasn't exactly subtle in racking up a body count.

"Fine." Ito nodded to the two men and indicated that I was to follow them to the door. I noticed she shoved her gun into her purse before I turned around. "Let's go. Quietly."

I scanned the shop as I turned around and saw what I needed. Moving slowly, I timed my path to cross with another tourist and crashed into him. The two of us went down, and I reached out to steady my fall as I crashed into a display and palmed a small package of bobby pins that had big, plastic *I (heart) Spies* buttons on them. I tore off one bobby pin and the plastic piece before anyone could spot me. At least I could pick handcuffs now.

Quickly, I jumped up and helped the man I'd knocked over up. A clerk came over to see what happened.

"Sorry!" I apologized. "I tripped." I looked at the startled tourist. "Are you alright?"

The man nodded. "Sorry. I wasn't watching where I walked." The clerk glared at me as I left with my captors, probably pissed off about the mess I'd made. That made me memorable. That was good.

Once outside, one man held the door to a black SUV while the other shoved me into the backseat. Ito sat in the back with me, and the two men were up front. Ito's gun made an appearance again, and she trained it on me.

"What did you think of the museum?" I asked Ito, trying to sound casual.

She rolled her eyes. "Typical Americans—always bragging about yourselves."

"Well, when you're good at what you do…" I shrugged. I wondered if they would blindfold me or knock me out.

Ito said nothing but kept the gun trained on me.

"So, where are we going?" I asked as the car snaked through the streets.

No one spoke, but the man in front of me turned around armed with a hypodermic needle. Great. I hated being knocked out chemically. It was worse than coming to after a punch. Depending on the chemical used, I'd have one hell of a headache when I came to.

I didn't move as they injected me. There wasn't any point. Ito would have no qualms about shooting me inside of a speeding car, and I didn't want her doubling back to grab a couple of girls.

Within seconds, everything went blurry. Another few and I was out cold.

Something was off. I'd missed something important. What was it? My memory swirled like a violent storm. I'd never heard anything more about Chlotilde. Wait. That wasn't quite right. In fact, that was completely wrong. I knew exactly what happened to her. For some reason, I'd suppressed that information. But why? It didn't make any sense—but a nagging inner voice told me I needed to remember...

I read in the paper a few days later that a female employee of the German Embassy had accidentally fallen on the train tracks exactly when a train was zinging through. Chlotilde was dead. I shrugged it off. I couldn't do anything about it, and didn't push her.

Riley acted strangely after he heard the news. Maybe he was worried she'd committed suicide because he dumped her. That would be just like him. Arrogant bastard. Jealousy reared up inside me. Forget about it. It doesn't matter anymore.

I went back to work on my assignment, but it was going nowhere. Japanese officials were difficult to turn. Honor was a big deal here. My time in Tokyo was nearing an end anyway. They were going to ship me to Okinawa for a few days to follow a lead there.

The night before I was to leave, I was having dinner in my favorite restaurant downtown. I had this great booth way in the back, facing the door. The backs of the seats were high, so could duck down and hide if I needed to. But more importantly, they had the best Kobe steaks on the island. I loved a good, ju steak and was feeling a little homesick for Iowa, so I thought I'd have one more before leaving.

I was just polishing off some sake when I saw Midori Ito walk in with a huge entourage. Ducking down in my seat, I crawled under the table and sat in the seat with my back to them. I waited a few moments before chancing a glance. Great, they were sitting just one table over. I'd be here a while. As a gaijin, *I'd stand out like a sore thumb if I tried to leave now.*

"...took care of the German bitch..." Midori said. I didn't catch all of it.

My radar went into overdrive. Were they talking about Chlotilde? I shifted a little lower into the booth and strained to listen without looking like I was listening. Not an easy thing to do.

"Interpol trying to involve themselves in our business." One of the men at the table snorted. "Tried to get the CIA to do their work for them."

Were they talking about Chlotilde trying to get me to work for her? How could they know about that? Did that mean they knew about me? I wasn't even involved in investigating the yakuza. At that moment, I was very happy I hadn't taken the German Interpol agent up on it.

"...not even German...American..." Midori snapped.

What? Chlotilde wasn't even German? Damn. She had the accent down. I was impressed and horrified for her at the same time. Could she have been one of ours? It was always possible that I wouldn't know her. My handler, Riley, owed me no explanation. He didn't have to make any of his field agents aware of the others who worked for him.

"...CIA a problem?" someone asked.

"Not anymore," Midori said with a laugh. "You took care of the Limey...keep an eye on Americans...anyway..."

I guess they killed the British mole too. And they were going to watch us for a little while. Maybe I should tell Riley about this.

After that, they lapsed into a discussion of the drug trade. I stopped listening. Not my assignment. Curiosity about cases they weren't involved in got many spies killed over the years. I wasn't going to be one of them.

I had a bigger problem in that I was basically trapped. they knew Chlotilde had tried to recruit CIA agents, then they probably knew about me. Why did I have to call that number? Now I was screwed by appearing to be involved in something I wasn't involved in. I shouldn't have been surprised. This stuff happened all the time. Of course people were killed for this reason.

The only way out of the restaurant was on the other side of Midori's table. I had to stay. They were there for four hours. By the time I made it out of there, it was very late.

Riley met me back at my apartment. He was pacing in the sparse living room, clearly agitated. I told him what I'd overheard in case it was involved with something else he was pursuing. When I mentioned the assassination of Chlotilde, he turned deathly white. It was unnerving. I'd never seen Riley ups before. Not even when I'd dumped him.

But this was beyond my pay grade, so I didn't pursue it. If he'd lost an agent, he'd need some time to deal with it. Instead I packed my duffel and the next morning, flew to Okinawa. We never spoke of it again.

I was right. My head felt like it was being hit over and over with a sledgehammer. Imagine having being hit so hard you saw stars. It was like that, only my brain was pulsing instead of getting punched.

There was no point in giving away that I was coming to so I kept my eyes closed and tried to remain still. The silence was broken by the booming pain in my head. I couldn't identify any movement or voices. My hands were bound in front of me and so were my feet. Pain washed over my extremities as I very gently tried to flex them. My arms and legs responded by screaming at my brain for daring to attempt such a thing. I ignored it, and my fingers gently probed my front pocket. Yes! The bobby pin was still there! I had one advantage my captors didn't know about.

Very slowly, I opened my eyes to slits. When nothing happened, I opened them all the way. Bright white light flooded into my swimming vision and also complained to my brain about instigating pain.

The first thing I saw was my wrists. Damn. Not

handcuffs. Zip ties. Well, that screwed the idea of picking the lock. I knew how to get out of zip ties, but it took a lot of movement and strength to pull it off. Right now my body hated me, so I was pretty sure I wasn't going to get much of that.

Zip ties were excellent restraints for normal, everyday people. There was a psychological terror associated with them because you immediately assume you won't be able to undo them. That wasn't true, but most people didn't know that and usually gave up just at the sight of the thick, plastic straps.

Right now, my mind was begging me to stop thinking. It assumed I was torturing it with pain just for fun. I took deep gulps of air. An influx of oxygen could help diminish headaches, although in this case it just made me feel like vomiting. To distract me from that, I turned my attention to my environment. I was in a plain, cement room. No windows, one steel door, and no video cameras. It was a pretty good lockup. I appeared to be all alone in the room with no one watching, which was fine with me.

Very slowly, I tested my strength only to find out my arms and legs had decided suddenly to take on a rubbery quality. I brought my wrists to my mouth and was rewarded with searing waves of pain. Working through the pain without puking was a challenge, but I forced the ties to my mouth and worked the little plastic buckle to the front, right between my wrists.

I slumped against the bare wall and closed my eyes, exhausted from the effort. This would all have to be done in bits and pieces until I recovered. What in the hell had they dosed me with? Whatever it was, they obviously used too much. If I got out of here, I would use it on them.

I listened carefully, my head throbbing against the cool, cement wall. There were vague murmurs on the other side of the wall, but there was no way I could make them out. How long had I been out? I wiggled a little in an attempt to see if my phone was in my back pocket. It was. What terrible spy-craft! Leaving me with a phone? But then they probably thought with my hands bound in front of me, I'd never be able to use it.

What were my options? I'd need to stand to break my wrist restraints, which would be difficult to do considering my ankles were bound as well. That and my body had made it pretty clear it wasn't going to be cooperating anytime soon.

So, I was all alone with just my thoughts for company. The vague remnants of a dream swirled around my brain, and I reached for it. I'd had several dreams since Riley had called and asked for help. All relating to that time in Tokyo. Until now, I'd assumed it was because Riley and Midori were kind of foremost in my mind.

But maybe it was more than that. Maybe my memory was trying to tell me something. But what? It didn't make any sense. The closest I'd ever gotten to Midori was that one time in that restaurant. And why did Baby Ito think I'd had anything to do with her mother's murder?

Okay, I did…a bit. Ito Senior turning up dead in my kitchen kind of connected me. But the murder part happened before she got there. Kelly knew that.

Kelly! Rex said she'd been in labor! She must've had her baby by now! And I had no idea if it was a girl or boy! This sucked now for one more reason. I had to get out of here. No way I was going to die before congratulating my best friend.

Sitting straight up, I brought my ankles close to me. The pain was excruciating, and every nerve ending shrieked. Very slowly, I pressed against the wall and tried to stand up. My legs burned in protest, but I ignored it, concentrating all of my effort on getting my body to do what I wanted it to.

I inched up the wall about a foot before I crashed back down to the floor. Sweat streamed down my forehead in spite of the cool temperature of the room. This wasn't going to be easy. Once again, I brought my knees to my chest and started the climb. About halfway up my knees started buckling, but I pushed on. All of my attention was focused on getting upright. Then I could go on to the next step.

Wobbling, with only the wall for support, I finally stood all the way up. I allowed myself a few moments of leaning against the wall to regroup but only a few. Ito and her thugs could come through that door at any moment. Time was not a luxury I had.

I pressed my elbows together and brought my arms up over my head then slashed downward, separating my arms at my hips, breaking the lock and popping the zip ties off. Ignoring the pain in my wrists, I undid the bindings on my ankles. I was finally free.

I examined the door. No hinges or locks were visible on my side. There was a doorknob, and I very carefully tested it. It turned, and I was able to open it. Who did that? Who kidnapped someone and then left them in an unlocked room? Not that I was going to argue with them. Their stupidity would make my escape possible, so yay me!

The hallway was brightly lit and seemed to go on forever in both directions. I pulled my cell from my pocket. No service. I might've been underground. No access to Wi-Fi either. Ito must've figured I wouldn't be able to use it, so she ignored it. That was stupid. What was going on? Why were they making so many mistakes?

I froze for a moment. This could've been an elaborate trap. If they thought they wouldn't get any information out of me, if I developed a false sense of security, maybe I'd spill. Now you could see why paranoia is a good thing in a spy.

At this point, it didn't matter. I was going to have to get moving. Staying here wouldn't do me any good. *But which way should I go? Right. I'll go right. If I don't find anything soon, I'll double back and go left.*

This was the kind of mind game I was used to. In my experience, it was best just to push through and take your chances. I broke into a light jog down the right hall. As I moved my muscles loosened up, and the pain started to drift away. It was extremely quiet. I'd heard voices earlier, back in my cell. And while that could be either good or bad, I decided to run away from them. Rescuers usually shouted instead of carrying on conversations in a normal volume.

The hallway ended in a T intersection, and I had another decision to make. Which way this time? Wasting time thinking about stuff like this could get me killed, so I decided once again to go right. At least then it would be easier to backtrack if I needed.

Funny…I hadn't passed a single door in all this time. What kind of place was this? It kind of felt like an underground bunker. But a bunker with only one door? My mind raced as I picked up speed. If I didn't find anything soon, I'd have to retrace my steps.

Was Riley being held here? It would make sense if he was. This place seemed pretty vast though. I wasn't sure I could find him. In fact, I wasn't sure he should be my mission here. Getting out alive would be nice. And if I did get out, maybe I could return with help.

I stopped running. It was a dead end. The hallway just ended. There was nowhere else to go. Now I felt a little like a rat in a maze. Like I was part of an experiment to get me to find the cheese. Only in this case, the cheese was Riley.

Turning around, I started running faster. When I got to the T, instead of turning left to go back to where my cell was, I decided to clear this hall first. I didn't panic much—it was a huge waste of time and caused you to make mistakes. Stupid mistakes. When I was fresh out of the academy and on my first assignment, I got trapped underwater in a cave. I freaked out and was promptly attacked by bats. And while I wasn't really afraid of bats, their swarming me only made things worse, not better. Since then, I'd always tried to keep my fears under control.

Besides, Maria probably had the CIA looking for me, and my dad probably was doing something similar with whatever resources he had. I wondered if Rex was on his way. Who would he have looking after Philby and the kittens? Hopefully someone nice who I wouldn't have to kill later.

Another dead end. Okay, I thought as I turned around, that narrowed things down a bit. I raced back to where I'd been held and this time took the hallway to the left. Good thing I had comfortable shoes on. I couldn't imagine running around in high heels.

Have you ever noticed how often that happens in movies? The heroine runs around forever in stiletto heels without complaining once. I'd complain. There was no reason to do that. One time, when I was at a formal party at an embassy, I just took off my high heels to search the building, putting them on when I had what I needed. And yet, moviegoers are subjected to the belief women are comfortable running long distances in four-inch high heels. What is the point?

Wow. The hallway was going on forever. Seriously, where was I? This building had to take up at least two city blocks underground. Even for Washington DC that seemed a bit excessive. Just walking around would take forever. Oooh! Maybe they had Segways! I'd always wanted to try one of those.

The hallway banked sharply to the right, and I kept going. The throbbing in my head was receding, probably due to the influx of oxygen in my lungs. The muscles in my legs had finally stopped whining, but I started to slow down a bit. No point in running out of breath. What if I had a fight coming up? It would be better to save my strength.

A door was coming up on my right, and I slowed to a stop in front of it. It looked similar to the steel door of my cell, meaning it probably housed another prisoner. Pressing my ear to the steel, I listened for any noise that would indicate more than one person inside. When I heard nothing, I reached for the doorknob and turned.

Unlocked! Unbelievable! Okay, so I should've been grateful my captors weren't bright, but I was really starting to question their ability to be dangerous. The room was very dimly lit. I stepped in, taking off my shoe to prop the door open in case it tried to lock behind me. The room was the same one I'd been in. Except that in the corner there was a huge lump of rags.

The rags moved—something they didn't usually do. I froze. Then they groaned. These weren't rags. It was a living thing. I kept my distance and got into a defensive position. It could've been a person. But it could also have been a tiger. You shouldn't laugh. That happened to me once in India. Fortunately for me, it had been chained up, and I realized it was a killing machine just before I stepped into range. You couldn't take anything for granted in this business.

"Who are you?" I said in my sternest, most intimidating voice.

"Wrath?" a man's voice croaked weakly.

I ran to the lump of rags and carefully turned it over. In spite of the blood and bruises on his face, I knew who it was. I'd found Riley.

CHAPTER SIXTEEN

———

I scanned the room as I helped him sit up. No cameras. That was good.

"Yes, Riley, it's me!" I said quietly. "It's Merry."

Riley opened two swollen eyes and studied me for a moment. He didn't look like he was happy to see me. In fact, he looked alarmed. He must be in shock, I thought.

"Oh no!" His eyes were wide open now, and he grabbed my arms. "What are you doing in this place? You shouldn't be here!"

"What are you talking about?" I asked calmly as I checked him for traps. "You called and asked me to help you. Don't you remember?"

He froze, his eyes going up and to the right, indicating he was thinking. I removed the torn blanket I'd found him in. Underneath, he was wearing khakis and a black golf shirt—both of which had seen better days.

Riley shook his head. "I never called you. I didn't want them to know you were involved!"

My mind reeled back to the phone calls. If what he said was true, then I'd spent this whole time in DC walking into one huge booby trap. The confidence I'd felt up until this moment deflated.

"They must've used recordings or something." Riley was more alert now. "I would never have called you. Never!"

So that's what happened. Ito wanted to know if anyone else was involved in her mother's murder. Somehow she'd tricked him into saying my name and Maria's, recording them, and sending them to me to see if I'd take the bait. And like a big moron with half a brain—I had.

I started to pull him to his feet. "We'd better get out of here."

My mind was racing. It was possible they'd been watching me all along. They wanted me to find Riley and somehow admit that I'd been involved in Midori's death. As I helped him up, I noticed his left wrist. He was wearing a device I'd never seen before. It looked like a video watch.

Those bastards were watching and listening. That also meant they were probably on their way right now.

"Can you move?" I asked as he finally got to his feet.

Riley ran his fingers through his hair and noticed the thing on his wrist. Suddenly, he started clawing at it like a madman. I slapped his other hand away and took a closer look. It appeared to have a locking latch mechanism that held it in place.

I pulled the bobby pin from my pocket and began working the lock. If we were going to run, I saw no reason to take them with us. It felt like a giant stopwatch was clicking beside me as I struggled to unlock the mechanism. Riley could barely hold still. He was trembling violently. That wasn't good. Finally, the lock sprang, and we dropped the band to the floor where I immediately stomped it to pieces.

"Let's go!" I said, yanking his arm toward the door.

Riley and I made it out the door and turned left to run down the hallway. He kept up pretty well for a man who'd been nearly beaten to death. I didn't let go of his arm, dragging him with me as I ran.

The hallway ended in a door, which I flung open and ran through. We were in some sort of stairwell. I pushed Riley in front of me and told him to go. If he was weak, at least I could catch him from behind. We took the stairs two at a time. Riley seemed to get stronger with every step.

We ran up two flights before we saw another door. There was no sign, no markings to tell us if this was the ground floor. I didn't want to come out on another underground level, but I didn't want to overshoot the first floor either. That was our best option of finding our way outside and escaping.

"We'll go this way," I decided as I opened the door and shoved Riley through it.

This level had carpeting and multiple doors. Very

slowly, too slowly, it dawned on me that we were in the Japane
Embassy.

"Keep moving," I whispered. I told Riley where I
thought we were. He nodded and kept going.

The PA system came to life. "Ms. Wrath, Mr. Andrews
please turn right and join us in the conference room."

"Like that's going to happen," I hissed, pushing Riley
further down the hall. We were getting out of here.

The two suits who brought me here appeared at the end
of the hall. Both had guns trained on us. A door on the right
popped open, and Leiko Ito stood to one side, waiting for us to
enter. We had very little choice. I could rush one of the guys, b
I didn't think Riley had it in him to take out the other.

We entered the room to find the table laid out with fooc
and drinks. That was unexpected. The two goons joined us and
took up positions on either side of the only door, guns still
drawn. Riley and I sat down. We would have to do what they
wanted until we came up with something better.

Ms. Ito sat across from us, pouring herself a glass of te
and picking up a donut. Looking at her svelte frame, I wondere
if her body would reject the donut and throw it across the room
Sadly, that didn't happen. Once she took a bite and had a sip of
tea, I reached for the pitcher and poured glasses for Riley and
myself. *Always fuel up if offered the opportunity.* James Bond
never turned down martinis from the bad guy, even if he knew
they were poisoned—which, now that I thought about it,
probably wasn't the best idea.

We ate and drank in silence for a while. Clearly Ito wa
expecting me to say something. Probably a full confession on
how I kidnapped her mom, brought her to the US (violating he
being on the No Fly list), and murdered her in my kitchen. We
I wasn't going to because I didn't do it.

"Mr. Andrews has been our guest for a while now,"
Baby Ito said. "We're so happy to have you join him."

"Yeah," I said, "about that…neither of us wanted to be
your guest. So I guess now that that misunderstanding is cleare
up, we will be on our way." I got to my feet.

"Sit down!" Ito barked. "I was just being polite. If you
want blunt, I'll admit that you two are our prisoners. That is, u

we get what we want out of you or we kill you."

"What is it you want out of us, exactly?" I asked.

Ito laughed. "I think you know what we want."

I shrugged. "Not really, so why don't you tell us?"

Riley said nothing. He just sat there, eating and watching. He was building his strength back up and sizing up the situation. The man had been here for a long time, but I'd bet he wasn't as damaged as he'd led them to believe. That meant he could spring into action if the time came to do so.

Riley knew what they wanted to know. The question was, had he told them already?

Leiko Ito sighed heavily before getting to her feet. "What I want is for you to tell me how and why you killed my mother."

It was kind of refreshing, really, to hear that question finally spoken aloud. Oh, I suspected that was the thing. But it was still nice to hear it outright.

"We didn't kill your mother," was all I said. Important spy tip—never give more information than they asked for. People tended to blather on when they thought their life was at risk. She didn't need to know that Riley and I had found her mother's lifeless body and dumped it two and a half hours away in Chicago.

"You are lying," Ito said. "We know you disposed of her body. Therefore, you must have killed her."

I shook my head. "Nope. We didn't kill her. Sorry for your loss, by the way."

"Yes." Ito's face was turning an alarming shade of purple. "You did. And I want to know why before I kill you."

Riley looked at me for a moment. He was trying to tell me something with his expression, but I had no idea what it was.

"Then we are at an impasse," I said. "Because we can't tell you something we don't know. And you won't listen to anything other than what you want to hear."

It might sound like I was calm and collected. I wasn't. I was very concerned. We were technically on Japanese soil. These people didn't look like they were going to let us leave alive, even if we told them what they assumed was the truth. I needed a plan.

Ito Jr. snapped. She started pounding on the table and swearing in Japanese. The two men covering the door looked startled. I knew Leiko was extremely dangerous and more sadistic than her mother had been. At some point, she'd just torture us until we gave her something. And then she'd probably still kill us. The odds weren't stacked in our favor.

She looked at the men with guns. "Shoot her. Then maybe he'll talk."

One of the men raised his pistol and aimed it at me. This wasn't good. I nudged Riley's foot under the table, and he gave me a brief nod. Together we dropped down to the floor, flipping the conference table over, and started shoving it toward Ito and her men.

The table jammed the three up against the wall hard. One of the goons dropped his pistol, and it landed on my shoulder. I snatched it up. Before the other guy could aim, I trained the gun on his chest. To my surprise, he handed his weapon to me. I passed it to Riley.

Ito stood there fuming as the two of us walked around the table. I kept my gun pointed at them while Riley—who was now on an adrenaline surge—yanked the table back from the door.

Just as we were about to walk out, I saw Riley give Leiko a hard uppercut to her chin that made her head snap back. She fell to the floor, unconscious. We ran out the door.

We encountered no more resistance as we fled the embassy and ran toward the street. Maria pulled up in the van, and we got in before she squealed away.

"Thanks," I said. "Nice timing."

Maria nodded. "I knew you were in there. But we have no jurisdiction in the embassy, so I waited outside, hoping you make it out." She looked back at Riley.

"He's alright," I said. "But we can't go back to the hotel. And the girls aren't safe there."

"They're at the Irish Embassy," Maria said with a grin. "I figured the Japanese weren't likely to invade Irish territory, so that was the safest bet. Liam's giving them a tour."

"You have the girls here?" Riley roared from the backseat. "What were you thinking? You could get them killed."

Riley had a small soft spot for my troop. He'd been mobbed by them last time he visited. While he wasn't the settling-down type or even the type who liked kids, he seemed to make an exception where they were concerned.

"You knew I was bringing them for a trip. You had to know I was here when you first called," I said.

"I already told you, I didn't call you. They must've made a mash-up recording of my voice. I would never have called you."

"But that means you said my name to them. You implicated me somehow."

He shook his head. "I didn't implicate you in any way."

"I want to hear the whole story," I said. "But first, we have to get somewhere safe."

Maria smiled. "I'm already on it. I've got just the place. I'll park you two there and go back for the girls."

I nodded and leaned back in the seat. My body gave up the ghost. I was too tired to move. The adrenaline rush was over. Maria was in charge now. I closed my eyes and tried to rest until the van came to a stop.

"You've got to be kidding," I said as I opened my eyes. "We're staying here?"

We were parked in front of The USS Enterprise. Not the spaceship. A fantasy suite hotel for Trekkies. I remembered reading about this. There'd been some controversy when it was built. The rooms were all designed to look like they were part of a spaceship but with Jacuzzis and swimming pools. Trekkies flocked from all over the world to stay here, and I'd heard rumors of a *Star Trek* swingers group that rented the whole place a couple of times a year.

I got out of the van and opened the door for Riley. "How did you get us in here? I heard it's booked two years out."

Trekkies were nothing if not the first to mob the newest thing.

"I had a little pull." Maria smiled as she handed me a set of keys. "My sister-in-law works here. You go ahead and get Riley inside and cleaned up. You're in the Federation Starfleet Suite."

We walked into the lobby, and immediately the

concierge gave us the split-V Vulcan greeting. People moved around dressed in the original series garb. Most of the staff wore blue or yellow costumes, but occasionally we spotted a red shirt. I wondered if they had a high turnover.

The suite was on the second floor, and as we entered, I realized this must have been their version of the presidential suite. The furniture was all chrome and futuristic. The walls were curved upward with weird ductwork crisscrossing overhead. In front of the giant flat-screen TV were two recliners that looked like Captain Kirk's command chair. The remote control was a phaser gun. That was kind of cool.

"You'd better get in the shower," I said as I shoved Riley into a bathroom designed to look like Dr. McCoy's sickbay. "The kids will freak out if they see all that blood." Okay, so they'd probably be more fascinated than freaked out. But he didn't need to know that.

Riley closed the door behind him, and moments later I heard the shower running. I explored the rest of the suite. I didn't see any of the fabled swimming pools they supposedly had, but there was a Jacuzzi big enough to hold an Andorian star cruiser. Yes, I was a bit of a Trekkie.

I gave silent thanks to Maria for dropping off my suitcase so I could change into a swimsuit and ease my creaking bones into the warm, oscillating water. Grateful for the opportunity to relieve my sore muscles, I wiggled out of my clothes.

The cell in my back pocket immediately buzzed, and I answered it.

"Maria just told me you're alright." Dad sounded exasperated, and I felt bad for having Rex call him. Since I couldn't squirm into my swimsuit while holding a cell phone, I threw one of the complimentary robes on. It was blue, with the triangular Starfleet insignia on the left breast pocket. Nice.

"I'm fine. And I found Riley. And I kind of caused some trouble inside the Japanese Embassy," I said.

There was silence on the other end.

"Remember when you joined the Agency," Dad said, "and I asked you not to tell me about all the times you'd been in danger?"

"Yes." It had been the only condition my parents had. They didn't want to worry obsessively about me, so they came up with their own fantasy where I had a nice, safe job. A few years ago, I overheard Mom tell a neighbor that I was a math teacher. A month later, Dad told Aunt Clara that I was a process engineer for a farm equipment manufacturer. Parents.

"Well, that goes for fighting other people too. Especially when it's political. There really is such a thing as plausible deniability."

"Right. Let me start over. I'm fine, and Riley's safe. We just got back from a stroll through the Japanese Embassy," I said.

"I'm glad you're okay," he said. "But I do have to warn you about something..."

Dad was interrupted by a knock on the door. I started toward it.

"No problem, Dad. Really. Everything's okay," I said as the knocking continued.

"Well, I think you might be a little angry with me," he said.

I came up to the door and looked through the peephole.

"I kind of flew Rex out here," Dad said.

I already knew that because standing out in the hallway, angrily pounding on the door, was my boyfriend, Rex.

CHAPTER SEVENTEEN

———

What was a woman to do in a situation like this? Well, obviously, answer the door, but I was kind of hoping for a typhoon to suddenly hit, my troop to show up, or maybe Bigfoot to wander through the room arm in arm with Mr. Spock.

No such luck. I did hang up on Dad…that felt a little bit better.

"Rex!" I said as I opened the door. "What are you doing here?" So I knew Dad just flew him out, but he didn't know that knew.

The gorgeous Iowa detective stormed into the room and threw his arms around me. His lips met mine, and all the pain in my body turned into something wonderful.

Rex pulled away, "You're alright! Good! Because now can be mad at you!" He was frowning. I didn't like it when he frowned.

"I'm fine. Dad shouldn't have brought you out here," I insisted. "It's all under control."

He put his hands on his hips. "Your dad told me everything. At least, I think he told me everything. But you'd better start at the beginning."

I nodded. "Okay. I owe you that much."

I filled him in on everything, leaving nothing out, because I was an awesome girlfriend. To hide something now would have been stupid. I was busted. Time to confess. So I told him everything. Starting with Midori's murder. He didn't seem like that part. I mean, what police officer would? I'd basically covered up a crime right across the street from where he lived.

Rex's body tensed, but he said nothing. Once the adrenaline wore off and he was over me being in danger, I had no doubt I'd get a lecture. To be fair, I didn't know him then. He had just been a local cop. I'd have to remember to tell him that. He listened quietly to my entire story, looking angry each time I mentioned the girls or danger. But he listened. He got props for that.

By the time we finished, we were sitting on a couch that looked like it was made of tribbles. It was a very uncomfortable sofa. Who made a couch out of a hundred stuffed, furry balls?

"Why didn't you tell me the minute it started?" Rex finally said. He didn't sound so angry anymore, which was good. "I know your background requires classified information, but I could've helped."

He was right. I had nothing. So I shrugged.

"Hey..." Rex started looking around. "What's the deal with this place? Looks like the deck of the Starship Enterprise." He pointed to the bubbling hot tub. "You were about to get in?"

I nodded. "I kind of had a rough day." I made my fingers into a gun and fired.

Rex relaxed. He was probably still mad at me, but at least he was getting over my treachery. He got to his feet and started walking around the room, checking out the weird décor.

"I'm a bit of a Trekkie," he said.

I faked shock. "That may be worse than what I've done." He didn't need to know I was one too. It was too early in the relationship for that.

"Oh, I doubt it..." Rex frowned again. "Seriously, Merry, you have to keep me informed on this kind of thing. And we are going to talk about it more in depth later. You're not off the hook yet." He closed the gap between us and pulled me into his arms. "I was very worried. And you just, out of the blue, say you're in trouble, and I need to call someone." He looked into my eyes, and I was lost. "I should be that someone. I should come to your rescue."

And then he kissed me again. I leaned into it, giving in completely. My beyond-gorgeous boyfriend wanted to be my knight in shining armor. Granted, I didn't really need one, but here he was anyway. It was a romantic, mind-numbing gesture.

Rex had dropped everything and flown halfway across the country just to make sure I was safe. I'd have to get used to that, but it was awesome to have someone feel that way about me.

I pulled back to get some air and smiled at him, like a goofy, lovestruck puppy. This was definitely *the* guy. How did get so lucky? When I was forced into early retirement from a jo I loved, I thought nothing good would ever happen to me again. was wrong. And for once I didn't mind being wrong.

"Are the girls sharing this room with us?" he said softly "Or can we use that hot tub right now? I'm pretty sure I can eas those aches and pains."

Wow. My body temp went from cold and bruised to ho and bothered in seconds.

"I didn't ask," I said, kicking myself for not asking Mar what the arrangements were. "They could walk in any second. But maybe we could go on a little trip of our own after we get home."

Rex pulled me tight against him, and I melted. "I'm going to hold you to that." He looked at the door. "I forgot my bag. It's in the hall. I'll just grab it."

I reluctantly let him go and watched as he turned the door lock inside out to prop the door open. Wow. I'd really dodged a bullet there. Rex had every right to be furious with m At least he was less so now. And with a few more kisses, I was pretty sure I could melt that fury away.

Rex walked back in, pulling a small rolling suitcase behind him. He was wearing a formfitting black T-shirt and jeans. I couldn't help sighing. Rex was athletic but lean like a cowboy, and it was totally hot. Riley was more muscular…

Oh damn. I knew I'd forgotten something.

"Hey, Wrath." Riley stepped out of the bathroom wearing nothing but a towel around his waist. Water beaded o his muscular chest and shoulders.

"You should see the shower. It looks like that teleporti thing they had on *Star Trek*!"

Rex froze, his face hardening into a mask. Riley spott him and actually had the nerve to blush. Huh. I'd never known him to do that before.

I was in trouble. Big trouble.

"Rex." Riley reached out to shake his hand. "How're y

doing, man?"

Rex took the hand and shook it out of politeness.

"I know how this looks," I stammered. "But it's not what you think. I was going to get into my swimsuit before getting into the hot tub. But then Dad called, and you knocked, and I didn't have a chance."

Riley nodded. "Nothing happened." But did I detect a little hint of regret? Had Riley wanted something to happen?

Rex took in the bruises, gashes, and swelling on his rival and relaxed a little. I'd told him earlier about rescuing Riley. He was putting it all together. That made him a good detective. They didn't jump to conclusions but let the facts speak for themselves. And it saved my butt this time.

"Okay, Evelyn is helping the girls settle in next door." Maria burst into the room. She took one look at me in the robe, Riley in the towel, and Rex glaring at both of us, and she started laughing.

"Oh, my God!" Her body shook from exertion. "This is so classic! How did I miss this? I should've been here!" Maria doubled over with hysterical giggles.

"You must be Rex!" She laughed even harder. "This is good. Too good!"

The three of us relaxed as we watched her collapse under the hilarity of the moment. I guessed it was kind of humorous. Like the kind you'd see in a movie. Only it was happening here. To me. That made it a little less funny.

"I'm just going to..." Riley pointed at the bathroom behind him and started backing up. "I'm going to put some clothes on."

Maria tossed him a tote bag, and without asking what was in it, he disappeared into the bathroom, locking the door behind him. I left Maria and Rex to get acquainted and ran into the bedroom to throw on some clothes. When I emerged, Riley, Maria, and Rex were sitting in the living room. They were smiling.

Maria tossed her curls a little before dazzling Rex with a smile. Hey! Was she flirting with him?

"So," I announced myself. "What have you been talking about?" I shot Maria a look, and she laughed.

"Rex said you brought him up to speed, and Riley told me what happened at the embassy," Maria said. "Did you really shoot those guys? I mean, I'm glad you got out okay, but that's pretty international-incident level stuff."

I sat down in the Captain Kirk chair. "What happened after Ito took me?"

Maria told me I was gone by the time they hit the gift shop. She bought each girl a little something in the shop to distract them while she called her supervisor at Langley. Riley seemed to flinch at that. Fortunately, Maria's boss was golfing a St. Andrews and didn't believe a word of what she said. I knew the guy. He was a total kiss-ass who wouldn't dream of ending his vacation for a mission. Maybe that was a good thing.

So Maria had herded the girls into the van and driven them to the hotel to pack, deciding that they needed her protection more than I needed her help. After leaving Evelyn with strict instructions on locking the door, she drove to the embassy, and we ran outside and into the van.

"No one did anything?" I asked in shock. It wasn't unheard of. The CIA sometimes chose not to act—especially o domestic soil.

"He said either I was pranking him, in which case he'd look bad." Maria scowled. "Or Riley had gone rogue, which wasn't the Agency's problem."

Riley said nothing. He was wearing a white, button-down shirt and khakis.

"Maybe it was a good thing." I sighed. "But your boss an asshat."

"Agreed." Maria nodded.

"So Maria and I are the cavalry?" Rex asked. I felt a pang of jealousy as he said Maria's name. I really needed to ge over that.

"I guess so." I shrugged. "Maybe we should ship the girls home first thing in the morning."

Rex agreed. "You're right. If Ito retaliates…"

I interrupted him. "You mean *when* Ito retaliates. She doesn't lose. And she thinks Riley and I killed her mother. She keep coming after us with everything she's got until we're dead or she is."

Riley finally spoke up. "We need to go after her first. She might decide to fly in some more backup."

I'd forgotten about the third man. I ran to get the photo and showed it to the men.

"The girls should be safe here," Maria said. "No one knows they're here, and I think it's safe to say that no one will expect them to be staying at a place like this."

"Hold on." Rex held his hands up. "This is all over her mother's murder?" He shot me a look that said *we are soooo not done talking about this.* "If you didn't kill her, who did?"

I stared at him. "If? If I didn't kill her? Rex, I told you—I didn't kill her!"

"Bad choice of words," Rex apologized. "What I'm trying to say is, who did kill her?"

"No one knows," Riley said. "And we destroyed the crime scene and removed the body, so it's impossible to find out."

I remembered the autopsy. "That's not totally true. The autopsy they did in Japan stated she was murdered before she was bludgeoned."

Riley's mouth dropped open, and I realized we hadn't had a chance to bring him up to speed.

"How," I asked him, "did Ito Jr. know you were involved?"

He shook his head. "I don't know. She never said. And unless you or Kelly told her, which I don't think you did, by the way…" Riley had the good graces to hold his hands up defensively.

"Kelly!" I shot to my feet. "She was in labor! That means she had the baby!"

I ran out of the room and grabbed my cell phone. There were no messages or missed calls, but I wasn't going to let that stop me. I dialed Robert, who answered on the first ring.

"Merry! I was just going to call you!" My best friend's husband sounded like he'd just won the lottery—if they gave babies away as lottery prizes.

"Well?" I asked, not intending to waste time talking.

"It's a girl!" I could feel him smiling through the phone. "Seven pounds, nine ounces, and twenty inches long!"

"You act like I know what that means," I said. "How is Kelly? Did everything go okay?"

I'd only witnessed one live birth in my life, and that was in the mountains of Ecuador. The baby was breech—at least that's what they said—and I was told that was bad. I watched as the midwife rotated the baby inside the mother, and then I fainted dead away. When I awoke, there was this screaming infant named Pilar.

"She had a little trouble but nothing big. Kelly and the baby are fine." If he could've reached through the phone line, I believe he would've handed me a cigar.

I felt the tension slipping away. Everything was fine. "What did you name her?"

"We haven't decided yet. But we should have a name picked out by the time you get back." I heard someone talking to him in the background. "Gotta go, Merry! See you when you get home!" He hung up.

"Kelly had a little girl!" I said as I joined the others.

Apparently, the whole troop had joined us while I was in the other room, and the place exploded with squeals of delight.

"What's her name?" One of the Kaitlins asked.

"Why is Rex here?" Inez asked.

"Did he bring the kittens?" Lauren started searching under the furniture.

Evelyn was openly staring at Riley, who, in spite of his injuries, still looked like a Greek god.

I held up my hand, making the quiet sign, and the room went silent.

"Wish I could use that with reporters," I heard Rex say to Maria.

Ignoring the twist of envy, I addressed them. "No name—they haven't decided yet. We should know before we get home tomorrow."

Betty frowned. "But we don't go home tomorrow. We home Friday." The other girls nodded and looked at me.

"I have some business here I need to take care of," I said. "So we're cutting this trip short." I flinched inwardly, waiting for the cries and pleas.

"She must have spy stuff to do." Hannah nodded.

What?

"Are you going to kill somebody, Mrs. Wrath?" Another of the Kaitlins asked.

I felt my whole body go hot. How did they know? I looked at Maria and Rex, but they looked as startled as I was. I decided to play stupid.

"I don't know what you guys are talking about," I lied.

"You know…" Inez said. "The CIA stuff you do."

"She can't tell us, idiot!" Betty shouted. "It's a secret mission!"

A third Kaitlin said, "We totally understand, Mrs. Wrath."

A sea of tiny faces looked at me expectantly. Evelyn's jaw had dropped open. Apparently, she was the only one who didn't know my background.

"Ladies, please." I held my hands up. "It's nothing like that. I just have some paperwork to do. Boring stuff."

"Right…" Hannah winked at me.

"Okay, guys!" Maria stood up. "Time to go back to the room and order dinner! Who wants Vulcan pizza?"

The girls cheered unanimously and filed out the door. Evelyn grudgingly followed, giving Riley one last glance before the door closed behind her.

"That didn't exactly go as expected," I said, staring at the door.

"How did they figure it out?" Riley ran his fingers through his hair. "You sure you didn't tell them?"

I threw my arms up in the air "No idea! Honestly! Maria and I never talked in front of them. There's no way they should know!" I slumped onto the tribble sofa. "Now what?"

Riley picked up the hotel phone. "First, I'm going to call a buddy I have at the airlines to switch the girls' flight. Then, we're going to take care of Leiko Ito once and for all."

Something popped up in my mind. "Rex! What did you do with Philby and the kittens?" Somehow in this whole mess, I'd completely forgotten about my cat.

Rex fidgeted nervously with his belt. "Oh. Well, I didn't have a lot of time. I had to call in a favor." He was avoiding eye contact.

"Who?" I asked, not at all sure I wanted to know the answer.

"Just an old friend, Merry. It's no big deal."

I folded my arms across my chest. "Who? They're my cats. I'd like to know who has them."

Rex sighed heavily. "Okay. But like I said, I had very little time to find someone. And I know you don't want to board them. So I called the first person I could think of who liked cats"

"Rex? Are you going to tell me who?" I was using my angry-spy voice.

"Juliette Dowd. She has the cats."

.

CHAPTER EIGHTEEN

———

"That crazy psycho? You let the one person who hates me more than anything on the planet watch my cats?" It felt like my head exploded.

Juliette Dowd was my nemesis. Maybe my worst.

"If she hurts Philby and the babies, I'm going to break out the thumbscrews and work her over like a pit bull on 'roid rage!"

"She likes cats." Rex defended himself. "And she likes me. She wouldn't hurt them. I swear she wouldn't."

I wasn't so sure. True, she still carried a torch—a great big torch—for Rex. But she hated me in a way people usually reserved for political pundits. I pictured her tormenting the cats just to get back at me.

"Look." Rex took out his cell and dialed. "I'm going to call her now to make sure they're okay."

He paused, waiting for the flame-haired Satan to pick up. "Juliette! Just thought I'd check in to let you know I made it okay."

Rex blushed, and it was all I could do not to grab the phone and let out a series of expletives that would destroy a crusty sailor.

"Um, that's very nice of you," Rex said. He seemed uncomfortable. That made me feel a little better. "No, that's really not necessary. No really, you don't need to. Okay, we'll talk about it when I get back." He hung up and looked at me like a television evangelist about to be indicted on prostitution charges.

"What's really nice of her?" I asked.

"She said the cats are doing well. They're eating and

fine." He avoided eye contact.

"Rex? Please answer the question, or I will torture you with a pair of pliers."

"It's really nothing…" he stammered. "She's just making my favorite casserole and wants to have me over for dinner."

"That is not happening," I said.

"And she might've done all my laundry and made me a red velvet cake…" His voice drifted off.

"Hey!" Riley said. "Is that the cute redhead?"

"She's not cute," I said through my teeth. "And we will discuss this later!"

Maria came back in and sank onto the sofa. She looked from me to Rex and asked, "What did I miss?"

After glaring at my boyfriend a few more seconds, I shook my head. "It's nothing. How are the girls?"

"Fine. They're eating pizza and watching the old *Star Trek* series on TV—which appears to be this place's answer to HBO. I think Evelyn is in shock, but oh well."

The girls I was sure I could handle, now that they knew Evelyn was another thing altogether. I wasn't sure I wanted the parents to know that I used to kill people for a living. Hey…maybe I could use that to my advantage as motivation for next year's cookie sale…

"If we're all done with whatever the hell is going on, I think we should start putting a plan together to stop Leiko Ito in her tracks, because I do not want to go through all that again," Riley said.

He told us how he came to be kidnapped. A few days ago, he'd gone out for coffee at his favorite organic cafe. Spies usually avoided having favorite restaurants or routes to work. Even a favorite color could get you in trouble. But Riley, the health nut, really liked this place and made sure he went different routes every time and at different times of day to throw off anyone following him.

Getting into a routine should've made a secret agent far more aware of their surroundings. In these circumstances, Riley should've kept a careful eye on everything going on around him.

He hadn't.

As he'd walked out the back entrance in a weak attempt

to avoid being followed, someone had thrown a bag over his head and injected him with the same cocktail I'd been given. They had kept him in the cell where I'd found him, beating him to get him to confess to Midori's murder and to get him to name me as coconspirator.

"I never gave you up," he said, running his hands through his thick, wavy blond hair.

"Somehow they figured it out. Probably because you called me." I showed him the record of his calls on my cell.

"I didn't know I'd called you," he said sadly. "They must've drugged me. I would never implicate you. Not willingly."

Rex studied him for a moment before looking at me. "I believe him."

Truth was, I did too. I just didn't want to let him off the hook yet.

"Anyway," Riley continued. "They gave me food and water and a thin blanket and left me alone after that. I didn't see Ito again until in that conference room."

Maria said, "They thought Merry had killed Midori. That's why they gave up on you."

I nodded. "And they took me and let me find you in hopes I'd say something admitting I killed her."

"I think so," Riley said.

"So let me get this straight," Rex said slowly. "Besides you guys covering up a murder and tampering with the body, which I'm still pissed about by the way, now you might have created an international incident at an embassy without the knowledge or blessing of the CIA."

"That sounds about right," I said. "But I don't think the embassy will do anything about it. They'd look bad for having yakuza on staff, let alone torturing American citizens in the basement."

"Ito's not dead," Riley said. "She's probably sent for reinforcements from Tokyo, but it will take a day or so for them to get here. I think we've got her right where we want her."

I shook my head. "She's not the only yakuza in this country."

I told them about Elvinia and our trip there. Rex tried to

control his anger at my running full tilt into such a dangerous situation.

"But you said Elvinia is part of the Okinawa family and hates the Tokyo branch," Maria said.

Riley shook his head. "In the grand scheme of things, that doesn't matter. If Ito calls for Elvinia's aid, she'll have no choice but to come. They have an elaborate code that relies heavily on a sense of familial duty."

I sighed and reached for the room's landline.

"What are you doing?" Maria asked.

"Ordering room service. This is going to take a while, and I'm starving."

An hour later, as we were munching on Klingon Fries and Mr. Sulu Burgers, we were no further along in planning. The food helped though. And I got a kick out of seeing diet-conscious Riley react to the cheddar and bacon Scotty Sauce drizzled over the fries. When I dipped them in ranch dressing he almost had a heart attack.

"We can't invade the Japanese Embassy," Maria said. "That's the equivalent to invading another country."

"So, we lure her out somehow," I said.

"And just how are we going to do that?" Riley asked. "She's pretty embedded there. She just has to wait for more troops to come."

I thought for a moment. "We'll just have to promise her something she can't refuse."

Rex asked, "And what exactly would that be?"

"The truth about who murdered her mother," I said.

"How can we do that when we don't know?" Maria asked.

I shrugged. "She doesn't know that. She's always assumed Riley and I are guilty. So let's pretend we're going to confess in an attempt to end this feud."

"When?" Rex asked.

"After we're sure the girls are on their flight tomorrow. Then we launch this plan and hope we can pull it off."

"What plan? We don't have a plan, unless I've been asleep during this conversation," Riley asked.

"The one we're going to make right now, duh!" I said.

"But first, I need to make a quick phone call."

I excused myself to the other room and dialed. Maybe, just maybe, I could pull this off. If not, we were probably going to our deaths. I figured we had about a sixty/forty chance of survival. Okay, maybe it was more like forty/sixty. I just wasn't going to tell my team that.

CHAPTER NINETEEN

———

Riley had gotten the girls on a six a.m. flight back home. Evelyn didn't look very happy about being the only adult, but I promised her she'd never have to go with us again, and she grudgingly agreed.

"Mrs. Wrath?" Lauren asked as the girls lined up to go through security.

I knelt before the girl and waited.

She pulled a small baggie filled with shortbread cookies out of her pocket and handed it to me.

"What's this for?" The bag was warm. I wasn't sure I wanted to know if she'd had it anywhere else.

"For a snack. In case you get hungry." Lauren hugged me and then ran to catch up with everyone else—who were now going through security.

I tucked the baggie into my back pocket and shook my head. Those kids were so awesome. I'd have to tell them that when I got home.

We waited at the airport until we saw on the monitors that the plane had taken off and then made our way back to the hotel to launch *Operation Avoid Dying at All Costs*. Sure, we could've come up with a sexier name, but all our creative energy went into making the plan in the first place.

Riley called the Japanese Embassy and asked for Ms. Ito. To his surprise, he was connected. He gave her some instructions and an address, indicating that he would tell her the whole story of Midori's death. She agreed, probably because in her psychopathic mind she believed him. We still had no idea what had happened, but she didn't need to know that.

We didn't tell her to come alone or unarmed because t

was just something they did in the movies. It was unrealistic to think that spies or crime bosses wouldn't bring weapons and would show up on their own. Past experience had shown this to be a naïve suggestion and quite a few spooks had lost their lives in the field by truly believing the bad guy would honor the request.

Maria called in a couple of favors from Ahmed and Jenkins. Zeb Jenkins jumped at the chance to finally see some action, and Ahmed was bribed with a lifetime supply of cookies. Everyone, and I mean *everyone*, had a price.

We set up the rendezvous point to be at an abandoned warehouse that used to be an Agency safe house in the Maryland countryside. The huge, steel-sided building was the only structure in the middle of a barren field. We'd be able to see anyone coming miles before they arrived. If we were lucky, we could get out of this alive and get home in time to rescue my cats from the evil clutches of Juliette Dowd.

"I can't believe we're doing this," Rex grumbled as he checked his .45 one more time.

"I'm so sorry," I apologized. Not only was this completely illegal, I'd dragged my boyfriend, a police officer, into it. And it wasn't his jurisdiction. He could end up fired or imprisoned.

"Maybe you shouldn't be here," I said finally. "You could go back to the hotel and wait until it's over."

Rex shook his head. "I don't see how I could do that. There's no way I could live with myself if you got hurt."

My heart went all squishy inside. How lucky was I to have a man like this?

"But Rex," I argued, "you could lose your job or go to jail if this turns south. I don't want that to happen to you. Especially when this is all my fault."

His mouth hardened into a stubborn line. "I'm doing this whether you like it or not."

Yeesh! Fine! So touchy. Okay, I was reacting out of guilt. If Rex wanted to stay, there wasn't much I could do to change his mind. I walked over to Maria to check on her.

"Are we all set?" I asked. Ahmed and Zeb were in the corner, loading magazines and practically trembling with excitement. "Are those two going to be able to handle this?"

Maria rolled her eyes. "Oh yeah. Their part isn't very big, just backup. I just hope they remember that and don't do anything stupid."

"Yeah," I said, "because I'm the only one who gets that distinction."

Maria laughed. "I wouldn't say that. You did really well with snagging Rex. He's wonderful. How'd you find a guy like that?"

I shrugged. "You just have to change your name and appearance, move to a small town in Iowa, and have a hottie detective move across the street from you. It's easy."

"Go check on Riley." Maria smiled.

Riley was fifty feet away in the back corner surrounded with monitors that watched the approach to the warehouse in every direction. We gave him that duty as punishment for getting us all into this in the first place. He didn't argue. I was sure he felt bad about it.

"Hey," I said as I walked up behind him. Four monitors—one for each direction—sat in front of him in a horseshoe formation. "All set?"

Riley turned toward me, and I started watching the monitors for him. "I'm so sorry, Merry. This really got out of hand. And I ruined your trip."

"Normally, the nice, Midwestern girl in me would argue with you to make you feel better. Unfortunately, she's armed and dangerous right now, so that's not gonna happen."

Yes, it was harsh. And it was tough to see Riley flinch my words, but he needed to know that I was upset about it.

"I deserve that," he said. "I had no idea I'd called you. was under some serious drugs, but that's not much of an excuse"

"Wow," I said drily. "Who are you? Where's Riley?" T old Riley was more selfish than that. Maybe he'd learned a little something here.

"I shouldn't have gone to the coffee house more than once." He looked duly chastened. A look I'd never seen on him before. "It was stupid and sloppy."

"Now you know why we have those rules in our line of work," I said, my eyes scanning the monitors every few secon

"But there's nothing we can do about that now. I'm grateful for the apology though."

Riley looked into my eyes, like he had more to say. I waited, but no words came out. I got that. Sometimes you just felt like nothing you said would make a difference. And it wouldn't. The yakuza believed Riley and I were involved in the murder of their leader. Chances were, they'd have come to Who's There, Iowa, looking for me anyway. At least this way, my hometown was safe.

"Forget about it," I finally said to break the uneasy silence. "We're good. And as long as this works, we all get out of this alive." Always look on the bright side when attempting a dangerous plan.

"I should also apologize for what happened in Japan," Riley said quietly. I took my eyes off the monitor and looked back at Rex, who was now deep in conversation with Maria.

"Forget about it," I said, but there was a hard edge in my voice. I guess I was still mad at myself for screwing around with Chlotilde.

Riley shook his head. "I'm not sure you understand..."

I nodded. "Yes, you shouldn't have been holding another woman in your arms when I walked in on you. But that's water under the bridge. Besides, if I hadn't caught you snuggling up to that German bimbo, I would've found you with someone else later."

I guess I wasn't over it. The image of walking in to see Riley holding Chlotilde against him still hurt. But a snake couldn't change its stripes, so better then than later.

Riley stared at me with his mouth open. He probably didn't think I'd actually say it out loud. Oh, well. This was a learning experience for him. And I was kind of proud of myself for saying what I should've a long, long time ago.

"Merry, I don't—" he started.

I held my hand up to silence him. "Save it." I pointed at the monitors. A black sedan was rocketing toward the south end of the warehouse. The yakuza had arrived.

CHAPTER TWENTY

———

"Showtime!" I called out, and everyone went to their predetermined locations. Maria and her two wannabees took up positions behind rusted machinery. Rex nodded and went to the monitors, where he took up a sniper position behind some old, rusty barrels. He'd keep an eye on the screens just in case anyone else joined us. It would be just like Ito to have a second wave come in when she thought we were distracted.

Riley and I moved to the middle of the room, in plain sight, waiting. We were armed to the teeth, but you wouldn't have known it to look at us. I had a pistol in my waistband against the small of my back and another one in my jacket pocket. I also had a throwing knife up the sleeve of my right hand and another in my left sock. Riley was similarly outfitted.

The warehouse was air-conditioned, or we'd look completely weird considering it was so hot outside. I was pretty sure Ito would see through this façade, but on the off chance she didn't, it was best to be prepared.

"Well," I said under my breath. "Here goes nothing."

Riley took my hand and squeezed it, dropping it as the door opened in front of us.

Leiko Ito walked in, flanked by the bald guy from the photos and, to my complete surprise, Elvinia and her boys, Cletus and Earl. I hadn't thought of that. I mean, I knew she'd ask Elvinia, but seeing the mountain men with her surprised me a bit. It shouldn't have. And there it was—a flaw in the plan. I prayed there weren't more things I'd overlooked. I wondered where the two thugs we'd encountered at the embassy were, but they probably got sent back home in shame.

Ito Jr. walked up to us, stopping about twenty feet away.

She was dressed tactically, wearing long, black leather boots, leggings, and a tunic covered with pockets which probably hid a million different ways to kill us.

Elvinia and her boys carried shotguns. Their faces were expressionless. I wondered how she felt being dragged into this. Question was, should I tip my hand and address Elvinia directly? Ito didn't know we knew each other. I decided to do nothing.

"Ms. Wrath, Riley..." Ito nodded.

"Leiko," I said. "And company."

Ito sneered. "Oh, I know you are acquainted with Elvinia and her friends. I'm not an idiot. But you need to know that when you're in the family, your loyalties are cemented."

I shrugged. "Okay."

"Okay?" Ito started to turn purple with rage.

"Yes. Okay," I said. "You want to play icebreaker games and get to know each other better, or do you want to settle this once and for all?"

For a moment, I thought she was going to shoot me. Although in her mind, she was planning to do that anyway. She just wouldn't get the answers she wanted if she played her hand too early. I watched as she managed to bring her fury back under control.

"You have something to confess, I believe?" she asked calmly.

I looked at Riley then back at her. "I can tell you everything we know." I stepped forward to show I was in control of this standoff. "We didn't kill your mother."

"Liar!" Ito reddened and started to shake. "I know you did it!"

I shook my head. "We didn't kill her. We did find her body and dispose of it in a disrespectful way. And for that, I'm truly sorry."

I explained what had happened, leaving out details like where I lived or the fact that Kelly had been there. No way was I dragging a new mom into this. Ito listened but maintained her level of anger. When I finished explaining, I apologized one more time.

"Again, we are so sorry for the way we handled it. That was wrong."

That was it. I'd told her everything I knew. It felt good, to be honest. Now the ball was in her court to figure out if we were telling the truth.

"Why should I believe you?" Baby Ito asked through clenched teeth.

"Because that's what happened." I shrugged. I could understand her disbelief. If I was still a spy, I'd totally lie to her. She didn't know that since I'd gone citizen, things had changed.

Where in the hell was Riley in this? Why was he letting me do all the talking? Here he'd apologized for being a cheating jerk back in Tokyo, but he was letting me do all the apologizing and explaining here. I was kind of pissed, but maybe I should've expected that.

Ito shook her head. "No. You lie. You lured her to the United States and then killed her. I know you did."

"I have no idea how she got here. That's the truth. Whoever killed her obviously brought her over and murdered her to frame me." *Come on, Riley. Jump in any damn time.*

"You expect me to believe that?" Ito stormed.

I sighed heavily. "I know it's hard to believe. I'd have a hard time buying that story if I was you. But I'm not lying." I looked at Riley, who continued staring at Ito.

"In fact, I'd like to make a proposition," I said, taking us into phase two. "I'd like to help you find out who actually did kill your mother."

"And why would you do that?" Leiko spat. "You're just trying to confuse me!"

I shook my head. "No, I'm not." This time I turned to Riley and smacked him with my left arm. He needed to participate in this little showdown.

Ito turned to look at her right-hand man, who was staring hard at me. I noticed that while Clem still had a solid grip on his shotgun, Elvinia had lowered hers a little. That was interesting. I knew Maria and her two clowns were covering us, as was Rex. Hopefully, Ito didn't know that.

"I need a moment," Leiko said, catching me off guard.

"Take all the time you need," Riley answered. Finally. What was up with him anyway?

We watched as Ito Jr. walked back to the big guy she'd

brought with her. They started whispering to each other. It was impossible to hear them. I concentrated on Elvinia. Clem wasn't a weak link—he was probably looking forward to shooting someone. But Elvinia knew me. Granted, we weren't BFFs by any means, but still, she had tried to set me up with her nephew, so there had to be something there, right?

Elvinia's face was passive, but the way she carried her shotgun said a lot. She was thinking, trying to sort out if I was telling the truth. In the end, would she act based on her own assumptions or on Leiko's?

Honor and family loyalty were huge tenets of the yakuza code. Elvinia would be expected to go with whatever Ito decided. On the other hand, Elvinia was her own woman. Her yakuza husband was dead, and she was pretty far removed from the Japanese syndicate. On more than one occasion, she'd told me how much the Okinawa family despised the Tokyo branch. The woman was a wild card. Which way would she go?

In order to keep their locations hidden, I didn't glance in the direction of Rex or Maria. Instead, I turned to Riley. His face was unreadable. In fact, he was frowning. That was strange. Riley was usually so laid back. Most likely, his guilt was killing him. He'd hated dragging the girls and me into this. He was probably very concerned about what would happen next. I should have cut him a little slack.

"What do you think?" I whispered.

"No idea," Riley replied softly. "It's a total crapshoot at this point. Mostly because Leiko has a reputation for being wildly unpredictable and a bit unstable."

"She hasn't killed us yet," I mused. "And she's had plenty of opportunity."

He nodded. "That's true. Like I said, unpredictable."

Minutes ticked by. What was taking her so long? I thought about the car she came in. Five people were here, so the sedan couldn't have carried more people. And if another car were coming, Rex would let us know.

Ten minutes passed, and Ito and her man were still talking. If Elvinia and the boys could hear her, they weren't letting on. This was getting ridiculous. The only reason they could be conferring so long was that they were waiting for reinforcements. Right now, we outnumbered them by one person. Another vehicle full of gun-toting criminals would put us at a disadvantage.

"Time's up," I said finally. My radar was going off. Something was wrong.

Ito turned to face me. "I thought you said we didn't have to rush?"

"I did say that. But this is taking too long. Either you believe us, or you don't. What's it going to be?"

"Why are you in such a hurry?" Ito sneered.

I shrugged. "I've got tickets to a performance at the Kennedy Center tonight. I'd like to change before I go." It was a lie, and she knew it. There really was a time for snark, and maybe this wasn't it. But I wanted this over. It just seemed like the yakuza was playing with its food.

"You're in a hurry to die?" Leiko stepped forward.

"Let's just get it over with," I said.

"Come on, Ito." Riley finally spoke up. "Time to decide."

Leiko smiled. That woman really could go from zero to crazy in seconds. She pulled her gun and leveled it at me. Immediately, Riley and I pulled our guns, aiming them at her and her dude. So this was how it was going to be.

"I can't. I don't know if you're telling the truth or not. So I might as well kill you."

I shoved Riley out of the way and dove in the opposite direction as the shot rang out. Riley fired, hitting Ito's man in the leg. Clem and Earl began firing their shotguns at us.

Elvinia raised her arm, and to my unbelieving eyes, both men lowered their shotguns. That was a good sign, but I didn't take the time to appreciate it. I fired at Ito, but she dodged it, shooting directly at me. The bullet barely grazed my shoulder, but I didn't have time to react.

Rex came up behind Ito. "Drop it," he growled.

She turned, and he knocked the gun from her hand. I was already on my feet, running toward her, when she pulled a knife on my boyfriend and lunged for him. It was like watching something in slow motion. Rex blocked the arc of her knife arm and held the gun to her head.

What he didn't know was that wouldn't stop Ito. She was flat-out insane and would fight until she won or died. I screamed as her knife arced up and sliced into Rex's side. He dropped to the floor, squeezing off a shot that missed.

I tackled her from behind, bringing both of us to the floor. Oblivious to anything else that was going on, I rolled on top of her and punched her in the face. Unfortunately for me, Ito had some martial arts skills and threw me off her. As she straddled me, she started bringing her knife down toward my throat.

I'd like to have said that was no problem. But that would be a lie. Leiko was much stronger than I was, and even though I was holding her off with both hands, the knife was getting dangerously close to my neck.

"I'm telling you the truth, dammit!" I shouted. It meant nothing. Leiko was lost in her blood lust and wouldn't be satisfied until I was dead.

Other shots rang out around me, but I dared not take my eyes off my attacker. She'd stabbed Rex, but I couldn't risk a look at him. I could only pray that he was alright. Right now, I was fighting for my life.

Clunk.

Ito's strength stalled, and she looked confused, just before falling to the floor, unconscious. Elvinia stood there, wielding the butt of her shotgun.

"Thanks," I said as I rolled to my feet and jumped up to survey the scene.

Riley was tying up Ito's colleague, and Ahmed and Jenkins were holding Clem and Earl at gunpoint. Maria was tending to Rex, who looked at me with relief before passing out.

"I never liked the Tokyo branch," Elvinia said as she stood over Baby Ito's inert body. "And I'm an American first, bitch."

"You mean we don't get to shoot anyone?" Clem sounded disappointed. Elvinia had better keep an eye on him in the future.

Ahmed and Jenkins were giddy with delight. They'd gotten to be part of a big operation. That was all they needed.

"How is he?" I asked as I knelt down beside Rex.

"Just grazed him," Maria said. "He'll just need stitches."

"Thank God!" I said as I kissed my boyfriend on the forehead.

I got to my feet, adrenaline pumping, and may have accidentally kicked Leiko a few times. It was over. Somehow I' have to convince this woman that I didn't kill her mother, or she'd just keep coming after me until I was dead.

Ito awoke to find her accomplice tied to a chair. To her credit, she didn't even struggle. That was nice. I crouched down in front of her with Riley standing behind me.

"We are going to stay here until you believe me," I said calmly. Maria and the guys had taken Rex to the hospital. Elvinia left, promising to stay out of it. I knew she would. She seemed pretty pissed that Ito expected her to kill me, what with me and her nephew Knob being almost sort of engaged and all.

"I'll never believe that!" Ito spat. "I'll keep hunting you until I kill you! And then I'll kill everyone you know!"

I stood up, realizing that this was far from over. This lunatic had already stabbed my boyfriend. Now she was threatening to come after everyone from Kelly to my cats. And she had the resources to do it.

"I don't want to kill you," I hissed. "But I will not hesitate if I think you're still a threat."

To my surprise, I realized I meant every word. Here I was, ready to assassinate a woman illegally to keep her from killing my loved ones. I didn't even care if she killed me. It wa the others I worried about. There was no doubt whatsoever tha she'd keep coming back.

Vendettas were big in her organization, and some of them were handed down from generation to generation until th were sorted out. The yakuza would keep coming after Riley an me no matter what we did. And if our blood wasn't enough, they'd keep killing until they were satisfied. That was how it worked.

There were only two choices—let her go and keep fighting her for the rest of my life or kill her. I was no angel. Killing people had been part of my assignments on occasion in the field. Those deaths had haunted me—but not much becaus they were usually a bad-guy-or-me situation. This was something different. This was cold-blooded murder, and I was a citizen, not a spy anymore.

And, I realized, I didn't want to kill her. I hadn't killed her mom, and I didn't want to kill Leiko. But I would have to if it meant stopping her. This was a terrible problem. The only solutions were both inconceivable.

"I swear on the blood of my mother," Ito started to scream. "My whole organization will come after you with everything we've got until you are dead!" She was becoming unhinged.

Ito got to her feet and stood in a defensive stance. Really? She was completely outgunned. This psycho wasn't going to quit.

"It's over, Leiko!" I shouted.

Ito then did something that caught me off guard. She turned tail and ran for the door. I ran after her.

Ito actually made it out the door. Everyone else had been convinced this was over, so nobody else was prepared to chase her. Ito cleared the doorway and made it outside with me hot on her heels. She was fast. Faster than I'd thought. The crime boss was slipping farther out of my grasp when I heard a weird screech.

Out of the sky, Mr. Fancy Pants soared downward like a mentally challenged American eagle. He got away again? Really? What was wrong with his keepers? I kept running after Ito but couldn't take my eyes off of the king vulture. Ito was still running and out of my range. I had to grab her before she got away—but she was faster than I was.

And that's when I remembered the cookies in my pocket.

I pulled the baggie out and crushed the cookies inside as I ran. Ito was slowing down a little now, and I was a couple of arm lengths away. I tossed my cookies (that's right—I said it) onto the fleeing yakuza leader. Fancy Pants' two googly eyes actually came together and narrowed in on the flying shortbread.

He landed on Leiko with a thud, his weight taking her to the ground. I caught up as he started pecking the woman with a glee usually reserved for a pothead who just moved to Colorado.

Ito screamed and flailed as I picked her up and cuffed her. Elvinia and her boys were trying to capture the bird. I didn't tell them that Fancy Pants would soon hulk out on a sugar high. did insist that they didn't hurt or try to eat him. They seemed a little disappointed.

I dragged Ito back inside and sat her down in a chair. I was panting and out of breath. I might be getting a little too old for this. Ito started screaming hostilities at us, demanding over and over that we confess to her mother's murder.

"I don't care where you take me!" Ito spat. "I'll get away and I will kill you for what you did!" She lunged in her chair toward me. What was I going to do with her?

I rubbed my face with my hands. There was no way out of this. I was innocent, but what I would do next would make me guilty. I looked at Riley.

"You won't need to," he said to Ito as he pointed at me. "She's completely innocent…like she said."

"It's no use, Riley," I said, suddenly exhausted. "She's not going to stop until one of us is dead." Would it be possible put Philby and the kittens in the witness protection program? Could I convince Kelly and Robert to bring their baby and go on the lam with me?

I raised my gun, pressing it against Ito's forehead and sighed.

"That's not true." Riley reached out and took my gun from me. Was he going to kill her to stop her?

"I killed Midori," Riley said directly to Baby Ito. "I drugged her and smuggled her into the country. I shoved a hat pin into her brain, then beat her on the back of the head and dumped her in Merry's kitchen."

"Riley," I said. "She's never going to believe I wasn't involved. Lying to this madwoman won't make a difference."

He looked right at me, wearing an expression I couldn't decipher.

"I'm not lying," was all he said.

CHAPTER TWENTY-ONE

———

"Stop it! She's not going to believe you. So why lie?" I asked. Riley had lost it. Maybe he had Stockholm syndrome from his time in Ito's clutches.

He shook his head. "I'm sorry, Merry. Really I am. But it happens to be true. I killed Midori Ito."

"What?" was all I could think to say.

Riley ran his hands through his hair. "Remember Chlotilde?" He waited for me to nod, and I did. How could I forget her?

"That wasn't her name. Her name was Rachael. And she was my sister."

"That can't be right. You never told me you had a sister. And I know what I saw!"

"No," he said. "You didn't see what you thought you saw. We were just hugging when you walked in. You totally overreacted."

Um…what? My mind reeled back to that night. I'd walked in and seen a woman in Riley's arms, head against his chest. I screamed at him and walked out. Omg! I totally messed that up. All this time, I'd thought he'd cheated on me, when all he'd done was hug his sister.

"Damn." I whistled. "And all this time I thought…"

"I never cheated on you," Riley said. "I wouldn't have done that."

Oh. So, I guess I had that all wrong. This was too much to wrap my head around. I'd experienced some weird plot twists in my life, but this won the grand prize.

And then it dawned on me. "So you killed Midori because she killed Chlotilde…I mean, Rachael!"

The memory hit me like a brick. I had gone to Riley with what I'd heard Midori say in the steak house. That she'd killed the woman I'd thought was a German bimbo. I felt bad about it now.

"Why didn't you tell me she was your sister?" I whined. "Why let me think that all this time?"

"I was going to explain it. Rachael was deep undercover with the Germans. She was even trying to turn you to make her look more legit. I wasn't under any obligation to reveal that to you, and I knew you wouldn't fall for it. So I was going to wait until the whole mess blew over. Except it didn't work out that way."

Because Midori killed Rachael. And everything else became secondary. My misunderstanding was sucked into the white noise that surrounded the huge issue of his sister's murder. How could I be so stupid?

The dreams I'd been having came back to me in waves. Little puzzle pieces that fit themselves together in my mind.

"By the time I recovered somewhat, you had moved on, decided it was better for you if you weren't in a relationship with me. But I always wondered what would've happened if I'd explained everything." He gently tucked a stray curl behind my ear.

Riley had been serious about us. He never cheated on me. Wasn't even a womanizer. And he'd given me up because he thought it was better that way…for me.

How had I missed all of this? For years I'd been completely wrong about him. One of the big rules in espionage was never to get involved with people you work with. It made you blind. I saw the truth in that now.

All this time, Riley and I could've been together. We might've even been happy. But I'd blown it by not confirming what I'd seen. What a terrible spy. And a terrible girlfriend. What had I done?

"I'm so sorry, Riley…" I stammered. "I'm a complete idiot. I should've let you explain…" I was starting to hyperventilate a little. This was a lot to take in. I'd been betrayed before but never by myself.

"It's okay, really," Riley soothed. "I didn't want to upset you. I just wanted you to know the truth."

I let that sink in. I took a deep breath.

And then I punched him in the face. "You put her body in my kitchen!"

Riley took a handkerchief out of his back pocket and wiped the blood from his nose. "I guess I deserved that."

"Hell yes, you deserved that!" I shouted. "Why put her in my kitchen? What were you thinking?"

"I wasn't. None of it was planned. I'd brought her to Iowa so I could torture her for killing my baby sister. Then stuff started happening to you, so I had to deal with it. I guess I thought since so many other bodies were piling up around you, one more wouldn't hurt."

"That's a terrible excuse," I said.

"Yes it is." Riley pulled me against him. "And I'm sorry."

"I hate to interrupt such a romantic story," Ito sneered. "But I'm still going to kill you!" She glared at me. "Even if you didn't murder Mother, you're still an accomplice. And for that, you are going to die!"

Riley pulled his gun from his belt and fired a single shot into Leiko Ito's head. Before I could even react, he shot her henchman.

"What did you do?" I croaked.

"I'm finishing what I started." Riley grabbed my hand and started dragging me out of the building. "You weren't here. You didn't see any of this. Go."

I stared at him. "But I did! I'm part of this!"

Riley shook his head sadly. "No. You're not. I'm going to deal with this. You were never here." He turned on his heel and walked back into the building, shutting the door behind him.

I met Maria at the hospital where Rex was getting stitches for "falling onto a fence." The nurse didn't look like she totally believed that but said nothing and stitched him up. We were back in the Trekkie hotel within an hour. Maria left with her lackeys, promising to catch up with me in a day or so.

"What happened at the warehouse?" Rex asked when we were alone.

I sighed, trying to decide what to tell him. "Riley is dealing with it, with the Agency's assistance." That was another lie. I doubted Riley was going to let the CIA know what he'd done. In fact, I didn't think he'd be on the grid for a long time.

"He should've done that to begin with." Rex grimaced as he adjusted himself on the tribble sofa.

"Don't move so much—you'll tear out your stitches," I said.

"Don't avoid the fact that Riley should never have involved you in this mess." Rex reached out and pulled me to his chest.

"I won't," I said, struggling not to cry. "But it's all over now."

We ordered room service and spent the night quietly watching a *Star Trek* marathon on TV.

A few days later, Maria met me for breakfast in the hotel café. Rex was doing better but still resting. We had a flight out scheduled for that evening. It was over, and we were going home.

"Riley has taken a leave of absence," Maria said as she took a sip of coffee. She hadn't asked me what happened. She was a good spy. She knew I'd tell her if I had to.

"I don't think we will see him for a long time," I said sadly.

"In spite of everything," Maria said after a moment, "I had fun with you and the girls. And I'll never forget Mr. Fancy Pants."

I couldn't help but laugh. "What happened to that bird?"

"They reinforced his enclosure. There's no way he's breaking out again." Maria grinned.

"Are your two guys going to keep quiet?" I asked about our only loose ends.

She nodded. "Jenkins is going to try for a field post…again. And you owe Ahmed four cases of peanut butter cookies a year for the rest of his life. It's all good."

I laughed. "Deal. I think I'm getting off easy."

Maria nodded. "Promise me the next time you come home we'll just go out to dinner and maybe a movie?"

"Agreed," I said.

We finished our breakfast and went our own ways. Maria was a good friend, and I'd been lucky to have her with me. I just hoped it would never come back to haunt her.

Rex and I flew home that night. We got in late and spent the night at my place. The next morning, he slipped out and collected the cats from Juliette so I wouldn't have to deal with her. He was an awesome boyfriend.

Philby and the kittens were oblivious to my return. I'd like to think they missed me, but it's hard to tell with cats. I played with them for hours before I took a shower and headed over to Kelly's house.

"It's about time!" Kelly said as I joined her in the living room.

"Sorry," I said as I gently hugged her. She was holding a tiny baby in her arms.

"Want to hold her?" Kelly asked then handed the baby to me before I could answer.

The infant was sound asleep. I stared in astonishment at her tiny features. I'd never really been around babies before. This was my first real experience. She didn't look real. I kissed her forehead, and she wiggled a little before sighing and drifting off again.

"She's beautiful!" I whispered.

Kelly laughed. "She won't wake up. She sleeps like a hibernating grizzly."

"What did you name her?" I asked, unable to take my eyes off the baby.

Kelly smiled at me. She looked so happy. Like glow-in-the-dark happy. I don't think I'd ever seen her like that. Good for her. She deserved it.

"We named her Finn. After you," she said.

For the first time in minutes, I took my eyes off of the baby and looked at my best friend.

"I'm not sure I deserve that," I said at last.

"Oh, you definitely don't," Kelly replied. "But we like the name, and it suits her. Just don't go thinking you're all that."

"I won't." I turned my attention back to the baby. "I definitely won't."

Rex made a full recovery and insisted he forgave me fo the whole mess. He did say he wasn't forgiving Riley any time soon. I understood that. Riley had put us in a terrible position. I forgiven him, but that was because I was pretty sure I wasn't going to see him again.

I didn't tell Rex the whole story. He didn't need to know Riley had killed Midori or her daughter. Cops operate in a different world than spies. What was black and white for the police had a million shades of gray for secret agents. I was prett sure it wouldn't translate.

I also left out the information about my previous relationship with Riley. To his credit, even though I thought he suspected, Rex never asked. Just one more reason I loved him.

Reconciling my feelings for Riley was far more complicated. I went through the typical stages of loss, because was mourning a relationship I'd ended prematurely. My head w spinning with what-ifs. And when I thought about Riley suffering alone for the death of his sister and the end of whatev it was we had, I felt awful.

Fortunately, there were cats, babies, and junk food. Th helped. It didn't make it better or even go away. It just helped. Sooner or later, things got better, with cats that looked like Elv and Hitler and a whole mess of Oreos.

CHAPTER TWENTY-TWO

———

Two weeks later, we had another Scout meeting – this time in my back yard with a fire blazing and lots and lots of s'mores. I'd missed this. It's not like we could've started a fire in front of the Washington Monument to roast marshmallows (which would probably have gotten us in more trouble than king vulture kidnapping). In the future, I'd prefer trips that ended with gooey, chocolatey treats, instead of stark-raving Japanese psychopaths and shotgun toting moonshiners.

Kelly brought Baby Finn, and I brought the kittens. The girls were delirious with joy. After the screams died down and everyone had a chance to hold the baby and at least one of the kittens, we all told Kelly about the trip. I think the parts about Mr. Fancy Pants were her favorite.

I dug into my pink backpack and brought out several boxes of cookies. For good measure, I made sure no sugar-mad king vultures were anywhere in the proximity.

There were still a couple of questions I needed answers to.

"How did you guys put together that I'd been a spy?" I asked as I tried to keep the Elvis kitty from leaping off my lap like a flying squirrel.

"It's pretty obvious," Betty said. The others nodded.

"Number one"—Hannah counted on her fingers—"you took us to the black box at Langley." Huh. They knew it was called the black box. Impressive.

"And then you added that embassy to the itinerary and vanished while we had the tour," Betty said.

"Don't forget the International Spy Museum!" Inez said.

"Where you vanished into thin air," one of the Kaitlins

said. "Not to mention the fact we had to suddenly switch hotels.

"Like I said"—Betty commandeered the conversation— "pretty obvious."

"When you add that to all the other weird stuff that's happened over the last year, we figured you had to be a spy," Lauren said.

These girls were smart. Too smart. And I loved them to death for it.

"One more question, and it's for the Kaitlins…" I asked

The four little girls perked up, a little flattered that I'd singled them out. Philby was curled up on one of their laps, purring menacingly in case I did anything that would disrupt th massage fest she was getting.

"Which one of you is Evelyn's daughter?" I asked straight out. I'd been too embarrassed this whole trip to ask. It was kind of awful that I didn't know the parents of my girls.

"What do you mean?" one of the girls asked.

Ugh. For smart kids, they could sometimes be a little dense.

"Evelyn Trout—the other adult with us on the trip," I explained.

The four Katilins looked at each other curiously. Mayb whichever one it was, was clearly too embarrassed to admit tha the bored, middle-aged housewife belonged to one of them. I guess I could understand that.

"Evelyn isn't any of our moms," one of the girls said. The others nodded.

"What do you mean?" I asked, repeating their earlier question.

Another Kaitlin spoke. "She's not a mom. Not of any c the girls. We thought you knew that."

I felt a twisting in my gut and a wash of cold fire beneath my skin.

"Is she an aunt or family friend of one of you?" I aske

All twelve girls shook their heads in unison. They did know her. Evelyn Trout was a complete unknown to them. Ke and I froze as we exchanged looks of complete shock.

Uh-oh.

But at long last the nightmare of Midori's murder was

over. As for Evelyn, well, that would have to be another mystery for another time. Right now, I was happy to be home. My troop was safe, and life could go on. As I chewed on my fifth s'more, I couldn't help but search the sky, just to make sure Mr. Fancy Pants hadn't followed us home.

ABOUT THE AUTHOR

Leslie Langtry is the *USA Today* bestselling author of the *Greatest Hits Mysteries* series, *Sex, Lies, & Family Vacations*, *The Hanging Tree Tales* as Max Deimos, the *Merry Wrath Mysteries,* and several books she hasn't finished yet, because she's very lazy.

Leslie loves puppies and cake (but she will not share her cake with puppies) and thinks praying mantids make everything better. She lives with her family and assorted animals in the Midwest, where she is currently working on her next book and trying to learn to play the ukulele.

To learn more about Leslie, visit her online at:
http://www.leslielangtry.com

Enjoyed this book? Check out these other reads available in print now from Gemma Halliday Publishing:

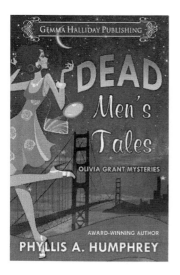

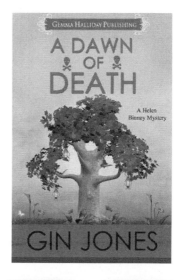

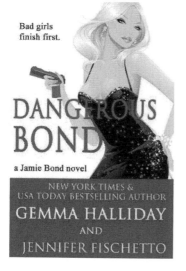

www.GemmaHallidayPublishing.com

Made in the USA
Middletown, DE
10 April 2023